SHAMELESS KING

MAYA HUGHES

To my sisters who have been my workhorses for this release! I love you both so much and I don't know what I'd do without you <3

PROLOGUE - DECLAN

The Rittenhouse Prep prom committee had gone all out again this year. Limos and luxury cars lined the entrance to the building. Those cars cost more than my house was worth, but you couldn't tell that from the way people called out our names as we walked by. Me and the guys who'd had my back since our first practice together freshman year, The Kings, were State Champions—again.

I'd been to every prom since freshman year. It seemed even senior girls had no problem being seen on the arm of a freshman, as long as it was me. The thumping of the music guided us through the entrance of the building with a slightly fishy smell. Being right on the water, the building had a distinct salt-and-sea tinge to the air.

My rented tux fit well. Working my magic, I'd done a deal with the shop. Told people where I got mine from, and the shop rented it to me and had it altered for free. It was a pretty sweet deal. I figured if I was going to be uncomfortable in the thing, at least I'd look good.

And from the way heads turned as we walked in, I knew I did. Lots of guys walked in with their custom tuxes, but I didn't care because all eyes were on me and the rest of the Kings. Rittenhouse Prep Kings and state hockey champions in the flesh. People on the dance floor clapped and cheered when we came in through the double doors of the ballroom.

"Declan!" Someone whooped from a few tables away. A bunch of woo-hoos and Kings' chants later and we could finally leave our spot at the door. If Ford got any redder, he'd be ready to explode. He tugged at his collar. They'd had to special order his tux. But he had that strong silent thing chicks went wild for. Jet black hair, serious scowl that melted away in an instant. He hated the attention; that was fine. I could soak up more than enough for all of us.

The warm buzz from the pre-prom drinks we'd had at Emmett's meant I was feeling good. Nothing too crazy. We didn't want to get kicked out, but just enough to kick up the fun a notch.

"What did I tell you? We don't need dates." I grinned, and my eyes swept over a few of the more plunging necklines of some of the dresses our fellow students wore. We moved through the room, and people's heads turned as we walked past some classmates already seated. High fives were doled out for all of us as we strolled by.

"Declan, guys, this way, I'll show you to the table." One of the bubbly juniors rushed up to us and looped her arm around Heath's, tugging him forward. I rolled my eyes. Heath never had to bat an eyelash to get the women to fawn all over him. Blond hair worked for guys as well. He was easy to spot with the surfer look on the East Coast.

"We took the liberty of putting your tent cards on the table already. We didn't want you to have to find your names." She had a mountain of blonde hair piled up on top of her head. The curls were so tight it looked like she could bounce around on her head like Tigger.

Our spot was a prime location in the center of the ten-seater tables dotted around the dance floor.

"I have a feeling we're going to be dancing a lot," Ford grumbled, elbowing Colm as he took his seat. He looked as uncomfortable as I felt. The fabric of his tux was stretched to its limit on his shoulders—if he wasn't a gentle giant, who'd mastered the art of chilling the fuck out, I'd swear he was ready to Hulk out at any second.

"Don't worry, big guy; I'm happy to intercept any dance requests someone might throw your way." I lifted my glass of water to him as a toast.

Colm slid his flask across to my lap, and my eyes got wide. He was our resident mischief maker lately. Having your life thrown into chaos had a way of making people act not quite like themselves. Emmett by far got into the most trouble out of all of us, but with his parents' power and influence he never really had to worry about the consequences. Heath, Ford, and I were scholarship kids who knew how to toe the line. "Is this the older brother breaking all the rules?" I covered my mouth in fake outrage.

"Shut up. Olivia's not here, so what she doesn't know won't hurt her." Colm had become the guardian of his younger sister when their parents died earlier that year in a car accident. He'd always taken on the protector role, but that had gone into hyperdrive now that Olivia relied on him.

I drained the water and put my glass under the table, pouring some of the vodka into it.

"Declan, can I have a dance later?" A girl, Hannah—or was it Anna?—asked as she passed by on the arm of her date.

I winced and shrugged my shoulders at the guy. *Sorry, dude.* I'd convinced the guys to go solo. Well, except for Emmett. He'd of course brought, Avery. They'd been joined at the hip since sophomore year. But Heath, Ford, and Colm were by my side at our table. Blue light skated over the room from the massive fish tank that took up one entire wall.

Not many people got to say they had their prom at an aquarium. A group of other students crowded around one end of the tank where a fish that looked almost as big as Emmett hung near the glass. All it was missing was the giant bushy beard.

This was one of our last nights all together. The prom, the big pep rally, a final blow out at Emmett's, and then we were all off to college. Bittersweet in a way. Leaving most of the guys behind. Heath and I would be playing locally at the University of Philadelphia. Colm and Ford would be up in Boston, and Emmett was being cagey with his plans for next year.

A few hors d'oeuvres and a shot from the flask later, and the prom was really in full swing. Emmett arrived with Avery on his arm, beaming like he always was whenever she was near him. Dude had it so bad and he didn't even care. We didn't even give him shit about it anymore, that was just how it was. Avery meant everything to him, made sense when you had parents as shitty as his.

The room heated up, and I shrugged off my jacket, draping it over the back of my chair, ready to get back on the dance floor. While most people would have expected everyone to be uptight, it seemed that the dim lighting and fish as an audience meant everyone was ready to show off their moves.

"Holy shit!" someone behind me said, and my gaze darted all over the place to figure out what they were talking about.

I'd been hit in the chest with a puck before, but nothing quite compared to this feeling. Across the room, standing in front of the entrance, was a breathtaking sight. I don't remember what the hell color her dress was, all I knew was I couldn't take my eyes off her.

She stood there fidgeting with the small bag in her hands and glanced around the room.

"Wow, looks like the Ice Queen has finally thawed out a bit."

A slight murmur rippled through the people around me. My stomach dropped as my mind whirred trying to place her. And like a slow motion reveal, Makenna Halstead slid those horn-rimmed glasses she'd worn every second I'd ever seen her back on.

Avery spotted her and raced across the room, wrapping her arms around an incredibly uncomfortable-looking Makenna. It was like now that she knew all eyes were on her, she couldn't handle the pressure.

It wasn't just the glasses that were missing. It was also the telltale bun and the talk-to-me-and-I'll-kill-you stare. Normally, she walked with her shoulders square and a stomp that could shatter bone. I'd never seen her look so...nice.

She bit her bottom lip. It was the first time I'd ever seen her look unsure. I'd have never thought her barely strawberry-blonde hair was that long, since she always wore it up. She also swore up and down that dances and other stuff like this were a waste of time, so seeing her here had taken my brain at least a little while to piece it together.

Avery dragged her over to our table. We had a couple seats free. Mak gave the table a small wave.

"No, you're not wearing those tonight. You don't need them." Avery tugged the glasses off her face and shoved them back in her bag.

"Actually, I kind of do." Makenna reached for the bag as Avery smacked her hands away.

"Nope! I'm sure one of these strapping young men would be happy to lead you around like your very own seeing-eye stud if you do need to go anywhere."

The corners of her mouth turned down, but this time her lips were all soft and shiny. Deep pink brought out the fullness I'd never seen before. I shook my head. This was Mak the Ice Queen we were talking about.

She sat on a seat beside Ford, who seemed completely content to be sitting beside someone who was also happy doing her best mute impersonation.

"If you don't dance to at least five songs tonight, I swear I'm tanking our final project on purpose."

Mak gasped, like a real-life hand-to-chest gasp in horror at Avery even suggesting it.

"They would never find your body, Avery." Mak grinned up at her with her arms crossed over her chest.

I laughed into my napkin, and Mak turned her glare on me.

"I'm sure Emmett would. He's like a bloodhound when it comes to me." Right on time Emmett slid his arms around her waist and planted his nose in her neck, letting out a sniff loud enough for everyone to hear.

"I smell someone who needs to get out there and dance." Emmett led Avery away from the table. Avery held out her hand, flashing a five at Mak over and over. I grabbed the flask from the spot Colm had stashed it and had another drink.

A long, slender hand slid its way down over my shoulder, stopping at my chest. "You promised me a dance." The smell from Anna's hot breath against my neck told me we weren't the only ones who'd snuck in a little booze tonight.

It was not a good smell on her, and my skin crawled. Out of the corner of my eye, I caught the pissed-off face of her date. I did not want to have a fight tonight.

"Listen, I'm sorry. I would, but I already promised Mak a dance, and you know how she gets when she can't get what she wants, and it looks like tonight she wants me."

Mak's eyes got as wide as saucers, and her mouth hung open. Slipping out of the grasp of the date-ditcher, I rounded the table and held out my hand to Mak.

Glancing behind me at the very pissed-off Hannah or Anna and her even more pissed-off date, Mak perhaps sized up the situation and didn't want to be in the middle of a whirlwind of haymakers or thrown drinks, so she took my hand. A small jolt shot straight up my arm the second my skin touched hers. It was that same feeling you got standing in line for concessions at a movie you'd been waiting for forever. I shook my head. This was Mak we were talking about, and she didn't look one bit affected by my fingers wrapped around her.

"And tonight I want you?" She lifted an eyebrow at me as we walked out onto the dance floor with the corners of her mouth turned up the tiniest bit.

"I improvised. I know how people get when they don't get a piece of me." I grinned at her, but she just rolled her eyes.

"Probably for the best. Hannah can be a real bitch when she doesn't get what she wants, which probably means Edgar is in for a rough night. Poor guy." She glanced back over her shoulder to a very irate Hannah standing with her arms crossed over her chest.

People parted out of the way to give us some room. The moderately fast-paced song switched up to a slow one almost as soon as we found our spot.

We stood there staring at each other. I took a step forward, and Mak hesitated before looping her arms around my neck. The sensation was back now and worse than before. Staring down into Mak's eyes, I really saw them for the first time. They were the brightest blue I'd ever seen. Maybe it was the room or a trick of the lights, but I'd never seen so many blues in one spot.

It was the soft stroke of her fingers along the hair at the nape of my neck that made my hands tighten on her waist. The way she stared into my eyes, I don't even know if she realized she was doing it. Like her hands had a mind of their own, trying to soak up a little bit more of me. And I figured that was how she felt because my fingers had the same idea as I pulled her in tighter against me. Her lips parted, and her eyelashes fluttered.

The thud of my heart pounded as we moved to our own rhythm under the dim lights at the center of a sea of people. Electricity buzzed through my body, but I knew it wasn't just the vodka. It was all to do with the woman in my arms who usually drove me up a wall.

"I don't think I've ever seen you without your glasses before."

"I don't think I've ever seen you in a tux before." Her pink tongue darted out to lick her bottom lip. The wetness left behind drew my gaze to it, and I wanted to have my own sample of her lips.

"You've never been to prom before." My hands pressed into the small of her back, closing the tiniest of gaps that had been between us. *Why did she feel so good in my arms?* The blues and greens from the fish tank washed over us like a spell had been cast and we were living in our own little underwater bubble.

"Almost didn't come to this one."

"Why not?" I leaned my head back, savoring the trail her fingertip blazed along the base of my neck.

She never let herself have any fun. Normally, it also meant no one else could have any fun and it irked the shit out of me, but tonight I just wanted to hold her close on the dance floor all night.

"It's not really my thing, but I figured it's a rite of passage and all, so I decided to come." She shrugged her shoulders.

"I'm glad you did."

Even with the pretense of her helping me out of a dance with the devil—aka Hannah—gone, we stayed out there through a string of slow songs. At least I think they were slow songs; our tempo didn't change. It was the first time we'd probably had a civil conversation with each other in years. So weird that it would happen now. It was like one of those high school movies I swore I never watched, but I had at least a few times, where the big thing happened between the two nemeses.

My head dipped down slightly. It was like the warning sirens blaring on a submarine. My blood pounded in my veins, and I needed to taste her lips like I needed my next breath. It was an uncontrolled dive, and I didn't know exactly what I was doing, but she wasn't pulling back. She wasn't pushing her hands against me or cocking her hand back for a slap; if anything, she leaned in even more.

Her eyes almost fluttered closed as my lips parted, so close to hers. Her body went stiff, and her eyes snapped open wide. "Are you drunk?" She pushed back in my arms.

I let them drop. "No, I'm not drunk. I've had a couple drinks, but that's it." I took a step toward her, and she took a step back.

Before I could say anything else, a booming voice came out over the squealing PA. "And now it's time to announce our prom king and queen." One of the prom committee girls grabbed me by the arm. "We need you up front, Declan."

With a strength I didn't think someone of her size could possess, she pushed me from the middle of the dance floor. I glanced behind me at a stone-faced Mak with her arms crossed over her chest. She was back at our table and had her glasses back on her face. Things were back just how they'd always been.

The bright lights hanging from the ceiling shined in my face as they went through whatever the hell they were doing up onstage. I kept my eyes on Mak with the corners of my mouth turned down as she slowly made her way toward the double doors.

"And this year's prom king is Declan McAvoy!" Someone placed a crown on my head, and everyone cheered. The doors closed behind Mak, and I couldn't help but feel like that was the end to something. The end of something that hadn't even really started. But I know one thing. If I'd known how long it would be until I got to hold her again, I'd have held on a bit longer.

2

MAKENNA

The man who held the key to my financial survival on campus squinted at me from across the table. My stomach clenched tight as he gave me the once over again.

His furrowed brow dissolved, and his face brightened. "I know an overachiever when I see one. You've got the job." He held out his hand.

I slid my hand into his and pumped it up and down so hard he winced. *Way to dislocate your new boss's shoulder, Mak.*

"Plus, I need someone who won't flake, can keep calm under pressure, and won't mind taking the shifts no one else wants. You don't happen to like hockey, do you?" He raised an eyebrow at me.

My hand froze mid-shake, and I whipped my head from side to side as the pit in my stomach grew. Hockey only brought back memories of high school. Of the prom and the only school dance I'd ever had. Of all the fanfare around the Kings and *he who shall not be named*.

"Absolutely not."

"Excellent. We need someone here to help with the rush after the hockey games. Everyone piles in here, and no one ever wants to work." My stomach churned. *Hockey players here?* At least two of the Rittenhouse Prep School Kings went to this school. My smile faltered.

"That's not a problem, is it?" Larry's eyebrows pinched together, and I slapped my smile back into place.

"No problem at all. I can do it."

"Great, come into my office, and we can fill out the paperwork and get you your schedule."

"Perfect!" What were the odds that Declan would be there or that we'd even see each other? There had to be other bars on campus. If they needed more people, the place was most likely packed, so the odds of running into him here were slim. I took a deep breath, tried to push down the churning in my stomach and chalked it up to not eating anything all day.

∿

Me: I got the job!

I texted Avery the second I got out to my car.

Avery: Excellent! Should be fun. Free bar food, right?

Me: Not exactly a selling point.

Avery: Free is free...I'll have to come visit you sometime when I can get some time off and Alyson has a sleepover.

Avery was one of my friends from high school. She'd stayed behind in our Philly suburb when everyone else headed out to college. Being back in the area, I hoped we'd get to see more of each other.

Me: Yes, you should. You could come to campus and we could have a fun weekend. Bring Alsyon!

Avery: My shifts are insane for the next few months, but maybe I can swing a dinner or something.

Me: Nice.

An hour later, I drove through my childhood neighborhood. The sprawling front lawns framed the bright and pristine houses that were just different enough that no one felt like they were living in a cookie-cutter manicured existence.

Nothing had changed much in the three years since I'd left, but so many things were different. Coming back for summers and breaks wasn't the same. I was back for good now.

Climbing the steps to the sprawling neoclassical house, complete with white columns, I put my key in the front door. The trumpets and old school synth music blared straight through the solid wood.

Seventies music. I pushed the door open, and a mouthwatering aroma hit me, which was enough to put a smile on my face. Turning the corner into the living room, my smile faltered. My throat tightened as I watched them glide across the living room floor. Mom's head pressed tight against Dad's chest. Their hands clasped together as they hummed the tune. Tears welled in my eyes before I blinked them away.

They were so different. Not like the broken shells I'd been so eager to leave behind when I left for college. The house was clean and organized, dinner cooking away in the kitchen. No pots left unattended on the stove, boiling over. No half-abandoned meals I had to finish. And they looked happy.

As happy as I was for them, part of me crumpled inside, like a kid looking in through a window on a happy home they'd missed out on being a part of. The joy radiating off them and out of this house made it hard to breathe. I hadn't known it was possible for them to act like this again. *Why couldn't I have had this for those last years I was home? Why did it take me leaving and my dad's diagnosis for them to remember they were still alive? That I was still alive?*

Pictures that had been hidden away for years were all out on full display. Me and Daniel building sandcastles, sitting on Santa's lap, running around in the backyard. Happy memories tinged with sadness that had threatened to swallow us all. The last bits of the setting sun streamed in through the wide-open front windows, casting a warm orange glow over them.

"Mak's home," Dad said, twirling Mom away and dancing toward me. I couldn't hold back my bark of laughter as he grabbed my hand and spun me. His strong arms steadied me as he twirled me around the room. Mom, not to be outdone, jumped up and started her own solo dance moves right beside us when a dance number came on.

We finished out the song doubled over with laughter. I wiped away the tears streaming down my face, and Mom squeezed me tight. The music started up again, and Dad grabbed for my hand.

"Oh no, I think Mom's ready to take back over." We all looked up as a ding sounded in the kitchen. "You two get back to funky town, and I'll go check on the food."

"It's okay. I can get it." Mom tried to move past me, but I spun her around and right into Dad's arms.

"I've got it, Mom." I bolted from the room before they decided to have another dance battle like they'd had last week. My muscles had taken a few days to recover. Grabbing the oven mitts, I savored the normalcy of it all. *Was this what life could have been like back in high school?* Then came the guilt. I had no room to feel sorry about any of it. At least I was here.

I battled against the beat blast from the oven and a slippery roasting pan to wrangle the thing out of the oven without burning the crap out of my arms. *Why was this pan so heavy?* Mom had taken to making heartier meals lately. Rebalancing my grip, I slid the pan onto the counter.

The smell brought me right back to being ten again. Mom always used to cook pot roast every Friday. Daniel and I would run in after school and help her peel potatoes, using the peelers like swords and fighting in the kitchen until Mom kicked us out again.

We'd run back outside and play until she called us in. Having pot roast again every Friday this summer had brought those old memories slamming right back into me. I'd been running from them for three years. Trying to keep myself busy enough that the quiet moments were never long enough to think about everything I'd lost and would continue to lose. It was only a matter of time before they came back with a vengeance.

I set the potatoes on the counter next to the roast and stared out the kitchen window into the backyard. Even that was tidy. The neat lines of the freshly mowed grass made it look like something out of a magazine. Our old swing set sat abandoned in the backyard, but it didn't look like a relic of the past. The metal gleamed, and the wood had been restained.

"How did the job interview go?"

My heart jumped into my throat as Mom sneaked up behind me. She grabbed a cup and filled it with water and took a few ice cubes from the freezer.

I turned from the sink and dropped the towel onto the counter.

"It went great. I got the job. I'll be working a few nights a week. Not too bad."

"That's good. I'm glad you're getting everything settled, but I still don't know why you didn't stay at Stanford, sweetheart. You only had a year to go."

"I know." I stared down at my canvas high-tops, rubbing one sole over the toes of my other sneaker. But it would have been longer than that with the pre-med joint program. Two more years before finishing med school and we didn't have that kind of time.

"Not that we're not happy to have you close by." She came over and wrapped her arms around me. I squeezed her back and breathed her in. Her smell was like I remembered from middle school. A floral perfume mixed with Dad's cologne. For so long she'd smelled like nothing. Like she'd ceased to exist.

I hadn't been back more than a month, and I'd be moving into my on-campus apartment after the weekend.

"But I hope since you're not halfway across the country, you'll stop using the distance as an excuse not to have a little fun."

"I have fun." I dropped my arms. Not this again.

She eyed me suspiciously and gulped down some of her water. Dad would be back soon, ready to punch her dance card again.

"What? I definitely have fun. And I'll be working in a bar. I'm bound to have some crazy stuff happen working there."

"I'm talking about experiencing some life that doesn't revolve around the library or watching other people have drunken make-out sessions in bar booths. Maybe someone getting felt up." She gave me a look that told me she knew exactly what she was saying.

"Not what I want to hear." I cupped my hands over my ears, torn between laughing and barfing.

"What? Making out? It's something people do, Mak. Please tell me you're not still a virgin." She snapped my butt with a kitchen towel.

"Mom!" I yelped with my eyes wide. Her grin made me want to grab the dish towel and hang myself right there in the kitchen.

"What? I'm just asking. I know things were hard for you before." The sadness was back in her eyes. The one I'd gotten used to for so long it was second nature not to look into her baby blues because of the pain she'd worn plain as day. It had been so heavy at times it threatened to suffocate you where you stood. She cleared her throat, and the sadness wasn't as raw anymore.

"We weren't the best for a long time, and you held things together. I...I don't want our mistakes to stop you from having the life you deserve."

"I'm fine, Mom. I swear, and if it will make you feel better, I'll have you know I lost my virginity at the end of sophomore year to a handsome and kind junior. We were both tested beforehand and used condoms the two times we did it." I said it smugly, expecting it to be her turn to cover her ears and go running from the room; instead, she rolled her eyes.

"Make me a promise." She grabbed my hands. Her warm hands were softer than all those times she'd held my hand when a doctor came into the hospital room, bracing ourselves for the news to come. Her skin was thinner than it used to be. She was getting older and so was Dad. There was so little time left, and it stole my breath away.

"Try not to play it so safe, okay? Not with the protection part." She waved the thought away as a foregone conclusion.

"And I hope whoever you're with is kind to you, but please don't stay in your safe little bubble for the rest of your life. You need to get out there and get messy and make some mistakes. No one can be perfect all the time."

She tucked a few strands of hair back behind my ear and left her hand on the side of my face. Her warmth soaked into my skin. I had my mom back.

"No one." She stared into my eyes with all the caring and love that had been missing for so long. When you could barely take care of yourself, it was hard to have anything left for anyone else.

Tears filled my eyes, and I blinked them back. When you shouldered the weight of someone else's life and dreams, it was hard to let go and not worry. I wasn't just doing this for me. I was doing it for Daniel. He hadn't had these chances. I wouldn't throw away the opportunities he'd never get to have.

"Where are my two best girls?" Dad's voice boomed from the doorway to the kitchen as he smacked his hands together. "Smells good. Are we ready to eat?"

Mom squeezed my hand one more time and let me go.

"Ready!" Mom spun around and smiled at Dad with all the brightness back in her eyes. She was staying strong for him. It was better than the alternative.

We put all the dishes out on the table. Passing the food around, the delicious smells made my stomach grumble. I added some extra green beans and roast to my plate. With college cafeteria food right around the corner, I needed to load up on the good stuff while I could.

"Are you excited to start up the new semester?" Dad sliced into his beef and a slight tremor shook his hand.

"I'm ready. I worked hard at Stanford; I can work hard here. It will all be fine. I'm glad I'm closer too. I can drive over most weekends as long as I don't have an exam coming up." I took a bite of my mashed potatoes and caught the two of them sharing a look. My stomach dropped.

"What? What is it?" I dropped my fork as my heart leaped into my throat. Mom reached across the table and put her hand over mine, squeezing it. Everything I ate threatened to come right back up.

"Nothing is wrong, sweetheart."

"I'm fine." Dad crossed his heart with his finger. My shoulders relaxed an inch, and I glanced between the two of them.

"Then what is it?"

"Well, your father and I thought that since we don't know how long we'll have with him mobile, that maybe we should go out and have a little adventure. His doctors have given us the go-ahead and his medication is working. So, we're going on a road trip." She gave me a small smile.

"Surprise," Dad said gently, shaking his imaginary pom-poms.

"You're leaving? For how long?" My voice jumped an octave.

"We'll be back a week or so before Thanksgiving, if everything holds steady." Her hand moved up to my shoulder.

"Oh." The tightness was back in my chest. I'd transferred schools, uprooted myself from one of the best colleges in the world to be closer to my parents, and they were leaving.

"We can cancel the trip, honey. We didn't know you were coming back when we made those plans," Dad offered, taking my other hand.

I stared down at my plate before taking a breath and slapping a smile on my face.

"Don't be silly. I'll be fine. You guys should definitely go on this trip. Of course you should. I'll be here when you get back, and driving back and forth to campus was a silly idea. It will be good for me to focus and stick to campus."

They exchanged looks. I slid my hands out from under theirs and took a hearty bite of my food although it tasted like dirt in my mouth. It figured that me moving back would be when they decided to leave for a trip for a few months. I guess that's what I got for not clueing them in on my plans before I moved back.

Staring up at my ceiling in my bedroom after Mom and Dad slow danced their way to bed, I glanced over at the frame on the nightstand beside the bed. For a long time, the picture in my room had been the only one in the whole house—well, the only one anyone could see.

Daniel at nine before our lives were turned upside down. It was easy for Mom to say to live my life and go out and make mistakes, but how could I when he couldn't? How could I when it was my fault he wasn't here anymore? Going out and screwing up was a slap in the face to his memory.

Being the best I could be was the only way I coped. The only way I hadn't let myself fall apart like Mom and Dad. Even if I hadn't been able to save him. If he couldn't be here, I'd be the best I could so that no one ever thought the wrong Halstead had lived.

3

DECLAN

With my helmet firmly strapped onto my head, I powered across the ice. Sweat poured from my body as I whipped around, changing direction, controlling the puck as I stopped at the mid-rink line. This was where everything made sense. My skates dug in as I flew around the ice, stick loose in my hand as we raced from one end of the rink to the other.

The drills were meditation. Out here, under the pads and jersey, the world faded away and there was nothing but the brotherhood between me and my teammates. This was my home turf, and the guys had my back.

I waved to some of the fans who came to watch us practice. Somehow they managed not to freeze their asses off in tops that low, not that I was going to complain. It certainly made practice a bit more interesting.

I skated past the edge of the ice, staring up at the rows of blue chairs stretching to the roof of the stadium. One of the women came right up to glass, practically pressing her tits up against it, giving everyone a superb view. I shook my head, and the corners of my lips turned up. *Fucking love enthusiastic sports fans!*

Coach Mickelson blew the whistle, and we all crowded around him, grabbing our water bottles off the ledge. Heath smacked me in the back of the helmet, and I rammed my shoulder into him.

"Focus is essential," Coach said when we all made it to the bench. He and the team captain, Preston, shot us both a look. Heath became incredibly interested in the giant lights hanging over the ice, and I noticed the tape on the end of my stick needed to be redone.

"Now is not the time to get cocky. It's not the time to slack off. Being national champions for the past three years is enough to make anyone's head bigger than it should be. But letting up and not being dedicated to every practice, every game, and every class is when slipups happen." Preston's head whipped around to mine, and I gritted my teeth.

"Scrimmage. Usual teams." He blew the whistle, and we took off into our positions.

Pres skated in front of me. "You need to stop slacking, Declan. If you're trying to actually graduate, you need to get your head in the game, and I don't just mean the ice."

"I don't think the Flyers give a flying fuck about my GPA."

"Maybe not, but you should."

The assistant coach dropped the puck on center ice, and I leaned into Preston, our sticks and gloves smacking into each other as we warred for control of the puck. I got possession and spun around him, the stick loose in my hand as I sped away from him. The comforting sound of skates scraping across the ice was drowned out by my sharp breaths. Preston raced into my peripheral vision. I passed the puck to Heath and went into defense mode to help clear his way to the net.

As cocky as coach and Pres thought I was, being a team player was never an issue. If I had the shot, I was going for it, no holds barred. But if I didn't, I wasn't going to hog it and lose someone else the shot.

This team was my life. My teammates, past and present, were the closest I had to brothers. Heath, doing what he did best, handled the shit out of the puck and slapped it into the back of the net, outskating everyone, me included.

He loved to pretend he was the chill laid-back guy, but the minute he put his skates on, it was easy to see why he'd been scouted for professional play right out of high school.

Sweat poured off me as we wrapped up practice. Coach pushed us harder and harder as the start of the season approached. We still had two months until our first game, but he made sure we left every practice winded and drained. Maybe he hoped we'd be too tired to get into any trouble after. *Fat chance.*

Some of our spectators came down from their seats and buzzed around the bench as Coach gave us the rundown before we headed into the locker rooms. Rah rah, play hard, study hard, practice hard. I glanced at one of the chicks behind the glass. She was new. Maybe a transfer. Every new semester brought not only new and wonderful classes for me to work my ass off in, but also a brand-new buffet of women to sample.

"Declan!"

I whipped my head around to see everyone else clearing off the bench.

"Going, Coach." I grabbed my gear and headed for the door.

"Come see me in my office once you're all cleaned up."

Nothing good ever came of seeing the coach after practice. He used his after-practice bench sessions to ream out anyone who'd screwed up and set them straight. His office was for more epic fuckups that not even he wanted to air in front of the whole team.

I dropped my gear and got a shower in record time.

"Declan, you headed to Threes?" Heath called out, rubbing a towel over his mop of blond hair, pulling off the surfer-dude look even though it was probably forty degrees in here.

"I'll meet you there. I've got to meet with Coach."

A collective "ohhh" broke out across the locker room.

"Whatever. It's nothing." That gnawing pit in my stomach said otherwise.

"Right, and that's what Sunshine said before he was benched all season for getting arrested with that pig in the back of his truck. Been to any farms lately, Dec?" one of the other seniors called out, laughing as he slammed his locker shut. I glared at him before walking the long hallway to the coach's office.

I'd barely even been on campus after leaving the development camp. It had been my last shot to show the pro coaches they hadn't made a mistake. Archer's disapproving glare at my every move had been absent this summer, which meant I hadn't played like I'd only just put on my first set of skates. I'd dominated the summer development league and minors scrimmages.

Classes were fine for graduation. Practice, games, and traveling to others hadn't made excelling in my classes in the cards, but I'd held my own for the most part. The barbs thrown at me back in high school about fucking this up hadn't come true.

My mom had already gotten the day off almost nine

months from now and wasn't going to let any of her jobs get in her way of seeing me walk across that stage. At this point, I wished someone would pipe up about her missing work and I could tell her to quit. She wasn't working another day once I graduated. When I signed that pro contract, she was officially retired.

Wiping my sweaty palms on my jeans, I rapped my knuckles on the wood and glass door. It rattled, and I fisted my hands at my sides.

"Come in, Declan."

"Hey, Coach." I dropped into one of the chairs opposite his imposing dark wood desk that had been the stage for many chewed out asses and benchings over the years. He drummed his fingers on the manila folder under his hand. My heart pounded in my throat, and a thin sheen of sweat broke out across my forehead that had nothing to do with the intense session on the ice.

"We have a problem."

"I know you think I'm not focused enough, but I am. I'm doing what I need to do so I don't psych myself out. We can close out this season with a fourth national championship, and I want that just as much as anyone else." I said it all in a big rush, trying to head off any argument he might have had against my performance.

"It's not about that. It's about your classes."

I glanced up at him with a dumbfounded expression. "My classes?" I mean, I wasn't making Dean's List anytime soon, but I had an okay GPA.

"It seems your Sophomore Seminar grade was a fail, but the calculation on your GPA was off. They went back and did an audit." He slid the paper across the desk to me.

I heard his words, but my brain took a long ass time to put them into something I could understand. My pulse pounded and I got the watery mouth feeling. I grabbed the folder, my fingers numb.

Sophomore year had been a cluster. New course load, intense practices, the gnawing worry about being dropped from the pro development team—and something truly stupid everyone had warned me about. Trying to add a part-time job into the mix.

Archer sitting up in the glass club box, staring at me during the summer practices with eyes that matched my own hadn't helped either. Every time I saw him, I pictured his face in the back of the net. My stick delivering a painful blow, knocking his teeth right out of his head.

That searing hatred in the pit of my gut had made it hard to focus. Every missed goal with his eyes burning into me, gloating over my failure, made me want to throw off my gloves and shatter that glass. He could sit up in his ivory tower looking down on me, but I'd have the last fucking laugh. His career was over, and I'd show him I didn't need him, neither of us did.

On top of everything else that went wrong, Mom got hurt and couldn't work for a few months.

The money I'd made on my development team for the summer went straight to paying overdue bills. There wasn't anything left, so I did what I had to do.

Without telling anyone, I'd gone out and gotten a night job. Bonehead idea, but I could do everything off the ice on my own, right? *Wrong.* I'd barely passed with high enough grades to stay on the team. Actually, it looked like I hadn't. I stared down at the paper, crumpling it as I balled up my fists.

"One point. It's only one hundredth of a point. Are they seriously going to bench me over a hundredth of a point?" I raised my voice, staring down at a piece of paper that was about to derail every plan I'd had for senior year.

"You know how important graduating is." He held up his hand when he saw me ready to jump out of my chair. "I know you've been working out with a team for the past four years, but if you want your degree, be a part of this team this season and graduate, you'll need to retake the class."

"I need to be on the ice, Coach." I jabbed my finger out toward the rink. It was hard for me to catch my breath with this kick to the chest. I had that watery mouth, I'm-going-to-puke feeling going on.

"I know, son."

I bristled. I wasn't his son.

He pushed back his chair and rounded his desk. His hand was heavy on my shoulder as he squeezed it. Any amount of reassurance he was trying to give me wasn't working.

"I've talked to the deans, and we have a small work-around."

My head snapped up and my heart raced. I'd stand in the middle of the quad with an Easter bonnet on and nothing else singing nursery rhymes if it meant I was back on the team.

"What is it?"

"They are willing to let you rejoin the team, if it looks like you're doing well enough by October to get your grade where it needs to be. You still can't practice with the team, but I think you'd be able to find a few guys who wouldn't mind putting you through the ringer. Keep those grades high and do well in the class, and you won't miss a game."

I nodded sharply and stood on numb legs.

"I'll see you at that first game, because there isn't

anything in this world that's going to keep me from passing that class."

"Glad to hear it. You don't need to clean out your locker. Leave your gear in there and you can use it should you find the time to get on the ice when you're not studying your ass off."

It was like someone had filled my body with lead. My legs would barely move, and I tried to get the intense roar in my head under control. I was off the team. My hands shook as I wrapped my fingers around the cold metal bar running across the door. I pushed it out and winced against the blinding light shooting straight into my eyes from the setting sun.

It was like I was watching someone else move through the stadium and out to my car. I was a spectator in my own life. *What if Archer finds out about this*? I gritted my teeth. That SOB thought he was better than me. I'd fix this so I could join my place on the pro Philly team and make sure I picked his number for my jersey.

It would be like he was never there, erased when I did what I did on the ice, and they retired my jersey. That was my goal. Make everyone forget they'd ever heard of Archer Travis.

I sat in the driver's seat with my hands wrapped around the steering wheel, my knuckles so white it seemed like either the wheel was going to snap or my fingers were.

The blaring of "It's the End of the World as We Know It" jolted me out of my stupor. I picked up the vibrating phone and accepted the call.

"Hey, Mom."

"Hey, sweetie. You made it back to campus safely?"

"I just left practice."

"Great! I hope I'll be able to come to a few more games

this season. I switched up some of my shifts. I can't believe you're already a senior. I know you're super excited about skating, but you'll be the first in our family to graduate from college. I'm really excited to see you walk across the stage with that diploma in your hand." She said the same thing every time we talked, like she wanted to be extra sure I hadn't forgotten I was meant to graduate in eight months.

"I'm excited too." I tried to muster up as much happiness in my voice as I could. Guilt slammed right into my gut. She'd worked so hard.

Letting her down wasn't an option. The money I'd made in the development teams over the summer helped some, but not as much as a pro athlete paycheck. I wished she hadn't gotten my graduating so ingrained in her head. There was no way I could let her down.

"All those shifts and late nights and juggling jobs to see my baby out there on the ice and up on that stage. It's been a dream I didn't know if I'd ever see." Her voice cracked and managed to make me feel like an even bigger piece of shit than I already did.

"You will, Mom, and I promise I'll have a front-row seat for you at every game."

"Good, I'll be rushing to get there after I finish cleaning my last office of the day."

I jumped at the sharp knock on my window. Heath's face was pressed up against the glass. At least it wasn't his ass.

"I've got to go, Mom. The guys are here and they need me."

"Okay, talk to you soon. Love you."

"Love you too." I ended my call and opened the driver's side door.

"What did Coach want?" Heath piped up before I'd stepped foot out of the car. He leaned against the hood with his casual-guy look on, but the intensity was there in his voice. Some of the other guys from the team crowded around him.

"I'm not going to be able to practice with the team until the start of the season." I stared down at the ground and squeezed the back of my neck, bracing myself. The guys went off like a bomb.

"What?!"

"How can he do that?"

"What the hell did you do?"

"Get your shit together so you can get back out on the ice." That one came from Preston.

"You think I don't know that, Cap? That I'm not going to do what I need to do to make sure I'm skating beside you guys for the first game of the season?"

"We'll see how you feel about that tomorrow morning. This isn't just about you, Declan. This is about the team."

I clenched my jaw and stared at him as he climbed into his car. His words stung. He thought I didn't already know that. Like I wasn't sitting in my car trying to keep it together. Everyone watched Preston pull away and whipped back around to me.

"Three Streets." Heath leaned in, knowing exactly how to mellow this situation out.

I glanced over at Preston's car hitting the edge of the parking lot. *Fuck him.* "Yeah, let's do it." Classes hadn't even started yet. Tomorrow, everything would be different, and I'd work with a singular focus. Tonight, I was getting shit-faced. A solid hangover was a surefire way to put me off having a drink for a long while, and if I didn't blow off some steam, I was likely to have an aneurism.

Bring on the booze!

4

MAKENNA

They weren't kidding about needing more help with these shifts at Three Streets Bar and Grill. The tables gathered in the middle of the bar were lit by dim lighting and the flat-screen TVs strategically placed along the walls. There were various signed and framed sports jerseys hanging on the walls from championship teams of the past. Basketball, football, a few soccer jerseys, but hockey dominated the decor.

The green glass light fixtures hung from the ceiling, and the place was just run-down enough to feel homey but not seedy. It seemed like the kind of place college kids in movies would hang out. Earlier there were a few people in the booths that lined the walls, typing away on computers while they chowed down on cheesesteaks and soft pretzel bites along with other bar staples.

Three Streets was at the corner of three streets on the edge of campus. It was close to the sports stadium and had been around forever. The names scrawled on the brick wall outside went back decades.

Those first few hours of my shift had lulled me into a

false sense of security. I had no idea why the night before the first day of classes was so busy. Apparently, everyone had to have a drink right this moment. It wasn't even eight yet and the place was nearly standing room only.

I wiped the sweat from my forehead with a napkin and tugged my shirt away from my chest, trying to circulate some air on my skin. I prayed the sweat wasn't plastering the fabric to my back. I balanced a tray with five drinks on it and some nachos and rounded the bar. Dropping the glasses off at a table, I asked for their order before rushing back into the kitchen.

Working as a server was a hell of a lot different than as a barista. Fried carbs, grilled meat, and loads of cheese slid across the pass in the kitchen where the chefs put the food when it was ready for the front-of-house staff.

Weaving my way through the back-to-school crowds, I dodged flailing arms and bumps from customers. I dropped off the order at a table in the far corner of the bar after safely navigating my way there with minimal spillage. The first couple hours of my shift hadn't been so crazy. Steady but not insane.

I spun around, ready to check on my next table, when I froze like a bucket of cold water had been poured over my head. A crowd of newcomers barreled into the bar and headed straight for the one booth that had been cordoned off the entire night.

All heads turned at their entrance, and a few rounds of applause and whistles broke out from other people sitting and standing around. No one had even attempted to steal a spot there, and now I knew why. *Hockey players.* It was their spot. Their table, right in my section.

And right at the center was the one person I'd tried to convince myself I wouldn't have to face for a long time. His mop of light brown, curly hair bounced as he laughed with the other players.

His bright green eyes twinkled like he didn't have a care in the world, and why should he? Life was presented to him on a silver platter, and it was crazy of me to think anything would ever change.

He looked the same as he had in high school. *Yup, totally the same.* Not the tiniest bit different. Well, maybe a little different. He surveyed the bar, soaking it all in like a king surveying his domain. Like he'd walked off the pages of some high-fashion ad for real guys who played sports, had calluses and drove fast cars. He'd trimmed off every inch boyishness and replaced it with rock-hard hotness.

And I wanted to strangle him the second I laid eyes on him. His broad shoulders narrowed to a trim waist and strong thighs he worked out constantly on the ice. I wasn't even going anywhere near his ass. Somehow, I kept my eyes averted from that spot even though it felt like a tractor beam was trying to lock onto him.

The guys fell into their booth, and every eye was on them, including mine.

I headed back to the bar and slid in beside one of the other servers on for the night.

"Hey, Gretchen, wouldn't you like to maybe switch tables with me?" I nodded toward the new arrivals. She flipped her hair over her shoulder.

"I've been warned by Larry that I'm not allowed to serve their tables anymore."

My eyebrows shot up. I glanced between them and her. "Why?"

"Apparently dumping a pitcher of beer over the head of an asshole who doesn't return calls isn't good customer service." She made air quotes in what was probably one of the best uses of it I'd ever seen. Definitely not good customer service at all.

"Oh, okay." Fairly certain I was working with a psycho, I grabbed my tray off the bar and walked toward the surprisingly stoic bunch in the corner booth like a prisoner on the way to her execution. *Will he even remember me?* Part of me hoped he wouldn't, and the other part thought he'd better.

Holding my tray in front of me like a shield, I stood at the end of their table and glanced at the other guys. Heath's bright blond hair stuck out among the other darker-haired guys. He smiled wide in that sleepy way of his when he saw me, showing off his perfectly white teeth. Everyone always said he skated as fast as he did because he didn't want anyone to screw up his smile by getting any of his teeth knocked out.

"Well if it isn't Mak." Heath propped his chin up on his fist, his grin even bigger as Declan's head whipped around. His eyes were wide as he stared at me like I was the ghost of Christmas past.

"Makenna Halstead." He bit it out like a curse.

"In the flesh. Can I take your order?" I shifted from foot to foot as Heath grinned at me. Declan stared with a glint of anger and something else I couldn't place in his eyes, but it made my skin tingle. I stopped myself from looking at him. Dealing with him was not on my list of things I wanted to do ever, let alone tonight. The rest of the guys kept looking between them and me, trying to figure out what was going on.

"If you're not ready, I can come back." I dropped my tray and took a step away when thick, calloused fingers grazed my hand like he was going to reach out and then remembered exactly who I was. I snatched my hand back and wrapped my fingers around my notepad.

"What can I get you guys?" I turned to everyone else at the table.

They put in an order to overfeed an entire village some-where, and I jotted it all down. The whole time I felt Declan's eyes burning a hole into my chest. Gritting my teeth, I repeated the order back and scurried away to the kitchen to hand it off. The bar filled up even more as what seemed like the rest of campus arrived. Not too much longer left in my shift. Table service ended soon. *Thank God.*

The music was turned up, and it got harder to hear the customers over the roar of the crowd as they watched replays of last season's hockey games. Practically crawling up onto the tables, I got my final orders before heading to my last customers. *His table.* I'd managed to do drive-by orders at Declan's booth, dishing out drinks and food rapid-fire like the floor surrounding their booth was lava.

"It's fine. Maybe you'll find some undiscovered territory in the class."

The guys all laughed before quickly gulping down their beers when they spotted me at the end of their table. The booth had gotten a bit more crowded with a few new arrivals.

"Can I get you anything else before they close the kitchen?" I raised my voice over the din of the crowd.

"Ohh, snacks," one of the new arrivals said, grabbing the menu propped up on the table, her perfectly manicured finger running down each item. I tapped my aching foot on the floor.

"I just want like one chicken finger. Will you guys eat the rest if I only have one?" She batted her eyelashes at them, and I somehow managed not to roll my eyes so hard they'd permanently face the back of my head. I could kill a basket of chicken fingers right now. Hell, why stop at the fingers?

I'd devour the whole thing. My stomach was already growling.

A faint murmur came from the back of the booth from one of the other women wrapped around Declan's arm. I gritted my teeth and tried to keep my smile on. It didn't matter what he did or who hung all over him. I was thrown back into high school all over again. It wasn't my business, and I didn't care.

"I can't hear you." I cupped my hand over my ear.

"I'm not being caught dead ordering that drink. You better speak up!" Declan laughed and picked up his beer gulping it down until there was nothing but foam left. His Adam's apple bobbed, and I averted my gaze as he tried to hypnotize me with his broad shoulders straining under his t-shirt. *Damnit, stop looking at him!*

I leaned over the table, trying to get her order and get the hell out of there. She giggled and put her hand on Declan's shoulder to bend over the table and get closer.

"I'll have a Buttery Nipple and a Sex on the Beach." She twirled her finger around her hair and plopped back down in her seat next to Declan, licking her lips and staring at him like she wanted to mount him right there.

"Coming right up."

I gathered the rest of the food and drinks, wove my way through the intense crowd, and dropped them off at the table.

"But what do you mean you're not going to be practicing?" came a high-pitched wail from the booth. It seemed like she had the ability to speak over the volume of a hummingbird when she wanted to. Declan glared at Heath, who shrugged.

"It's fine. I'll miss a few until I finish a class requirement thing." Declan elbowed Heath, who brushed it off like he'd always done with everything. Crazy how so many things changed, but some always stayed the same.

It looked like the Kings didn't always come out on top. I slid the baskets of chicken fingers and fries and their drinks across the table, feeling vindicated.

"Looks like your slacking has finally caught up with you." I couldn't hold back the comment or my smirk.

He whipped his head around. Heath ducked his head and was incredibly interested in the basket of food slid under his nose. Declan's eyes turned icy cold as he glared at me.

"Hey, don't say that about him! He's amazing out on the ice!" His fan club piped up, but he lifted his hand, silencing them.

"Did you flunk out of Stanford, Books? Is that why you're here serving us beers at the same school you wouldn't even deign to apply to instead of out in California soaking up the sun." His fist was clenched tight on the table.

"My transfer was a choice, Declan. And I don't need groupies to fight my battles for me. You going to send them out onto the ice when you don't make the cut?"

One of the guys spit his beer out, showering the girls in the hoppy brew.

"Hey!" one of them shouted. I slid the check onto the table, fully expecting to get stiffed and definitely no tip, but I was willing to pay that price.

The look on his face had been enough to make it a successful night for me. I hummed my way back to the kitchen and ran through the closing checklist Larry had given me. I went back out into the bar, and Heath stood against the wall right outside the swinging doors with the check and some cash.

"You know, you two are always needling each other. I

think you're probably a lot more alike than you think." His blond hair hung down over his eyes a bit.

"Declan and I have nothing in common. Never have. Never will."

"Maybe. Maybe not. See you around, Mak." He handed over the check and disappeared back into the undulating mass of people that had taken over the place. I counted the cash to make sure I hadn't been shorted and was pleasantly surprised that there was a full 25 percent tip. My head shot up, but there wasn't a spot of Heath's honeyed hair anywhere to be seen.

Heath had always been a lovable guy, and it was nice of him to try to smooth things over between me and Declan, but that wasn't happening. Making enemies of regulars probably wasn't a good idea, but he got under my skin like no one else could. I'd never mouthed off, flipped off, or told off anyone else in my life, but for some reason it was easy with Declan.

The one time we hadn't been at each other's throats was because he was apparently drunk. It seemed that was the only way he could even think of getting near me. Touching me. I shook my head not ready for even more memories to come slamming home.

Grabbing a staff portion of food, I clocked out and headed to my car, parked out back. The smell of the cheesesteak and fries wafted out of the container, and even after being surrounded by it for hours, my stomach rumbled. I'd been too freaked out about my first day to eat anything. *Big mistake.*

Serving mountains of food all night was torture. Cheesesteaks were one thing I'd missed on the West Coast. I have no idea who told them that cheesesteaks had peppers in them, but they were dead wrong. Cheese, meat and grilled onions if you were feeling fancy.

Stealing a fry here or there wasn't going to cut it. I needed to go to town on a cheesesteak. My feet ached, and my back needed a serious crack, but I'd made it through the entire shift unscathed. My shoes were splashed with beer from the more than tipsy students as I'd finished up the evening. Maybe I should invest in a rain slicker.

Driving all the way to the other side of campus with this precious cargo was not an option. My mouth watered as I popped open the lid to the container. Glorious fries, ketchup, and the greasiest cheesesteak ever called my name. If I'd held the foil up to the side of my face, I swear it would have said, *Mak, we've been waiting for you.*

I sat sideways in the open driver's side seat of my car with my feet stretched out in front of me on the pavement. Shoving a handful of fries into my mouth, I could barely hold back my moan. Salt, carbs, ketchup. *What more could a girl ask for?* I slid my shoes off and wiggled my toes, resting them on top. The summer heat gave way to a taste of the fall temperatures to come this late at night.

My ears readjusted to the normal volume level outside. The parking lot wasn't too packed, which made sense since most people walked from elsewhere on campus so they could drink to their heart's content. Beer was still that one drink I'd never gotten used to. Trying it once or twice over the years had been more than enough for me to know it wasn't going to happen. Beer and I were mortal enemies.

A heating-lamp cheesesteak and lukewarm fries had never tasted so good. The greasy, cheesy flavor was what I needed. Even the bread was amazing. So good to be home. I did a happy dance in my seat as I devoured the whole thing.

I leaned back against my seat and let out a sigh. This was going to be a long semester.

The back door of the bar flew open, and a few people poured out. Their laughter bounced off the brick wall of the building and echoed out into the warm evening air. *Time to go.* Heels and sneakers clacked and squeaked as people wove in between the cars in the lot.

I crumpled up my cheesesteak foil and fry container and spotted a trash can a few feet away. Lifting my hand, I flicked my wrist, and watched the balled-up trash sailed through the air and hit the rim of the can. It ran along the edge before the satisfying *thunk* as it fell inside.

"Yes!" I pumped my fist overhead with a round of mock crowd applause.

"Nice shot, Books." I jumped in my seat as I peered up at my ghost of high schools past haunting me in the parking lot with his mossy green eyes, sun-kissed freckles and sleek muscled body, which were hot if I were into that kind of thing. *Who the hell was I kidding?*

I bent down and slid my aching feet into my borderline destroyed sneakers.

"What? I can't give you a compliment?" He leaned against one of the cars parked nearby.

I tugged the tongue out of the high-tops and didn't even bother lacing them up.

"I would have thought compliments fell outside your self-absorbed personal bubble that doesn't extend past the hockey rink."

"Glad to see you've upped your levels of snark over the years."

"Glad to see you haven't changed one bit since the last time we saw each other." His words ringing in my head, *"Go off and have your perfect little life, and I can't wait until it all comes crashing down on you."* He had no idea what it was like to struggle and watch the people around you suffer.

"I wouldn't say that. While I know I was built like a Greek god back in high school, I've definitely improved the mold since then." I glanced up as he flexed one arm, annoyed that I'd noticed the same thing only a minute ago. He might have been hot, but that was where it ended.

"Is this your attempt at being friendly or something?" I tilted my head to the side, trying to figure out his angle.

"And why would I be doing that?"

"I have no freaking clue. You're the one out here making small talk."

"I found it, Dec." One of the girls from the booth popped up from behind the car he leaned against. "I wouldn't want to forget this for tonight."

I didn't even look up to see what it was. If I was lucky, it was a butt plug for Declan, and he'd be in for a rough night. He pushed off the car, glancing behind him as I slammed my door shut. Not wanting him to think I was run off by his little groupie, I rolled down my window.

"I'm working here now and I'm going to school here too, but that doesn't mean we have to see each other any more than necessary. If I'm your waitress, I'll be as nice as I am to any other customer, but if you see me walking on campus, don't be shocked if I turn around and go the other way." He continued to stare at me like he was trying to use my old laser vision trick against me, and I squirmed a little in my seat. "No offense."

"None taken."

The girl from the car came around to his side and wrapped her arms around his waist, hanging on him like a Christmas ornament. "By the way," she said, snuggling into Declan like it was a cold winter's night, "you have some ketchup on your chin." She pointed to a spot on her face, mirroring the spot on mine, and my tongue shot out before I could stop it. Declan opened his mouth like he wanted to say something, but I rolled my window up, keeping my eyes straight ahead. Totally not pissed at all about trying to come off as a super bitch with my face drenched in ketchup.

The pair walked back toward the bar, and I flipped down my visor to check out the damage in the mirror. Grabbing some napkins from the center console, I shook my head. *Of course!* I rubbed the remnants of my cheesesteak off my face and rested my forehead against the steering wheel. At least I'd only have to see him after games if they came to the bar. Maybe I'd be on a shift with someone who hadn't gone full-on psycho ex on them and I could swap tables.

It would be fine, and I could totally handle Declan McAvoy in small doses. *Totally.*

5

DECLAN

The throbbing pounding in my head meant it took me a few minutes to realize I wasn't alone in my bed. I dropped back against the pillow and winced as pain shot straight through my skull. It was like someone took a metal trash can and whacked it as hard and as fast as they could.

My evening antics came filtering back to me through the hangover haze. The talk with Coach. That can't-breathe-because-I've-just-been-kicked-off-the-team feeling. The dull pit in the bottom of my stomach that Archer would find out.

Heading to Three Streets and running into Makenna Halstead of all people. Like the universe wanted to kick me when I was down, she'd swanned in with her big blue eyes behind those glasses and shooting her usual barbs at me. *Screw her!*

It was like senior year all over again, but her predictions were coming true. Truer than she probably realized. Spotting her back behind the bar sitting in her car destroying that cheesesteak had made me laugh. It was like seeing the queen trip or something. She was human. The glimpse I'd gotten of that back at prom came rushing back to me. She ate and smeared ketchup all over her face like a mere mortal. And she looked cute doing it—until she slipped right back into evil-robot mode.

I didn't need to think about her. I needed to get my head together and not screw things up even more. Going out to a club after the bar had not been a good plan, and bringing this chick home had been an even worse idea. Once the blonde in my bed found out we played hockey, she'd been relentless, practically giving me a lap dance in the club and suggesting I help her home in a taxi before conveniently being locked out of her place. It hadn't been my brightest of ideas. It was a mistake going out. I had class this morning.

Her hair brushed against my chest, tickling my skin. It annoyed the shit out of me. I pushed her head off me, letting it fall to the bed.

She groaned and rolled over as I slid out of bed, searching the floor for some jeans or sweats. Stupid to let her stay here. How far had the apple fallen from the tree? It was like I was trying to prove I was no better than Archer, letting myself get distracted like this. Now I had to get her out. I jumped into my sweats and checked the time on the clock on my desk.

Fuck!

Past eleven. I'd already missed my first class of the day. Not exactly getting into responsible mode. I took out a clean shirt from my dresser and slammed the drawer shut. She rolled over and stretched. No time for the sleeping beauty routine.

I raced around my room, swiped my bag off the back of my chair and flung the books I'd picked up at the bookstore into my backpack. My phone was nowhere to be found. I shifted everything around on the floor and desk, but still no phone. Maybe it was downstairs. With my workout clothes jammed into my duffel, I had everything I'd need for the day.

My head throbbed as I snagged my hat off my doorknob. I walked over to the bed, not trying to keep my steps light at all. Whatever her name was sat up with the sheet wrapped around her chest.

"Hey, you're up early." One of her fake eyelashes had come loose and gave her a double-eyelid look.

"I have to get to class. I'm already late." I adjusted my bag on my back in the universal I-have-somewhere-to-be move.

"I was hoping we'd have a little morning fun since we didn't get to have any last night." Her fingers grazed my belt loop, but I jumped back before she could get me in her grasp. Passing out while she stripped was probably the best thing that had happened to me yesterday. I figured she'd have left, but it seemed persistence was her strong suit.

"Listen, I've got to go to class, so it's probably best that you get dressed and head out." I backed out of the room, making sure there wasn't anything valuable or breakable out in plain view. "I'll call you later." I turned and headed down the stairs. A faint "But you don't have my number..." filtered after me as I took the steps two at a time.

I slammed into Heath rounding the bottom of the stairs, and his searing-hot coffee splashed all over my arms.

"What the hell, man?" My angry red skin throbbed to go along with the pounding in my head.

"Sleeping in?" He rubbed his bleary red eyes and yawned.

"Accidentally and now I'm late. Have you seen my phone?" I glanced around the living room.

"I think it's on the kitchen table. It was going crazy when I was getting my coffee." He rubbed his bleary eyes.

"Why didn't you come get me?" I stormed past him and into the kitchen. Notification after notification from Preston. Leaning my head against the cabinets, I closed my eyes as the room spun around me. This semester was off to an awesome start.

I shot off a quick message to Preston and grabbed a mug, filling it to the brim with the dark, piping-hot ambrosia. Heath slid a tall glass of cold water and a couple white pills along the counter.

"If you're going to make it through classes, you're going to need these."

"Thanks." I downed the pills and the water, slapped a lid on my cup and backed out of the kitchen. "By the way there is a half-naked hungover chick upstairs. Please make sure she doesn't steal anything or otherwise destroy the place. You're the man, bye." I slammed the front door in his wide-eyed face and gingerly jogged down the steps, heading to campus.

I made it to my second class of the day with seconds to spare and grabbed a seat at the back, trying to keep the nausea at bay. Without meaning to, I found myself checking out the room and watching the door, ready to bolt if Mak showed her face.

No way was I going to sit through an entire semester with her trying to roast me into kindling in one-hour chunks. My stomach threatened a revolt at least a couple times throughout our review of the syllabus and the professor's expectations. I sank in my seat with my hat pulled down low, riding out the rest of the class as the professor droned on. This was important stuff, but being present was as good as it was going to get right then. I'd go to the professor's office hours to make sure he didn't think I was going to slack during the semester.

The midday sun didn't send me scurrying back into the shadows like a vampire, so my booze-filled night was finally wearing off. My drunk legs were washed away with a burger at lunch, so the queasiness was gone.

My last class wasn't until almost five, which meant I had time to kill. I needed to burn the last of this hangover out of my system. Pushing through the first set of double doors of the gym, I was hit by the familiar smell of sweat and metal that filled the air. The worries faded away. The only place I could completely tune out the rest of the world was out on the ice, but the gym was a close second.

Heath burst through the doors, a wide smile on his face as always, even if he was drenched in sweat.

"Your mattress and sheets and the rest of your stuff were in a charred pile when you left this morning, right?"

My stomach dropped as he slapped me on the back, throwing his head back, laughing.

"Don't screw with me like that."

"Relax. That's what you get for leaving me to shepherd your leftovers out in the morning. You'll be happy to know the history major left without much of a fuss but did leave her number behind."

I wouldn't be using it. There was too much going on in my life, and I didn't need the distraction of female attention right now.

"I'll catch you back at the house. When's your last class?" I shifted my bag on my shoulder.

"It's at five, but I have to go to the greenhouse to check on a few things."

"Why weren't you a kinesiology major like every other athlete in this school?"

"It's those sexy buds. It's what gets me hard." He grabbed his junk and stuck out his tongue, walking backward to the doors leading outside. I flipped him the bird and pushed through the doors to the gym, coming face-to-face with the last person I wanted to see.

"Could have warned me,' I mumbled under my breath, glancing back over my shoulder to see Heath waving through the small window in the gym door. Preston dropped his free weights, the *clank* echoing in the sprawling room, and made a beeline straight for me.

I dropped my bag on the floor, took off my hat and braced myself for the impending reaming he'd had been gearing up for all day.

"I know. Before you start, I know. Not the best way to start off the semester. I needed to blow off some steam and things got a little out of hand last night."

"Out of hand? Do you want to stay off the team? Do you want to wash out after making it this far?"

I ran my hands over my face and into my hair, threading my fingers behind my head.

"What do you want me to say? I fucked up. It's what I do, right?"

He dropped onto the weight bench beside me.

"You have a shot, man. You're going to the pros one way or another—I've seen you out on the ice—but you didn't have to come to college. You could have gone to the development teams and the minors or gone straight there. You have this chance to get your degree and play the game you love. You're in the home stretch."

No one knew that getting drafted right away had been my plan. It had been a good plan until life in its infinite wisdom felt I needed a kick to the teeth that left me bruised and bloodied. Archer had been there almost every day, and every day I'd played like shit. I was lucky they'd kept me on this long.

Throw in my mom's face when she found out I'd made it into college and it made that small kernel of shame grow a bit bigger. If college was where I had to be, I was doing this for her, so she could see me walk across that graduation stage and finally stop working so hard.

"It won't happen again. I only missed one class, and the most important one isn't until tonight."

"Who do you have?" He handed me a set of forty-pound dumbbells.

"Alcott." I lifted them in bicep curls letting the muscle strain wash away the last of my hangover.

He let out a low whistle. "Be careful. That guy has a serious reputation when it comes to athletes. He will not take any shit, especially if he knows you failed that class before."

Exactly the kind of person I needed in control of my ability to play during the season.

"Noted. You going first?" I gestured to the weight bench with the hundreds of pounds of weights hanging above it.

"Hell no, Heath left without putting them back. I'd like to have use of my arms for the next few weeks, but be my guest. I'll see how your arms are after this workout, and maybe I'll let you spot me." He grinned and rested his hands on the metal bar.

"You're not even going to bench this? Why the hell would I?"

"Got to keep you in tip-top shape, right? Plus, I got here early and I'm almost finished with my workout. You have some serious mistakes to burn off. Maybe I should keep tiring your ass out with these unsanctioned workouts and you'll be so exhausted you won't even be able to think about partying."

"I can take anything you can dish out, Cap." I matched his smile and slid under the bench. I might not have been practicing with the guys, but at least Preston had my back. As much as he bothered the shit out of me and felt more like a nagging mom sometimes, at least I knew I was still part of the team.

What felt like twelve hours later, I finally tapped out. I glanced up at the clock; I'd barely made it seventy minutes under Preston's torture circuit. I never thought I'd long for Coach's sessions, but if this was how Preston was going to run things while I was benched, I needed to get back on the team yesterday. Everything ached as I headed into the shower.

There was enough time to grab some more food and check out when my next assignments were due before the last class. *Sophomore Seminar.* My first time around, I'd gotten back from the summer hockey session and my first run-in with Archer.

His voice came out deep and rough behind me as I left the locker room after showering up. "You think because you've got my blood pumping through your veins that you deserve a spot on this team?"

My head snapped up and my hands clenched into fists. "Does this mean you're acknowledging me as your kid?"

He made a gruff sound and glared at me.

"Why are you even here? Why do you care? You haven't cared for nineteen years; why show up here after every practice?" The words I'd gone over time and time again in my head disappeared the minute I came face-to-face with him. He would always lurk in the box or in the stands while I practiced with the team and leave the second my skates left the ice.

"You think you can do half what I did on this team? You think anyone will remember your name after you blow it?"

The urge to wipe his smug smile off his face nearly overpowered me. "If I do, what the hell does it have to do with you? You're nothing to me. You're no one." My heart hammered in my chest. I could fight with the best of them out on the ice, but when it came to Archer, the sperm donor who'd made my mom cry, it was like my body didn't want to cooperate.

"You sure as hell seem to care when you're always looking for me in the stands. You care, son."

"Don't ever fucking call me 'son' again." I clenched my jaw because he was right. And I hated that I even looked, that I even cared, but him calling me son... *I was seconds away from slamming my fist into his face.*

"You're right. A real son of mine wouldn't be out there fucking up his chance at the pros."

I took a step toward him, ready to lay him out.

One of the coaches popped his head out of the office and called to me. "Declan. Can we talk to you a minute? Hey, Travis, what are you doing here?"

My breath came out heavy, almost like a pant, as I stood toe to toe with my father. My hands clenched so tight my fingers ached.

"Nothing. Absolutely nothing," he said, staring straight at me before turning on his smug smile I'd seen a hundred times and walking off with his hands shoved in his pockets, whistling away.

Tears I never wanted to cry prickled the backs of my eyes. I vibrated with anger, blinking them back. I'd never let him see me cry. Never shed a damn tear for him.

So, I was making it to the pros if it killed me, starting with my next class. Whatever it took. I was going to do whatever it took and then wipe that smug grin off his face one way or another.

6

MAKENNA

My feet ached as I climbed out of bed, turning off my alarm. I slid on my sneakers, put my hair up into a ponytail. My hair was that weird in between where it wasn't quite red or blonde given the lighting. Checking out the window, I grabbed my phone and earbuds and headed out as the sun rose over the horizon. A run was the perfect way to start the day and get my head on straight.

Transferring as a senior had been a monumentally stupid move. I knew it when I did it, but there were some times when a stupid move made sense. At least in my head. What it didn't do was make graduating on time as easy as it should be. While I had more than enough credits from Stanford, there were certain required courses I needed to take at UPhil, even if I was way past them.

Plus, the BA/MD program meant I was taking some medical school classes since I'd been provisionally accepted. I'd gotten into a similar program back at Stanford. It meant it was only supposed to take me six years to graduate med school by combining some of the course work.

I'd managed to take care of a bunch over the summer, but there was one I had to take on campus. A special course offered only there. *Sophomore Seminar.* Talk about embarrassing. Being in a class full of sophomores as a senior wasn't exactly my idea of fun, but I'd made my bed; I had to lie in it. I'd done everything in my power, bringing in every syllabus from my old courses to show that they were similar and I'd covered similar topics. The deans wouldn't budge.

The circuit around campus took me past a few bleary-eyed people stumbling down the paths that crisscrossed the quad. The warm summer air breezed past me. I wove my way through campus and looked forward to the changing seasons. The vibrant colors of the fall leaves were something I'd missed in California.

Freshly cut grass squished under my sneakers as I took a shortcut back to the apartment. Birds chirped in the morning sky, and it was moments like this that were so perfect it made it hard to breathe.

Moments where I looked around at the flowers and squirrels running up trees and it was like the world stopped moving for a few seconds. The tears always came in those moments. I wiped them away with the back of my hand and picked up the pace past a few guys in rumpled clothes and girls carrying their shoes. Even on a school night, most of the campus had only come back the night before, so there were plenty of walk-of-shamers.

I got back to the apartment, and my roommates were still asleep. Tiptoeing into the kitchen, I made my egg-white omelet and fruit smoothie. There were a few emails from professors with some beginning of the semester notes. I scrolled through my phone, triple checked my schedule, and finished my food. Washing and drying my dishes, I tucked them back into the cabinets and went to my room.

This apartment had been a find. Each room had its own bathroom, which was pretty much unheard of for anywhere a college student would stay. It had been three single efficiency apartments that they combined into one giant one. Tracy and Fiona had needed a third, and I didn't seem like too much of a psycho, in their words, so I'd gotten the spot.

We were still in the I'm-trying-to-figure-out-if-you're-going-to-go-apeshit-and-smother-me-with-a-pillow-in-my-sleep mode, but so far so good. I took a shower, put on the clothes I'd laid out the night before and put on a little bit of makeup. My phone buzzed, and I checked the time. *Perfect.*

I triple checked my books, folders, and binders for each class and slid my backpack on. Glancing at myself in the mirror, I ran my hands over my skirt and pulled my ponytail from under my backpack strap. It was going to be a good day. Making this move had been the right choice. Fine, my parents were traveling across country in an RV and not close by if something happened to Dad, but that was fine. Everything would be fine. I was fine.

My morning classes all went as planned. Senior seminars and labs I needed to meet my graduation requirements were spread throughout the day. The professors had been interested in the work I'd done at Stanford, and there wasn't anything on the syllabi that freaked me out.

After grabbing some lunch in one of the dining halls, where I went over my calendar and put in timelines for completing my projects and lab work, I met up with Tracy, who was still wearing her sunglasses.

"He got everyone to give me a standing ovation when I rolled into class." She sipped out of her thermos, which I was only half sure wasn't filled with booze. "He said if I could make it to class looking like I did, there was no excuse for any of them. I mean, it's not *that* obvious I was super drunk this morning, is it?" She peered at me over her sunglasses.

"Your dress is inside out." I took a sip of my water, trying my best to hold back my laugh.

She glanced down and threw her hands up in defeat. "Damn it. Not again."

Tracy tagged along as I ran a few errands on campus. Somehow her class schedule didn't seem nearly as packed as mine. Stopping by the library before class, I requested a few books I couldn't find online that would help with some of my research during the semester. I also found out when I'd be able to grab a study room. The only wild card in my schedule was Sophomore Seminar.

I figured it would be no problem, but Tracy decided to fill me in. We strolled past people spread out on the lawn on towels even though the sun was setting. A few guys threw Frisbees back and forth without their shirts on, soaking up the last bits of summer we had left.

"Alcott is a notorious hard-ass. He's so pissed off all the time. He was a history PhD student for like ten years and figured once he graduated, they would let him leave the Sophomore Seminar behind. No such luck, so everyone is stuck with his perpetual anger and grouchiness." Tracy's warning came out in hushed tones. The way she spoke, it was like he was a feared sea creature put on the earth to sink a few sophomore GPAs like a kraken from the deep.

"I'm made for those types of professors. I've never had a professor or a teacher I couldn't work with. It won't be a problem." I hadn't maintained a 3.97 GPA by letting a few testy professors get in my way.

"He doesn't accept late work or excuses for anything," she said with her voice low.

I leaned in conspiratorially. "It's okay because I never turn anything in late." And I hadn't. Freshman year in California all on my own, I'd gotten the flu. I wouldn't have been surprised if I'd started bleeding from my eyes. Everything hurt, I could barely keep my eyes open but I managed to turn in my final papers before I drove home for the semester break.

"I'm trying to warn you. Be careful with this guy."

"Thanks for the warning, and I'll make sure I finish all his stuff extra early."

I walked into the room ten minutes before class began. It was usually a pretty good buffer, but the room was packed. My stomach dropped, and I triple checked the time. No, I was definitely early. It looked like I wasn't the only one who'd gotten the memo on Alcott.

The small room was stuffed with desks and fresh-faced sophomores who looked like they were about to be lowered into a vat of acid. His reputation most definitely preceded him. There were only two empty desks available, smack-dab front and center in the room.

The door swung open behind me. Before I could even turn around, something heavy slammed into my back. Tripping over my own feet, I grabbed on to one of the desks to steady myself as I was nearly bowled over by someone pushing me out of the way like I wasn't even there.

"Take your seats," came the gruff voice from the professor. My heart in my throat, I slid into the first empty desk and tried to settle myself. Almost taking a header in front of a class full of sophomores—or anyone, for that matter—wasn't exactly my idea of a fun way to start the semester.

I ran my sweaty palms over my skirt, smoothing it under

the desk. Sufficiently de-sweatified, I took out my notepad as the professor hefted his massive bag up onto his desk and took out thick packets of paper and slammed them down on the desk with an ominous *thud*.

Get yourself together! Things were fine. This was fine.

Until they weren't fine. Alcott finished his paper stacking and stood, staring down the whole class, ready to deliver what I could only imagine would be a soul-crushing speech, when the door swung open.

Like I'd conjured my worst nightmare to go along with the professor who already made me hate this class, the last person I ever wanted to be stuck in a class with swanned into the room smack-dab on the hour.

Declan strode into my final class of the day like he walked into every room, chest first. Even into a Sophomore Seminar where he should be hiding his face, he strode in like he owned the place. My spine went stock straight, and the hairs on the back of my neck rose as his gaze swept over the class and landed on me.

The one empty seat in the closet-sized classroom was beside me. *Of course it was.* He stopped and pivoted like he was thinking of walking right back out before a look of resignation settled over his face. It was probably the same one on mine.

The desk-chair combo scraped across the floor as Declan dragged it away, trying to get a few millimeters farther away from my seat. *Good luck with that.* The desks barely fit as it was.

"This semester because the administration has decided to yet again saddle me with this class, I'm changing things up." Professor Alcott looked every bit the part of a disaffected academic. He wore a tweed blazer even though it was at least eighty degrees in the pressure cooker of a room. The jacket was frayed and thinning in some parts.

"Since I don't want to read all your papers, I'm pairing you up. You will have a partner for the duration of the class. All your assignments will be completed together."

A creeping sense of dread settled over me. *Please not him. Please not him.* The professor called out the names of different students in the class, walking around the room and giving everyone a sheet of paper with their partner's contact information on it.

"Makenna Halstead." I raised my hand. "And you must be Declan McAvoy." He slid the pieces of paper onto our desks at the same time, and my stomach dropped. "Since you two are seniors and have somehow made it this far without passing this class, I wouldn't want to subject you to anyone else. Meet your new partners."

His dig for thinking I had actually failed a class didn't even land because whooshing blood pounding in my ears drowned out everything else except the words *new partners*.

"This is permanent. I don't want to hear any whining about wanting to switch or wanting to be with your BFF or bestie or whatever the hell you call friends nowadays. These are your partners. Don't come complaining to me about anything, unless they are actively trying to murder you. Past attempts don't count. Get the work done. That's the most important thing. In life, you don't get to do a lot of shit you want to do, but you have to make it work."

My hands tightened around the paper he'd sat in front of me. The gentle crunching as I crumpled the edges was the only sound other than the frightened breaths of everyone around me. I refused to look at Declan and kept my eyes on the professor trying to figure out what fresh hell he was ready to unleash on the class. This wasn't going to work. I could not be partners with Declan.

Glancing down at the wrinkled paper on my desk, I smoothed out the edges.

"What's the matter, Books? Afraid my irresponsibility will rub off on you? Look at you, already creasing your papers. Next you'll be coloring outside the lines and maybe even leaving the house without an emergency supply kit for a small village." He glanced down at my bag and backpack combo, and I reflexively followed his gaze.

The pen sticking out of his mouth clicked on his teeth, and my gaze narrowed, zeroing in on him, his mouth, and his disgusting habit. Yes, I carried around a lot of stuff, but it was the first day. Preparation was key.

Gritting my teeth, I sat up straight and waited for the professor to finish his droning speech. He handed out the thick packets sitting on his desk, and the mood in the room edged further into resignation that this level of suckage would only grow throughout the semester.

I could handle the workload. I could handle a hard-ass professor. I could not handle putting my GPA in the hands of someone like Declan. *My future.* I'd go to office hours the first chance I got.

"That's all. I'll see you next week after you've turned in your first assignment."

No one moved until the professor closed his bag and strode out of the door, the happiest he'd been since he walked in.

A hot and heavy presence pressed in close beside me as Declan rested his arms on the edge of my desk.

"When do you want to meet, Books?" he said around the chewed-on pen tucked in the side of his mouth. I took a few calming breaths and packed up my stuff.

"Let's try to do this through e-mail and a shared doc online. Maybe that's the best way to handle this." I put on a smile so weak a stiff breeze would have blown it away.

Declan made a *tsk*ing sound that fanned the embers of the annoyance that had been building since he stepped foot in the classroom.

"Check out the first line of the assignment." He slid it across my desk, and I glanced over at it. In big bold letters it read: *YOU MUST MEET IN PERSON. THE WORLD IS MADE UP OF PEOPLE MEETING FACE-TO-FACE. DEAL WITH IT.*

Thanks, Professor.

7

DECLAN

Sophomore Seminar was bad enough but ending up partnered with Makenna was a cosmic kick in the balls with everything else going on. But it was almost worth it to be Mak's partner for the look of annoyance on her face. She didn't want to be paired up with me any more than I wanted to be paired up with her, but I'd take pleasure in her irritation.

I held back my laugh as she crumpled her paper and tried to smooth it out. She was so tightly wound it would be a miracle if she didn't have a heart attack by the time she was thirty. Pointing out that we had to meet in person gave me some sick satisfaction that at least this class would be entertaining, if nothing else.

She packed up her giant bags like she was a Sherpa setting out to conquer the treachery of Mount Everest, and I was tempted to help her with them but I figured I might pull back a nub. Walking behind her as we left class, I followed as she rushed out of the building.

People walking by high-fived me or waved, and I waved

back but didn't stop because I didn't want to lose Mak, who was walking like someone had started a brushfire behind her.

I don't even know if she was leading us somewhere in particular or storming off, driven by her blinding rage. She might not even have known I was still there from the deep thought grooves creased in her forehead.

"Are we going somewhere in particular? Or were you trying to walk me somewhere private to murder me and secure yourself a new partner."

She jumped at the sound of my voice, so maybe she hadn't remembered I was there. Blow to the ego.

"I reserved a room in the library for after class. I need to be there before five minutes after six or they will give it away."

"Which library?"

"Samuelson."

"Why the hell did you book a library clear across campus when Harbin Library is right there?"

She made an exasperated sound. "Because I didn't know!" She threw her hands up. "I didn't realize the buildings were so far apart when I planned my schedule out for the day, and by the time I realized it, all the rooms in Harbin were booked."

I checked the time, and we had about two minutes to get there. Not really knowing what the big deal was, I didn't want to start things off on an even worse foot with her. Lumbering under the collective weight of a small mining town, she wasn't going to make it there.

"Here, let me help." I grabbed one of the bags off her shoulder without asking. She grabbed for the strap, but it slipped through her fingers. I slung her bag of bricks onto my back.

"Let's go, Books. We've got two minutes." I picked up the pace, and she scrambled behind me to keep up as we wove through the early evening dinner crowd crossing campus. The shining lights of the library up ahead meant the sweat trickling down my back was worth it. I swear she was training for some kind of Iron Man race with this bag.

We both dropped our bags onto the library floor at exactly six minutes after. I went in search of some water. Maybe I should have Mak weight train me. When I came back, the perky, curly-haired student worker behind the desk shook her head as Mak slid her ID card across the counter.

"I came all the way across campus. I need this study room." She held out her ID card to the person on the other side of the counter like she wasn't going to take no for an answer.

"The policy is five minutes."

I stepped up beside Mak, and the girl's eyes got wide. I glanced down at her name tag. *Amanda.*

"But what's a little rule bending between friends, Amanda. It's actually my fault. I was talking to a few people about the upcoming season, and Mak was waiting for me. I held her up, and that's why we were late." I threw on the smile that got me out of all kinds of shit, and she made that telltale giggle-snort thing that let me know I had her.

"What do you say you bend the rules a little and let her have the room?"

The girl glanced between the two of us and sighed.

"Okay, yeah, it's fine." She peeked up at me as she typed away on the computer and took Mak's ID card again. Mak grabbed her bags off the floor and trudged to the elevators after getting her room assignment.

Jabbing the button for the third floor like it had killed

her dog, she stood in front of the doors waiting for it to arrive. She crossed her arms over her chest, her shoulders looking like they were going to buckle under the weight of the bags.

"Do I get a thank you?"

"Thank you," she bit out.

"Don't sound so happy about it." I leaned against the wall beside the slowest elevators known to man. "So, what's the big deal about this study room? Why the rush?"

"It's a room reservation for the entire semester, and this is the closest library to my apartment. While my roommates seem fine now, I wanted a place I could go to study if they were too loud. And usually the graduate students snag these rooms early, so I needed to get one right away."

"Gotcha. You really cover all your bases, huh?"

I meant it as a genuine compliment, but she didn't seem to take it that way, glaring at me as the elevator arrived and the doors opened. I stepped in behind her, and she moved to the far side of the elevator like she'd climbed on board with a leper.

The elevator shook and groaned as it climbed to the third floor. The musty-paper smell was even stronger up here. Half the lights didn't turn on as we passed by. It was almost completely deserted, but the rooms lining the outside of the floor were already filled with stacks of books, personal items, and everything else a person who lived at the library would need.

Mak stopped in front of a room and used her ID card to open the door and stepped inside. The door beside hers swung open, and a blonde popped her head out. Her eyes got big when she spotted me, and her cheeks turned beet red.

"Hi, I'm Angel. It looks like we're neighbors." She stuck

her hand out. I hesitated and extended my arm. The stars were already in Angel's eyes, and I wasn't interested, not even a little bit. Our introductions were interrupted when Mak came back to the door.

"He's not your new neighbor. He's popping in for a quick visit." She glared at me and motioned with her head for me to go inside, spinning around and intercepting poor Angel's hand.

"Oh, right. Nice to meet you." She leaned in past Mak and waved to me. "And you too."

Mak closed the door and leaned against it with her arms crossed over her chest. When she leaned back like that, it had the unfortunate—well, not for me—consequence of pushing her tits up even higher. I found my gaze drifting down to them while trying to avoid the face-melting glare in her eyes.

Pushing off the door, she started digging through her Sherpa bags, unloading more books than one of the shelves in this library. I couldn't help but glance at her legs as she bent over to take things out. Nice legs, better than nice, even. Pretty spectacular. Too bad they were attached to someone so full of herself I was surprised she could barely see out her eyeballs.

I stared up at the ceiling because the thoughts I was having were not the thoughts you had about a woman who was probably going to do everything in her power to screw me over that semester, and not in a good way. The one time she'd been cool was one time I tried to forget. It was a mirage.

Maybe if she laid off the homicidal-thought daggers for a bit, we could make this arrangement more fun for the both of us, but I had no doubt in my mind that she would remove my balls with an ice cream scoop if I so much as hinted that I might be interested in anything more than the work.

"Our first assignment is due in a week. Why don't you tell me which parts of this you think you can handle, and I'll do the rest?" She slid the paper across the desk, and I slid it right back to her, my anger shooting up.

"You really think I'm a moron, huh?"

"Listen, we need to get through this. You're the one who's a senior in Sophomore Seminar. What am I supposed to think?"

"You're right there beside me in class, aren't you?"

"As a transfer. If I didn't have to take this bullshit class, I'd be able to graduate before the summer, so I'm not any happier than you are about this. We have to discuss the five strategies and approaches adopted to promote development and reduce poverty over four decades in the country of our choice, and the impact of those strategies."

"Fine. You take two, I'll take three."

"I'll take four, and you take one."

I clenched my fists against my thighs.

"So, you can complain to Alcott that I'm not pulling my weight?" My voice rose as she kept looking at me like I couldn't be trusted not to walk headfirst into a wall without enough warning. She squeezed the bridge of her nose.

"I'm trying to make this easy for you, Declan. Just like everything else in your life. You should be thanking me. I'm not going to rat you out to Alcott. I'm trying to get through this year and graduate as quickly as I can."

"And you see me as a barrier to that. Sorry we can't all be as perfect as you."

She glanced up at me, and something flashed in her eyes. I didn't know what it was, but it was still boiling from her endless digs. Her shoulders sagged, and she sat in the other chair in the room.

"I don't have anything against you personally."

I scoffed, and she peered up at me.

"Fine. I do. You don't know what it's like for someone like me to have my grades in the hands of someone like you."

My hackles rose as she pushed all my buttons.

"Someone like me? And how do you think I feel having my grades and future as a hockey player at this school in the hands of a perfectionist who would sooner watch someone drown than have it mess up their set schedule for life?"

She jerked back like I'd slapped her.

"It seems like we're both relying on someone we don't trust, so we might as well make the best of it and get this shit done so we can see each other for the least amount of time possible." I peered over at the assignment on the desk.

"I'll take two. You take two, and we'll finish the fifth one together. Maybe once you see that I'm not a walking, talking brain donor, you'll loosen the hell up, and we can have an enjoyable rest of the semester."

"Fine." The word barely made it past her clenched teeth.

We grabbed our computers and worked out which country we wanted to highlight and which issues to write about in our paper. With a basic outline for all the items, she seemed satisfied that I wasn't a babbling moron.

"We can meet to go over this stuff on Saturday and get it ready to submit on Tuesday, the day before class." She put her laptop back in the bag that was no longer bursting at the seams since she'd unloaded most of the stuff onto the small shelf above the desk in the study room.

"What time on Saturday?" I slid my arms into the straps of my backpack.

"Three?" She put her bags on her arms and no longer looked like she was going to keel over.

"Three works."

She opened her mouth and snapped it shut before turning to the door. I followed behind her and almost ran her over when she stopped short and whipped around with her mouth opening and closing again before she stared up at me.

"Spit it out, Books."

She shot me a quick glare, and the corners of her mouth turned down.

"I'm sorry if I made you think I thought you were stupid. I don't. I... This class is really important to me, and I need to do well."

I stared at her.

"I need to do well too. It's the only way I get to play with my team. I'm not going to screw this up."

"Then I think things will go well this semester." She held out her hand, which was probably the only time since that one night she'd ever willingly touched me. I slid my hand into her soft, warm one with her delicate fingers wrapping around mine.

The charged air between us shifted as we both let our guards down a little. The blue in her eyes behind those glasses seemed even brighter under the fluorescent library lights, and the pink of her lips was still shiny from when she'd been nibbling on them while we worked through our research.

"I think so too." We stood there, shaking our hands until one of the doors on the floor slammed shut. She jumped like she'd come out of a trance and whipped around, rushing from the room, and I once again had to chase after her. I didn't know how long we shook hands, but it was long enough that even as we left the library and parted ways, I could still feel her gentle touch wrapped around my hand.

I squeezed the back of my neck and shook my head as I caught a shuttle back across campus. If there was one person not to get any illusions about being anything more than study partners with, it was Makenna. The Ice Queen would eviscerate anyone who tried to get close.

8

MAKENNA

S tanding outside the professor's office, I shifted from foot to foot. It had taken me two days to build up the courage to even come near his office. I couldn't get the study session with Declan out of my head, and that was not a good thing.

When we'd shaken on it at the end and his hand enveloped mine. The calluses from his fingers had scraped against my skin and sent a shiver through me.

I'd noticed his freckles before, but up close the smattering of light brown flecks looked like they had been strategically placed for maximum impact. Like the cosmos created just the right combo to make unsuspecting women get lost staring at the pattern. The way they streaked across his skin reminded me of a lake on a warm summer's day.

The handshake had gone on for longer than it should have, and I didn't like how it made me feel. It made me want to laugh, like a giddy girl. Like Angel, who'd annoyingly checked in on my study space every time I was there, craning her neck to see if Declan had also stopped by.

With Saturday creeping closer through the week, my

anxiety had spiked. I'd even changed our meeting time twice trying to put it off a little longer. It was the dream I had the night before of our dance back at prom that spurred me into action.

I'd dragged myself down to Alcott's office. That giggly, bubbly feeling was scarier than any of the other shit going on in my head. Declan was everything I'd sworn I'd never be. He took everything for granted and never seemed to take anything seriously except for hockey.

Declan was a heat-seeking flirt missile. If there was a pulse, he'd turn on his charm to get what he wanted. I wasn't going to let him flirt his way into screwing up my graduation and med school plans. They were too important. Not just for me but for Daniel.

The office door swung open, and a girl with her hair in a braid came shuffling out, clutching her backpack straps. She glanced up at me with a scared look and trudged her way down the hall.

My hands were clammy, and my stomach threatened to revolt as I glanced from the door of doom to the girl who looked like someone had kicked her puppy and then kicked her. I took a step back, and my shoes squeaked on the floor. My shoulders hitched up around my ears, and I contemplated climbing into my backpack and pretending I'd never been there.

"I can hear you out there. Come in so we can get this over with." Professor Alcott's snarky voice boomed in the empty hall, and I glanced around, looking for a path of escape. Before I could fling myself out the nearest window, he popped his head out into the hallway and actually rolled his eyes when he saw me.

"I wondered how long it would take you to show up. Come in." He waved me into the office, and I walked like a tin soldier brought to life. My legs were as heavy as lead, and I swore the beads of sweat rolling down my back were forming a nice little swimming pool for me to drown myself in later.

Alcott dropped into his chair and leaned back, lacing his fingers together and sliding them behind his head. Kicking his feet up on the desk, he closed his eyes as I sat in the chair on the other side of his desk. The room smelled like old books and desperation, which was fitting because I'm sure that was the same thing people thought about me.

"If the first words out of your mouth are asking for a partner change, I can fail you both right now."

His words sent a bolt of fear through me, and my bouncing leg stopped immediately.

"Or did you come here for the amazingly charismatic company." He lifted one eyebrow.

"No. Of course not. I mean, I'm not here to change partners. I wasn't talking about the company part." *Is it hot in here?* It felt like the office had been launched into orbit around the sun. I barely stopped myself from tugging at the collar of my shirt.

Alcott dropped his feet down and tented his fingers on the top of his desk.

"Spit it out. Why are you here then?"

I opened my mouth and snapped it shut.

"I wanted to know if the noon deadline for the papers was Eastern Time or in another time zone." I cringed inside but managed to keep a straight face as he looked at me like I'd suddenly turned into an even more moronic little kid.

"It's all spelled out for you in the syllabus, but sure, why the hell not? It's twelve noon on the deadline day. I learned my lesson with midnight deadlines. Apparently, college students have a hard time figuring out which day midnight assignments are due. The portal shuts down at exactly 12:00:01p.m., and no late assignments will be accepted. Does that answer your question?"

I nodded and grabbed my bag. Standing, I slid it onto my back. He smirked at me with that smug look of his, and the pit in the bottom of my stomach grew.

This was it. I was partners with Declan for the rest of the semester. Taking a deep breath, I reached for the doorknob and opened it. Halfway in and halfway out of the office, I skidded to a stop when Alcott called my name.

"Ms. Halstead, if you had a truly compelling reason—and I'm talking incredibly exceptional reason—for changing partners, I might entertain it."

Frozen in the doorway, I thought of why I didn't want to work with Declan. High school drama and hating his attitude didn't feel like they fit the bill of exceptional in this case. Neither did *I get butterflies in my stomach when he touches me.* I turned around to face Alcott.

"Thank you for letting me know. I don't think it will be an issue."

"Good. Now close the door." And just like that I was dismissed.

Making my way across campus, I found myself back at the library like I was a homing pigeon, and this was my starting point. Climbing the steps, I wandered to my study room, opening the door when the one beside me popped open. Angel popped out with a wide smile. It dimmed slightly when she saw I was alone.

"Hi, neighbor," she said so cheerily I expected gumdrops to come pouring out of her mouth.

"Hi, Angel." If I didn't stand out there and talk to her for a few minutes, she would follow me inside. I'd learned that over the past few days.

"What are you up to this weekend?"

"Nothing. Working on my assignments. Going for a run. Sleeping." Taking a deep breath, I asked the question even though I really didn't want to. "What about you?"

"Oh, this weekend will be amazing. I'm going to a concert at the Electric Factory, and then I'm going kayaking with some friends. Then we're thinking we'll probably wander around the city looking for the best cheesesteak, maybe go dancing somewhere.

"I don't have everything planned out yet, but it will be awesome. I need to get all this energy out before the semester really gears up and I'm trapped inside." She said it all in less than two breaths and spent the entire time bouncing on her toes like she had to pee. I didn't really have much to say other than that. Her perpetual peppiness threatened to give me a toothache, but I envied her ease and happiness.

"That sounds really cool. I hope you have a great time." I mustered up my best approximation of a smile.

"You too, with your...run."

Yes, I knew my weekend sounded like the kind of weekend you had when you were being punished, but it would help me get a handle on what had already been a difficult new semester. She disappeared out of my doorway, and I finally felt safe enough to drop my bag and unload my stuff. Leaving Stanford had been a mistake, I'd tried to deny it, but there it was, and now I had to deal with it.

"She's a bubble of energy, isn't she?" A deep voice came from the doorway. My head whipped up, and there was a guy standing at my door, leaning against the door jamb and staring over toward Angel's room.

"That she is."

"I swear, I can hear her pep from across campus." He

was in a dark black T-shirt and jeans. Jet-black hair and dark brown eyes. He was like the polar opposite of Angel.

"I'm Seth." He stepped into the room with his hand out.

"Makenna." I shook his soft, strong hand and didn't feel like I was going to keel over any second.

"She's in my master's program. The poor professors don't really know what to do with her. Mechanical engineering programs aren't exactly built on the woohoos and excitement of other programs, but she knows her stuff, so..." He shrugged.

"She seems really nice. I'm not used to that much sunshine."

His rich chuckle filled the room. "Me neither. Listen, I'll leave you to it, but I'm right next door. If you ever need a rescue from happiness overload, let me know."

"I'll bang my head against the wall to alert you before I slip into a sugar coma." I smiled and crossed my arms over my chest, perched on the edge of my desk.

"Or you could give me a call. If you had my number."

Everything in the room stopped like someone hit pause on the remote. *Is he asking for my number? Is this flirting? How can I not even spot flirting?*

"If you wanted it, that is?" A look of uncertainty passed over his face, and he backed up.

I reached out and shouted louder than I intended. "No!" The red flush crept over my skin like a blanket ready to smother me with my awkwardness. I cleared my throat. "I mean, yes. Sure, I'll take your number, and you can have mine."

"Great." He slid his phone out of his back pocket, and I grabbed mine out of my bag, opening up a new contact. He did the same, and we traded numbers. There was a small flip in my stomach. It wasn't as big as the one I'd gotten with

Declan's hand in mine, but I brushed that aside. Seth went back to his study room, and I sat at my desk staring at my books.

After checking through my online calendar, I read over some more assigned pages for the next few weeks but focusing was nearly impossible. My restlessness threatened to boil over as the sun set, filling the study room with oranges and reds. I needed to run.

My assignments for the next week were finished. My part of the research for the Sophomore Seminar paper was long done and proofread twice. Meeting with Declan tomorrow meant my game face had to be on.

I needed to get outside and feel the breeze across my skin. Careful not to alert Angel that I was leaving, I stepped out of my door, only to see the rest of the study rooms completely empty. I checked the time again. After eight.

On the walk back to my apartment, my phone buzzed in my bag. I fished it out, wondering if maybe it was Seth, when relief washed over me.

"Hey, Mom, how's the open road?"

"It's great, sweetheart. I'll send you some pictures. We went to Disneyland yesterday."

I cracked a sad smile as I remembered our one and only visit to Disney World down in Florida.

"Did you get pictures with Mickey?"

"Sure did. Pushed some little kids out of the way to do it, and it was so worth it." Dad's voice came in over the line.

"Hey, Dad."

"Hey, chickadee."

"How are you doing?"

"I'm great. Never better. Your mom and I are going out for dinner and dancing tonight, and then we're off to Vegas tomorrow."

Dinner and dancing. It was like being put back into a time machine. They sounded so happy it almost hurt. I rubbed the achy spot in the center of my chest as I walked along the sidewalk to the cluster of apartments mainly rented by students.

"That sounds awesome. I'm so glad you two are having fun." I'd keep the brightness in my voice if it killed me.

"So are we, and I hope you're not working too much. You're always so hard on yourself. Don't be afraid to have a little fun sometimes."

"I'm not. I have fun."

"Running is not fun," Dad said, sounding highly offended.

"It's fun for me."

"Something not running or school or work related," Mom, unhelpfully, threw in.

I opened my mouth for a comeback, but I didn't really have one. Those things were my life. Pretty much all of it.

"I know we're not there, but we'll be back for Thanksgiving and if you haven't had any fun before then, we're going to burn your textbooks."

"Dad, that's like burning ten thousand dollars. I don't think you want to do that."

"I want you to let yourself live a little. Don't make us park this RV outside your apartment and make sure you have fun."

While the threat was ominous, I kind of liked the idea of them hanging out on campus. I'd be able to see them more, but it would get in the way of *their* newfound lease on life.

"I solemnly swear that this semester I will try to schedule at least a little fun and frivolity."

"You better. We love you!" they both said, laughing the entire time.

I still couldn't wrap my head around their change. Who knew it would take a diagnosis like Dad's to finally snap them out of their haze and rejoin the land of the living. Not that my way of coping was any better. *Perfect match.*

I shoved my key into the lock of my apartment, took a deep breath and closed the door behind me. Bright and playful chatter filled the place. Tracy and Fiona fought over the bathroom mirror at the end of the hall. Dropping my bag in the door, I leaned against the wall and watched them primp and preen, unable to control my smile.

"Makenna, you're back. We were wondering if we'd have to send a search party out to come find you." Tracy turned to me and waved the curling iron in my direction.

"I was hanging out at the library."

"On a Friday? You're not going out?" Fiona said from behind her with an eyeliner pencil precariously close to her eyeball.

"I'm going to go for a run."

They both turned to me with various beauty products clutched in their hands.

"But why?" Tracy wrapped the curling iron around her hair.

"Why are you two crammed into that bathroom when you both have your own?"

"Fiona's has much better lighting than mine." Tracy lined her lips and puckered up in the mirror. Leaving them to their prep, I went into my room and changed into my running gear. Snagging my phone off my bed, I slipped in my earbuds.

"I don't know how long my celibacy challenge is going to last," Fiona said, walking past my door.

"We made the challenge like eight hours ago," Tracy said from the living room. I tried to hold back my laughter and failed as the front door closed behind them. It would be an interesting semester for more reasons than I'd imagined.

After they left, I took off down the street until I made it to campus. Hordes of freshman wandered in search of the mythical college parties, though most people were still getting ready to go out. Always count on the freshman to be early.

My heart pounded as my feet slapped against the concrete, and I let my mind blank. There was nothing but the pavement and my muscles pumping as I wove my way through the streets surrounding campus. The tightness in my chest lessened and the weights of everything going on around me fell away as my legs loosened and hit their stride.

I don't know how long I ran, but I had to duck and dodge through crowds of people heading to the bars or out to beginning-of-the-year parties. Sweat poured off me as I walked back into the apartment. Music filtered in through the walls as other people had their own parties. After taking a shower, I curled up in bed and closed my eyes.

Tomorrow was another day. I'd be face-to-face with Declan again and I needed to make sure I didn't let him get under my skin, but part of me knew he was already there and had been for years.

9

DECLAN

My muscles ached and burned. I climbed the steps to the frat house feeling like I'd been hit by a truck. The stairs vibrated under my feet as the bass from the party flooded the street. Not that anyone would notice because thumping beats poured out of all the houses on the street.

Back to school meant everyone could party without worry since the semester had started. *Almost everyone.* I'd gotten all my work done for the Seminar because I was ninety percent sure Mak would castrate me if I screwed this up. Plus, I had a lot riding on it too. I wasn't going to flake.

Heath walked up behind me, jumping onto my back. I winced and chucked him off, running a hand over my shoulder. He landed on his feet like he was part cat, and I wouldn't put it past him for that to be true.

"Dude, what the hell? You know how many bench presses you had me doing this afternoon?" Heath always seemed to have a perpetual well of energy wrapped in his laid-back exterior. It was a trap. He lulled you into a false sense of security, and then your arms were boneless and you could barely walk after being in the gym with him for an hour. I thought Preston was bad. Totally wrong, I'd take a work out with Preston any day over Heath.

"How was practice with the guys?" The question I'd been putting off. Skating with Heath was good, but it wasn't being out there with the rest of the team.

"It was good. We're still working on the dynamics with you out of the mix, but it was fine." He smiled, but it didn't reach his eyes.

"I'll be back soon."

"I know. That's why I'm working your ass so hard. No one's going to think you missed a single practice." He squeezed my shoulder, and my knees nearly buckled.

I needed to stay sharp for the final verdict of the pro coaches. Skating around the rink with Archer's eyes boring into the back of my head, I needed focus. I couldn't let him throw me off my game like he had in the past. Why the hell did he have to watch? He wanted me to fail. Wanted to make sure I'd never be a rival for his shitty legacy.

I wasn't going to let him throw me off my game on my home turf.

"What's the matter, man? You miss a couple practices and you're already getting soft?" Heath walked backward across the wide porch with his arms spread open. People streamed past him out of the brick-front house.

"No, I just didn't realize you're a sadist. Now I know." I rubbed my sore arms.

A little distraction therapy for my current situation. No heavy drinking. No bringing anyone home but being cooped up inside all weekend would drive me insane.

I'd done my work. I'd meet with Mak tomorrow. I needed a little bit of fun while I could. Before I had to power through a semester of classes to make sure I graduated just in case and get back on the ice where my future would be decided.

"Did you hear the moon is supposed to be insane tonight? Something about the alignment of the moon and the other planets." He stared out into the night sky beyond the porch.

"I have no idea. Why the hell would I care about the moon?" Sometimes he confused the shit out of me. He was equal parts surfer guy, mystic, and party guy all in one. Heath and I stepped over the threshold and cracked wide smiles at the cheer from the partygoers. This was what I needed. Shrugging his shoulders, Heath spun around and walked deeper into the house a step before me.

"Planets and stars and nature, that's the universe's tricked-out special effects." He called out behind him.

What the hell is that supposed to mean?

"I'll take your word for it." The crush of the crowd quickly surrounded us. Heath's mop of blond hair quickly disappeared deeper into the party like a man on a mission. Someone shoved a beer into my hand before I even got to the keg. It was good to be king.

"Declan! Why weren't you at practice?" A girl sloshed a beer as she raced up to me.

"I'm doing some solo practices for a while, but don't worry, I'll be back with the team when it's game time."

Slaps on the back and fist bumps from everyone as I worked my way through the party.

"Dec! You're up for beer pong!" one of the football players shouted over the pounding music and crowd of people.

"I'll be there later." I cupped my hand around my mouth and called out into the group assembled around the Ping-Pong table covered in red plastic cups. Beer, pot, and liquor flowed from all corners of the jam-packed house. As I wove my way through my fellow classmates, there were more than a few hands deep in my pockets. The numbers were always overflowing after a night out. The *Hey, Declans*, notes, subtle breast brushes, and hair twirling meant I'd have my pick of whoever I wanted tonight. But I wasn't feeling it.

I'd come to get out of the funk of having the weight of my future hanging around my neck like an albatross, but Heath's workout had made me want to crawl into bed and sleep until midterms. That would be admitting defeat or that anything had changed, and I was determined it wouldn't. Temporary setback aside, this was my fucking senior year.

"Can't wait to see you out on the ice again, man." A guy I didn't know came up and gave me a handshake back-thumping hug combo. "Another national champion right here, everyone!" He lifted his hands, pointing to me, and sloshed beer on the girl beside him. I laughed into my beer and steered clear as she punched him in the arm.

I also needed to get out because my nerves were kind of a mess to see Makenna tomorrow. My cage was not easily rattled. I'd kept my cool in front of Archer—barely. I'd faced off on the ice against guys known to collect teeth and break noses at the drop of a hat. Skating off against them was never anything I had a second thought about, but man, Mak threw me off my game.

Not only because of our little moment in the study room, but because she'd be judging every single thing I did when it came to the class. Pretending I didn't care was fine and all, but I did. I didn't want her to think I was a complete moron. There were enough people in my life who felt that way. Failing the class had been a fluke.

I made it to the kitchen, and a few people called out my name and passed me some jello shots. Nothing like some boozy kids' snacks to distract me from the fact that a person who hated me had my life and career in the palm of her hand.

Downing the jello shot, I let the smooth burn slide down my throat. Someone put another full beer in my hand. I didn't even bother looking for Heath. He'd float around, wandering from spot to spot like a troubadour of happiness until he passed out somewhere. There would be a trail of women following after him like little ducklings, but he never looked twice. Well, maybe twice.

If he was feeling it, he might bring someone home, but that was it. He didn't do relationships, at least not ones he didn't have to work for. That was his thing. Go after the chick he had no business with, like our student teacher back in high school. He'd be relentless until she caved, and then he was finally satisfied.

If I weren't hanging with him most days, I'd swear he was high all the time from how mellow he was. He was a freak of nature that way. But on the ice, there was no one who skated harder or lasted longer. He left it all out there.

Another cheer came from the front of the house. Head and shoulders above most other people, Preston, the redheaded menace made a beeline straight for me with people pointing in my direction to lead his way. I glanced around the kitchen looking for a place to hide, but there were too many people between me and the back door to make a break for it. *Damn it!*

His hand landed on my shoulder as I stepped out the back door onto the deck. The warm summer air soaked up the noise from the other parties on the block, and the humidity clung to the side of my cup.

A lecture from Preston was not what I needed right now. That didn't mean I wasn't going to get it.

"My sister is in another one of Alcott's classes, and she said you guys have an assignment coming up."

"Are you my mother now?"

"No, but you know how important this season is, Dec. Don't throw away this time."

"I'm not throwing anything away. I'm having a little fun. I've done my work for the week. Mak and I are meeting tomorrow to finish our paper that isn't even due until Wednesday. She will ride my ass even harder than anyone can imagine, so you don't have to worry. I will not fuck up this semester. Although I'm sure you think I'll try my best."

"I'm glad to hear you have a responsible partner."

I nearly threw my hands up in frustration. He treated me like some little kid, and I was a month older than he was.

"You don't think I don't want to be out there practicing with you guys instead of Heath, who seems to have no issues with the two-a-day torture he's running with me." The stiff pain in my legs had transformed into a gentle ache after a few beers, but I had no idea how I'd feel in the morning.

Preston squeezed his hand along the back of his neck.

"I don't want something stupid to screw you up. You've got a shot not many people get." He looked at me, and the simmering anger melted away.

Preston wouldn't be going pro after graduation. He hadn't been picked up by a development league out of high school, and despite his talents and his leadership, for some reason he thought the pros were out of his reach. I didn't understand it, but I wasn't going to bust his balls over something he'd made his mind up about.

"I know." I leaned onto the worn and warped wooden deck railing. The kitchen door flew open, and the music and laughter burst out into the relatively quiet bubble on the deck.

People spilled into the backyard and scurried down the deck steps into the crab grass–covered, stamp-sized backyard. "Looks like it finally got too packed in there for them." More people flooded outside, and soon the party surrounded us.

"Hey, Preston. Hey, Declan!" A perky voice came from behind us. We both turned, and there was a petite, glassy-eyed girl teetering on her high heels, sloshing two beers everywhere as she tried to balance. "I got these for you!" she shouted. She had no idea how to meter her volume, thrusting the cups at us and pouring half the beer onto our shoes. We gingerly took the cups from her hands to avoid being drenched.

"I'm so excited to see you play this season." She swayed, and Preston shot out a hand to grab her arm. "I came to the practice, but I didn't see you there. Where were you hiding?" Her slurred words were matched by her droopy eyes. I scanned the people in the house behind her, looking for a girl herd that had lost one of their own.

"She is bombed, dude." I glanced over at Preston. He had on his best dad face, even more stern than the one he used with me, which was saying something.

"I know." My lips were a thin grim line. Getting buzzed was one thing, even drunk, but trashed meant trouble.

"I'm not bombed. I'm perfectly fine." She shrugged off Preston's hand and tried to walk down the stairs, tripping over the first one. Grabbing her around the waist, I pulled her back from the verge of a head and neck injury before setting her back on her feet.

"What's your name?"

"Tiffany."

"Where are your friends, Tiffany?" I tried to hold her bobbing-head, drunk-girl gaze. *Where the hell are her friends?* Wasn't that part of the girl code? Never leave a drunk chick to her own devices.

"They are inside." She pointed behind her, but the weight of her bird arm must have been too much for her because she stumbled backward. Tiffany was going to get herself killed if we didn't find her friends soon. Or some asshole might try to take advantage of her.

"Let's go find them." I looped my arm through hers, and Preston got the other. People parted as we nearly carried our new ward through the party.

"Lucky me. Look, ladies, I'm in the middle of a man sandwich!" She smacked her lips together as we walked through the house. Preston and I caught each other's eyes. It was a valiant effort, but he couldn't help but crack a smile. After about ten minutes of *who does this drunk girl belong to?* we got Tiffany reunited with her flock who promptly decided she needed to go home.

Tiffany fought them the whole way.

"But they were gonna bang me into next week!" she whined as her friends apologized and pushed her out the front door. A giant guffaw shot through the room so loud it made me jump over the thumping music. I whipped around to see Preston bent over with his hands on his thighs, laughing through the tears in his eyes.

"Finally!" I wrapped my arms around his shoulder.

"Finally what?"

"Finally, you're having some fun. Who knew all we needed was a pint-sized drunk girl to throw herself at you to loosen you up."

"Did you see the look in her eyes?" He wiped the tears from his face.

"Do you mean when she was dragged away kicking and screaming?"

"She seriously thought we were going to sleep with her... together." Preston wiped at his eyes as we both shuddered at the thought.

"I know we're close and teammates are almost like brothers, but it's bad enough almost seeing your balls in the locker room. I don't need to see them in action."

Preston shoved against my shoulder, trying to catch his breath from his laughter.

"The party hasn't even been going on that long. That girl must have started drinking at noon."

"I think she was a sophomore." I vaguely remembered seeing someone who might have been her during my Sophomore Seminar trek of doom.

"A sophomore?" Preston's head whipped up, and all the blood drained out of his face. "Becca's a sophomore. Do you think she's out? Is she drinking?" And just like that, fun Preston was gone as he whipped out his phone, ready to go into military tactical mode to locate his little sister. Poor girl would never have a wild night out until he graduated, and even then, I didn't put it past him to hide in the trees, keeping a watchful eye on her until she graduated. I bet she was regretting her transfer from a school down South right about now.

With the phone pressed against his ear, Preston rushed out of the house. I shook my head and went back to the kitchen to grab another beer. Someone thrust one into my hand, and then everyone pushed past me, flowing out the back door.

"Heath's on the roof." A couple girls giggled, racing out past me. *What the hell?*

Shouldering my way out the back door and down the

steps off the deck, I stood among the crowd staring up at the roof. It only took a matter of time for him to get an insane idea in his head, and then there was no stopping him.

Heath sat cross-legged on the roof of the house, staring up at the sky. He glanced down and smiled right at me.

"Declan, check it out!" Heath called down like I wasn't in a sea of fifty other people watching him up on the roof. He pointed back behind the crowd, and everyone tried to follow the direction of his finger. The tall trees behind the house were all anyone could see.

"You're going to have to be more specific, Heath," I said, cupping my hands around my mouth.

"It's the moon! I told you."

There were murmurs in the crowd about him being drunk, but I was ninety percent sure he was completely sober, just not completely sane.

"I'll take your word for it," I called out again, and he stood from his spot on the roof. Some girls leaned out the second-floor window. Apparently, none of the girl flock had decided to follow him out. They craned their necks to get a look at him from there.

"You should see this." He shook his head like I'd missed out on a trip from Vegas. Glancing down again, he stopped midstride, like he'd realized the backyard was packed with people. I started shaking my head before he even did anything, because I knew how much Heath loved to play it up for a crowd.

"Don't do it," I said under my breath, but I couldn't drag my gaze away as his arms went out in front of him and he bent his knees, throwing himself back and up in the air at the apex of the roof into a backflip. The collective gasp of the crowd when his foot slipped was only matched by the cheer that screeched through the night sky when he caught himself in a perfect surfer pose. The house was his board, and the world was his ocean.

Somehow I felt like the only sane one on the team. Preston was so tightly wound he might actually strain a muscle in his brain, and Heath was so chill he risked floating off into space.

Maybe I needed new friends...

10

MAKENNA

After checking my phone for the fifth time in three minutes, I gave up. The old, musty smell of the place did nothing to calm my rising anger. I should have known not to trust him. It was a good thing I'd planned for this and after we'd outlined everything, I'd done the rest of the paper anyway. Sick of hanging around in the study room when the library was a ghost town, I packed up my stuff and headed out ten minutes after the hour.

Sitting there for thirty minutes silently seething, wasn't exactly my idea of a good time. Relief washed over me as I stepped out into the humid late summer air and took the path leading to off-campus housing.

The walk back to my apartment was short and sweet. Having a library so close to the apartment was a bit of an occupational hazard. There was no excuse not to go study, not that I usually needed excuses.

The course work was already piling up, and what should have been my easiest class, Sophomore Seminar, was the one that filled my brain the most. Everything else was something I could control. The lab work would get done. The papers would be written, but I couldn't control Declan.

Sticking my key in the door, I opened it to what looked like a trail of glitter snaking its way from the back bedroom right out the front door. *What the hell were they doing?* Holding perfectly still, I craned my neck, and there was no movement in the place. I didn't even know if I wanted to find out what this was about. There was glitter all over the couches too.

I got into my running gear but didn't feel like leaving. Being outside, pushing through the droves of people on their way to parties, didn't hit near the top of my list just then. That was probably where he was. Our meeting forgotten as he did keg stands or played beer pong or whatever else he did to shirk his responsibilities. I flipped on the TV, tried to dust some of the glitter off the couch and searched for something good to watch. A sharp knock broke me out of my streaming video scrolling trance.

I hopped up and opened the door, ready to tell whoever it was that Fiona and Tracy weren't here, when the words died in my throat. Declan stood at my front door with his backpack on his shoulder. My shock turned to anger at the stormy-eyebrow look on his face.

"What the hell, Mak? Standing me up for our session."

The rage bomb I was about to drop on him stuttered and paused as I processed what he'd said.

"What? I didn't stand you up. I was there. I waited in the study room." I jammed my fist into my hip.

"For how long? I showed up at five minutes after because I had to come from across campus, and you weren't there."

"No, you didn't. I left ten minutes after. Don't lie to me." My fingers tightened around the edge of the door, and I was tempted to slam it in his face.

His annoyed look turned to confusion, and I'm sure it matched my own.

"I left at seven ten. You were ten minutes late."

"I was five minutes late for our seven thirty meeting."

"We were not meeting at seven thirty."

"Yes, we were. I had another study session that ended at seven twenty p.m. I told you that when you rescheduled this. Twice." He pulled out his phone and handed it to me. The calendar invite I'd emailed him showed up on a big block from seven thirty to eight thirty. I glanced from the phone up to him. His smug look was firmly back in place.

"Wrote me off that quickly, didn't you?"

I opened and closed my mouth a few times. The tips of my ears burned like they had been singed by the glowing satisfaction on his face.

"Sorry," I mumbled, feeling about two inches tall. *How did I screw that up?* "Come in." I stepped out of the way so he could walk into the apartment.

"Had a fight with a fairy?" He craned his neck to stare at my ass as he passed, and my cheeks were on fire. I turned my head to see what he looked at. The entire back of my body was covered in rainbow glitter. Trying to dust it off, my head snapped up at the clinking of bottles.

Declan produced a six-pack from behind his back and slid it onto the kitchen counter.

My gaze jumped from him to it as I tried to figure out what exactly he planned on doing with the drinks. Maybe for wherever he was going next. Until he took one out and opened and closed a few drawers in the kitchen like he had no trouble making himself comfortable.

"Where's your bottle opener?" He closed yet another drawer.

"I don't know. We might not have one."

"How does a college student not have a bottle opener?" He glanced up at me with his eyebrows pinched together like this was some Nancy Drew mystery. I was a second from throwing my hands up in the air and letting him off the hook for all the assignments.

"I don't know. Fiona and Tracy like the twist-off top, hard lemonade things and go out most of the time, and I've never had a need for one."

"I'll have to put one on my keys or something if we're going to be studying together this semester." His voice had a teasing edge that grated my nerves.

"We won't be needing these." I plucked the beer out of his hand, stuck it back in the carton, shoved it in the fridge, and slammed the door shut.

"Come on, Books, I always work best when I've had a beer. And it might help get your creative juices flowing." From the look on his face I couldn't tell if he was serious or not. I didn't want to give him the satisfaction of getting under my skin if he was joking, but I was sixty percent sure he seriously studied while having a couple beers.

"You're not really giving me a lot of confidence about what we're going to be going over today. Do you always do your papers drunk?"

"Getting drunk and having a beer or two are different things. Plus, getting plastered isn't how I do things during hockey season."

Glancing around the living room, we didn't have a place to sit. Not when the couches looked like a herd of unicorns had had an orgy. Chewing on my bottom lip, I grimaced, as that meant we only had one other option unless I wanted to lug all my stuff back to the study room.

"Come with me." I nodded and led him back into my

room where my computer, notebooks, and everything else was already.

"The expedition is getting their first glimpse of a rare sight. After much patience and persistence, the crew is finally able to film the Halstead in her natural habitat."

Declan's English accent narration from behind me as he stepped into my room made me crack a smile, even though it shouldn't. Putting on my serious face, I spun around and motioned to the other chair in my room.

Sliding into my rolling chair, I fired up my laptop and opened our paper.

"Do you want to email me your portion?"

I spun around and banged right into his knee, jumping at how close he was.

"Are you always so stealthy?" I rubbed the spot where his diamond-capped knee had rammed into my leg.

"My skills extend beyond the ice. I'm more than willing to show you how far." He grinned, and his little dig at me wasn't appreciated. I didn't even stop my eye roll this time.

"Let's get to work. The sooner we finish, the sooner we turn it in and can get out of each other's hair until the next assignment."

We sped through the portion of the assignment we'd both taken responsibility for. I read over his work and was pleasantly surprised that it wasn't a dumpster fire. It was actually pretty good. With a few tweaks it wouldn't be too far off what I'd completed.

The final point was where we locked horns. He threw up his hands and pushed out of his chair.

"What does it matter if they make these amazing scientific discoveries if they don't have a way to get those out to the world?" Declan paced across the room.

"They would be increasing the knowledge pool of their

communities."

"Again, if no one knows about it and they can't dissemi-nate the information, they might as well not have discovered it at all. They need the business and information infrastructure before they can jump right to science break-throughs." He sat back down and leaned forward in his chair.

"Sometimes learning and knowledge for the sake of itself is enough." It wasn't all about the fame and glory.

"How does that help lift the community out of poverty though? Isn't that the assignment? We're supposed to figure out a way to address it, not create a wonderfully educated bunch of people who have no way of improving their situa-tion because they can't get their ideas in the hands of anyone."

He stared at me with his arms crossed over his chest, and I racked my brain trying to come up with a counterpoint to his point. A few false starts and I admitted defeat by spin-ning back around to my computer and typing it out into our paper.

His smug face popped into my peripheral vision as he spun his chair around and sat on it backward. Always so smooth, if I'd tried that move, I'm sure a trip to the ER would have been in my future. As if the wide grin on his face wasn't enough, he hummed "Eye of the Tiger" like he'd gone toe to toe with an over muscled Russian foe.

"Fine, you made a good point." My jaw clenched so tight I could probably have cracked a few walnuts.

He threw one of his hands to his chest and made an exaggerated gasp. Lifting his other hand, he smacked the back of it to his forehead and pretended to faint. Fighting the urge to smile, I kept my lips in a straight line. The corners might have creeped up the tiniest bit.

"I appreciate you admitting you were wrong. I'm sure that took a lot out of you." His full lips were parted in a wide smile, and I tried to imagine what it would look like without teeth. Weren't hockey players supposed to have missing teeth? Broken noses and stuff? Look like they'd gotten into a fight with a grizzly bear?

"I never said I was wrong! I said your point was more applicable to this assignment."

"Potatoe, potato. I'll take what I can get. I feel like I'm one of those people on a documentary channel, making discoveries left and right. Next thing you'll do is tell me you secretly pole dance at night to make money for school."

"It's not too much of an open secret, and my stage name is Bentley." The sarcasm dripped from my voice, and it was worth it for the look on his face.

His mouth hung open, and he jumped back so fast he nearly toppled over the chair. A grin curled his lips, but I managed to keep a straight face.

"Was that a joke? Or do I need to start frequenting all the strip clubs in the area? Maybe you'd like to give me a little show right now."

And then my barely stifled grin was gone, and my teeth gnashed together. If I made it through this semester, I wasn't a hundred percent sure my teeth would. What made it even worse was the vision dancing through my mind of whipping my shirt up and over my head and how his hands would feel on my bare skin. I shook my head to banish those thoughts from my mind. His hands around my waist, trailing up and down my back. *Nope! Not going there!*

We wrapped up the last of our points in the paper, and I read them over silently while pacing my room as Declan scrolled through his phone. Every so often I'd glance up and catch his eye, but he'd quickly go back to his screen.

The visions I'd pushed aside popped back into my head every time our eyes clashed. A shiver raced down my spine like a mini torture session as I stared into his eyes. More than once I'd walked straight into the edge of my desk. Cursing under my breath, I rubbed the sore spot and hated that I was falling into his green-eyed, full-lipped, ungodly sexy trap.

"Your turn." I handed him the small stack of papers I'd printed after we finished the assignment.

"My turn to what?"

"To read it over. I never turn anything in without proofing it at least twice, so you can do the other one. I've marked up the things I caught. Here's the pen." I held the pen, and he stared at it with his eyebrows scrunched together.

"I trust you, Books. It's fine with what you got."

"No, this is an assignment we're doing together, so you need to look it over too. What if I've temporarily forgotten all the rules of English grammar, or I decided to throw in a few curse words?" I arched my eyebrow at him as he slid the pen out of my hand. A small spark of disappointment flared through me that he hadn't touched my fingers when he took the pen. I needed to get him out of here before my knees gave out and I went full-on mermaid, flopping around on the floor.

"I'd say whatever grade deduction we got for you throwing in a 'fuck' or 'shit' would be well worth it. Hell, for that kind of behavior from you, I might just be happy not playing all season." He had a huge grin on his face as he stood and followed in my footsteps, pacing the same track. I sat on the bed, bouncing a little.

It still hadn't sunk in fully that Declan was standing in the middle of my room. I ran my hands over the thick bedspread. The weather was turning quickly with a cold snap over the weekend. My gaze shot to the papers in his hand as he took the pen he'd been running along his lips, which drew my attention to the perfect vee above his upper lip. His cupid's bow was so mesmerizing I saw myself running my lips over it. He dropped the pen out of his mouth, and my gaze snapped to the paper as ran his pen across the sheet.

Had I actually missed something? I'd only wanted him to review it to ruffle his feathers a little and make sure he was pulling his weight. My fingers itched to get my hands on the paper so I could see what I hadn't caught.

I nibbled on my bottom lip as he paced. The light from my desk lamp caught the thick curls of his light brown strands. His biceps bunched as he held the papers up, flipping through them. And the pen was back to his full lips. I swore he was doing it on purpose.

I had half a mind to call him out on running my pen along his lip, but he'd entranced me with his pacing, and I couldn't stop staring.

"Take a picture, Books; it will last longer." He chuckled and peered down at me over the papers in his hands. "You think that by now I don't know when someone's checking me out?"

"I wasn't!" I blurted out way too quickly and loudly to not have been totally checking him out. My spine stiffened, and I ducked my head, examining the incredibly interesting rug I'd picked up before the semester. I'd never noticed that there was a little purple woven in there between the blue and green. The sheets of paper popped into my view as he handed them over to me.

I checked over the couple of suggestion he'd had, kicking myself for forgetting those commas, and slid back up to my computer to make the changes on the document. One final read through of the paper on my screen that was like pulling teeth and I hit submit.

A wave of satisfaction crested as I saw the confirmation email hit my inbox. Declan's phone pinged, and he got it too. We'd done it. First assignment done with minimal bloodshed. Maybe this semester wouldn't be so bad.

"We're good, right?"

"Yeah, we're good. I was thinking maybe we should work ahead and see what the next assignment is." I already knew, but I didn't need to tell him that. He already thought of me like a robot pretending to be a college student; no need to confirm it. Although I didn't think robots came with the kind of shitty life baggage I carried.

"I'd love to, but I got to go." He picked up his bag off the floor. And my stomach curdled like I'd asked him out on a date and he'd turned me down. It was a Saturday night. He was Declan McAvoy. The parties across campus waited with bated breath until he arrived.

"Of course, we've already run over the time we were supposed to meet anyway," I said, glancing at the clock on my desk.

"No worries, Books. It's cool. No need to go into shutdown mode. We can have a longer session next time. I didn't schedule out any extra time for tonight." His vagueness told me it was probably something that would erase the tiniest bit of respect I'd gained for him over the last ninety minutes.

Leading him out to the front door, I felt a small kernel of disappointment smack into my stomach, which was stupid. It wasn't like I expected him to hang out any more than needed to complete the assignment.

This was an Alcott-enforced requirement. It wouldn't be anything more than a study partnership, no matter what.

11

DECLAN

"How much longer until you'll be back with us?" one of the guys from the team asked after we placed our orders with the waitress, who wasn't Mak. I'd spotted that within ten second of walking through the door.

Not that I was checking on her or anything. At three weeks into the semester it felt like each day stretched on longer than the last. The first few days I got up and got ready with Heath like I was going to practice before it hit me. I wasn't practicing with them. My hands itched to get out there with the guys and skate side by side as we all fell into a rhythm on the ice. Instead, it was me and Heath running drills and one-on-ones until I couldn't feel my legs anymore.

I could see Archer laughing his ass off about my being kicked off the team. It made me want to punch something. I let him get under my skin more than I should. Hard not to when your biological father was campaigning for the end of your professional career before it even began.

The vision of skating out onto the ice wearing his number, replacing him with a better, faster version with the crowd yelling my name burned a deep satisfaction into my gut. I wanted that bad. I wanted to see his smug fucking face when I made my first goal, and he'd know it had nothing to do with him. I'd done it on my own, and I didn't need him.

Clinking glasses brought me back from that fever dream to the carefree people around me. The bar wasn't too busy because it was only seven on a Friday. Most people had come earlier for lunch or would show up later.

There were a few old games playing on the screens around the bar, and some of the people had their notebooks and computers out. Three Streets had a strict no-studying policy after eight on Fridays, lasting through the whole weekend.

The study and assignment sessions had gone smoothly since Mak had figured out I wasn't a knuckle-dragging moron. Working together when the other person wasn't under the assumption that you'd only learned to spell the week before made things easier. Her micromanaging had ratcheted down once she realized I could finish assignments on time and up to about eighty percent satisfaction for her. Our truce had been a silent one.

The way her eyebrows pinched together when she did her proofreading pacing always made me laugh. Maybe it was because she took her glasses off. She ran her hands over her eyes like she was recharging their powers and did a methodical back-and-forth pattern across the floor of wherever she was. I don't think she noticed that she took exactly ten steps in each direction, modifying her gait to hit the wall in any space we were in. I was tempted to take her out into a wide-open space to see if she'd break out into lunges to hit her ten-step method.

Why I noticed this? I had no idea. There were a lot of things I was noticing about her in such close quarters. Like how she rolled her pens under her long, slender fingers on her leg whenever she was thinking. Or how her lip was always shiny and wet when she let it out from between her teeth when she was deep in thought.

These were things I shouldn't be paying attention to when it came to her, but I couldn't stop myself. My gaze followed her the second she walked into the room, and all I wanted to do was run my hands along her skin and break the tension building every minute we spent together. I caught her looking at me just as much as I stared at her. Her eyes would dart away, and her cheeks got pink. She was driving me insane.

Pop music played in the background, and glasses clinked behind the bar. She would hate trying to study in this place. She loved her den of solitude back in the library where it was so quiet you could hear a mouse fart. I shook my head, clearing those thoughts away. *Why the hell do I care where she wants to study?*

Preston drummed his fingers on the table like he always did anytime anything got under his skin, which meant his fingers were practically nubs.

"Don't worry, Pres. He's got it under control. Relax." Heath smacked a glaring Preston on his back. The other guys at the table laughed at Heath's mantra to everyone: *relax.* He hadn't found a situation yet where *relax* wasn't his advice.

"He's right. Every assignment has been an A so far. If we ace the midterm, then there's no way I can fail the class." I rolled my bottle between my hands, coating them in cool condensation.

Preston rubbed his hands over his face and along his jaw.

"We need you, man. The junior they have in your spot

isn't cutting it. No offense," Preston said, turning to one of the other juniors sitting at the table with us.

The kid held his hand up and shrugged. "None taken."

And then Preston was right back in it. "The practice sessions have not been going well, and the fans are noticing. It will only be a matter of time before this 'special practice schedule' lie you've been telling is out everywhere. And if the fans know, then the other teams will know. They were gunning for us before; they will be out for blood if we step on the ice without you."

"You're making it sound all doom and gloom, Pres. I think it's an excellent opportunity for us to all step up our game and make sure that if we were to lose a man, we could still dominate out on the ice," Heath piped up, always trying to look on the sunny side of things. Preston glared at him.

Sometimes Heath's chill, it-will-all-work-out philosophy was annoying as hell. But I'd allow it in this case because Preston's nostrils flared and that vein on his forehead bulged as he tried to compose himself.

Heath lounged at the end of our booth like he didn't have a care in the world. I honestly didn't think he did. He was relaxed to the point that it sometimes put the people around him on edge.

Preston's beer *thunked* down on the table.

"If you're not back, there goes our streak and our record. You need to stay focused."

"Have you met Makenna? Do you think there is any chance in hell that I could do anything that wasn't up to her standards? She'd sooner disembowel herself with a rusty spoon than turn something in she hasn't proofread fifteen times and forced me to proof at least twice."

That seemed to satisfy Preston, and he sat back in the

booth. His lack of faith in me would have pissed me off if it weren't for the fact that I knew it only came off that way.

He was freaked out about leaving the ice permanently after graduating. Unlike the Kings, he hadn't been able to get a development team spot after high school. His school hadn't had the connections or visibility for scouts. He'd started on the team as a walk-on, and through unbelievable dedication and badassery, he'd become team captain for our senior year. I respected the crap out of him, even if his worrisome mother-hen routine got old sometimes. It came from a place of friendship.

"Well, don't piss her off. She could always tell the professor if she doesn't think you're pulling your weight, and then you're screwed." Preston drained the last of his beer.

"How do you know I won't report her for not pulling her weight? Maybe she's holding me back from my true Sophomore Seminar calling."

Heath laughed and held his hand up, trying to catch the server's eye to order another round.

"Speak of the devil, looks like her shift is starting." He turned, grinning at me. *Why is he grinning at me like an idiot?* Well, a bigger grin than usual. So what if Mak was starting? No big deal. I tramped down my initial reflex to scan the room for her.

I turned in the booth to see her hurrying past the bar. No matter where she was going, she was always rushing like there were only so many hours in a day and she was determined to cram an extra three hours' worth of studying into each one.

She shrugged off her coat. The buttons of her shirt gaped open a bit, and I caught a glimpse of a black bra underneath. My mouth watered as I imagined toying with her nipples and getting the peaks nice and stiff before teasing them with my tongue and teeth until she begged me to fuck her. She always smelled like books and strawberries. Like you were out reading in the middle of a field under the summer sun. I bit back a groan as she got ready to start her shift. These thoughts kept creeping up on me. Hitting me when I least expected it. Her lips when she asked a question. Her leg when she jiggled it while reading. Her ass when she bent over to pick up something out of her bag. Mak was a one-woman wrecking crew, and my self-control was slipping.

She greeted the bartender and other servers. It wasn't often I got to sit back and watch her. Wrapping a half apron around her waist, she darted into the kitchen, and I drifted back to the conversation the guys were having.

Coach had them go over tapes for the game coming up in two weeks. October was right there, and I needed to be on the team. Heath and I usually looked forward to a chance to go up against two Kings, Ford, and Colm, who used to play at Boston College, but they'd turned pro over the summer.

Everyone stopped talking and stared at the end of the table as baskets of fries and burgers passed down the row. Makenna had a tray piled high with our food balanced in her hand.

"Hey, your other server had to go. I'll split the tip with her, so don't worry about that, and I'll be right back with your drinks," she said, hurrying away, not making eye contact with me. Her ignoring me brought up some irrational, ugly feelings I didn't like. She was treating me like any other person, not like we hadn't been huddled together over the past three weeks for hours on end at her request, working away. The guys dug into their food, but I couldn't touch mine. She reappeared with our drinks, sliding them across the table.

"Books, I was just telling the guys how surprised I was that I was carrying so much of the workload this semester. I'd have thought coming from Stanford your work effort would be a bit more nose to the grindstone. She's always staring at me and getting lost in my eyes. Then she'll go off on tangents about how irresistible I am and how she can never really focus around me."

I grinned up at her as her eyes narrowed behind her horn-rimmed glasses. She slid my drink toward me with enough force that it hit my hand and sloshed half of it over the rim and directly into my lap. The guys burst out into guffaws as I grabbed napkins to wipe the beer off my lap.

"Whoops, sorry. I must have been lost in your eyes and got distracted." She made a poor attempt at stifling her smirk.

"By my eyes?" I tucked my hands under my chin and batted my eyelashes at her, and she rolled her eyes.

"No, by the giant booger in your nose." She gingerly rubbed her nose with the back of her hand.

My hand flew to my nose, and I glanced at the guys at the table, ready to give them hell for not telling me, and their laugher got even louder. I'd been played.

My gaze snapped to Mak, who stood there like nothing had happened. Like she hadn't busted my balls in front of the guys and managed to keep a straight face. And all I wanted to do was bend her over that table and show her how she could make up for my bruised ego.

"Let me get you some napkins." She spun around to the bar, but I didn't miss the smile she cracked and tried to keep under wraps. Laughing along with the guys, I took a sip of my drink, but my eyes never left her.

"You two bicker like an old married couple."

My head snapped at the junior's words as he crammed half a burger into his face.

"Yeah, she's pretty cute. Maybe you should ask her out," Heath taunted as he ate some of his fries. He knew our high school history and wanted to rub it in a bit more.

"Certainly wouldn't hurt your grade as long as you didn't break up with her until after the semester was over."

My gaze darted to Preston.

"Are you seriously entertaining the idea that I ask out and date Mak to help me get a grade?" I stared wide-eyed at him.

He shrugged. "All I'm saying is, if you decide to get your dick anywhere near her, you better make sure you don't fuck things up before the end of the semester. You need her a hell of a lot more than she needs you." He took a giant bite out of his burger like that was the end of that conversation.

The guys threw out a few more one-liners, and I laughed along. Makenna was not into dating anyone and definitely not me. I mean, even if she were interested, we were like oil and water. She was too uptight, and apparently, I was breathing, which was enough to make her not want to be around me.

That said, I found myself craning my neck as she moved around the bar from table to table. She had a kind smile for most tables and brought their food and drinks out quickly. No matter what she did, she always tried to do her best, which I respected, even if it annoyed the hell out of me sometimes.

One day she'd snap and lose it if she didn't have a little fun. Sometimes when we were staying in her cubbyhole of books, little bits of her hair would fall out of her braid. It was so strange how all together it looked red, but when those strands landed against her face, they looked blonde.

And when she took her glasses off to rub her eyes, sometimes she'd leave them off. Those little indents on the sides of her nose would stay there. She'd glance over, catching me staring, and her pink lips would turn down at the corners and she'd repeat what she'd been saying, but I would be lost for a second staring at her eyes. Like warm pools of water you couldn't wait to dive into.

I could barely drag myself away from staring at her ass. I tried not to think about her as anything other than my study partner, but my mind wandered to what she had hidden under her prim and proper exterior.

We finished up our food and got the check. She was rushing around as the crowds picked up. I should probably stop teasing her so much. Maybe I would, but it was so damn fun. If that was the only way to get her attention, then maybe I'd keep it up because I wanted to make sure she was thinking about me as much as she'd invaded my thoughts. Driving me out of my mind with the need to touch her bit by bit.

She grabbed the folio off the table and waved to me and the guys as we left the bar. I shoved my hands into my pockets as everyone split up after leaving. Heath and I headed back to the apartment. I zipped my coat up against the slight chill in the air. Summer was over.

He rambled on and on about some new plant species project he was working on in botany. *Why?* I would never know, but I kept zoning out and wanting to go back to Three Streets to maybe ask Mak in person when our next study session would be.

We'd only had one the night before and had one planned for right after class, but maybe I could needle her a little and get her to agree to one sooner. I'd barely put Heath's car in park outside our house when he jumped out of the car and rushed inside. Sometimes inspiration struck him, and he zoned out to the rest of the world. I shot Mak a quick message. She might not see it until after her shift, but that was cool.

I could wait.

12

MAKENNA

I stacked my papers neatly in the corner of my desk in the study room and put the caps back on my highlighters. My color-coded study method hadn't failed me yet. I tucked my index cards into the box where I had them all categorized by class and glanced at my phone, checking the time. He wasn't late yet, but he certainly wasn't going by my five-minutes-was-on-time policy.

It had been like pulling teeth to get him to go over the midterm this early. First a random text asking when our next session would be, which was weird, and then he was all evasive when I tried to nail down a date.

I wanted to wrap my fingers around his neck and squeeze until he stopped being so difficult. Maybe he had all the time in the world to do this stuff, but I was on a tight schedule. It was a relatively easy class, at least compared to my advanced pre-med courses. I couldn't let his worry-about-it-later attitude get under my skin and screw me up. My plans were set. All I had to do was not trip and the finish line was in view.

My phone pinged, and a message bubble popped up.

Mom: Having fun, honey. We hope you are too.

There was a video attachment. It was like they were trying to become YouTube stars or something. They'd sent me videos of them riding the rollercoaster on top of a hotel in Vegas. White-water rafting in the Grand Canyon, and the latest one was them bungee jumping off a bridge in Colorado.

It was a camera attached to their helmets as they shimmied to the edge of the ledge with their arms wrapped around each other. The grins on their faces were contagious. There was a countdown from one of the people beside them, and then the rushing whoosh of air as they leaped from the ledge screaming, "We love you, Makenna!"

I got a vicarious falling feeling, leaning back in my chair as the ground came rushing at them. And then it wasn't as they were snapped back up by the elastic cable attached to them. Their adventures were laugh-out-loud, scream-inducingly amazing. I was glad they'd gotten this time together before things took a turn. Tapping out a reply, my heart swelled with happiness for them. I put my phone on silent and went through some of my notes.

My other classes were piling up. I'd gotten special permission to take extra courses to try to keep myself on track for graduation. If I had less than eight credits to take in the summer, I could still walk during graduation. And then there was the matter of medical school.

I needed to get a 3.55 GPA here. They'd let me into the BA/MD program because of the strength of my course load at Stanford, but my GPA didn't come with me. I was starting over. A few of my classes hadn't had someone get an A in them for nearly a decade, so I'd have to be happy with an A-. This meant things would be tight grade-wise.

If I got anything lower than a B+ during the semester, I

was sunk. The first semester at Stanford had been rough. Leaving my parents and the memories I'd tried to hide from hadn't made adjusting as easy as I thought it would. Getting a B in any of my classes would mean I might not get to keep my automatic spot in the med-school program.

The promises I'd made myself and the promises I'd made Daniel on the gurney beside him fired up that extra bit of determination I needed to power through this and accept whatever I needed to, to achieve his goal—my goal. It was mine too, wasn't it? After all these years, it was hard to figure out if I was doing anything for myself anymore.

I checked my phone again. Exactly five p.m. At this point I was used to Declan always being a few minutes late. I adjusted my schedule to compensate.

Tapping my foot against the chair, I looked over our notes. Our midterm paper outline was almost finished, but we needed to go over a few last things. I slid my hand into the front pocket of my bag where I'd put my thumb drive. My stomach sank. It wasn't there.

My throat tightened like I was breathing through a straw. I grabbed my bag off the floor and picked it up, frantically turning it upside down. *Nothing.* Not even a crumb fell out.

That thumb drive had all my sources for this paper and data from my lab assignments. Some of the computers in the basement labs had terrible Wi-Fi connections, and we had to save to flash drives instead of saving them to the cloud. I backed everything up. *Everything.* Always, but I'd had a shift at work that I had to get to straight after and then I'd passed out when I got home.

I'd planned to save it when I got back to the apartment tonight, but it was gone. My mouth went dry as I scoured my desk. No paper, notebook, or regular book went unturned. *How could I let this happen?* Tugging at the collar of my sweater, I flopped down in the chair, squeezing my hands to the sides of my head trying to think. There wasn't enough time to redo the lab experiments before that assignment was due. My chest was tight, and it was hard to breathe.

The chipper voice from outside meant Angel had intercepted Declan. Taking a deep breath, I swung the door open and stopped short when I saw not only Angel out there with Declan, but Seth.

"Hey, Makenna." Seth gave me a small wave. "Angel and I were asking Declan how he thinks the season will be going." Seth's big smile dimmed a bit when I didn't smile back. I pushed down the panic, trying not to look like a maniac in front of everyone.

"Are you a hockey fan?" I crossed my arms and stepped into the doorway. Out of the corner of my eye I saw Angel's pink sweater-covered arm gesturing wildly like she was the conductor at a symphony. There wasn't time for this right now. I needed to find that drive.

"Huge fan. My dad and I watch the games all the time. I used to play when I was younger. Not at his level, of course, but a little." Seth's gaze darted to Declan with stars in his eyes. I fought the urge to race out of there without a word, leaving everyone behind. Trying to keep my face as neutral as possible and not show my annoyance and near panic attack, I turned to Declan and Angel. She'd moved on from just flailing her arms around to actually resting her hand on his arm as she talked.

I hated how that little flare-up of something hit me right in the stomach. I wasn't one of those girls. Catty. Territorial. Bitchy. I'm sure he'd had his run of many girls on campus, but this was our study time and I didn't want to be there any more than he did.

"I need to go to my apartment. We can reschedule this. I need to go."

His head popped up, and his eyes went wide before he nodded.

"I can go with you there. It's cool. We should tackle this thing and get it done." His easy and sudden acceptance at working on this almost pissed me off. Why couldn't he have been this cooperative before we had to send like fifteen messages to get this arranged? Every one of my texts had been met with another question, like he didn't want our messaging chain to end.

"Okay, I'll be right back." I let the door close behind me and nearly screamed in frustration. *Why did I say okay?* The urge to race out of there and get him away from Angel caught me off guard.

I thought about going back out there and saying never mind, but Seth and Angel were both still standing on the other side of the door. It would make me look even more like an idiot if I went out there and told him no. Packing up what we'd need for our paper, I jammed everything into my bag and left the safety of my study room.

"I'm ready. Bye, Angel. Bye, Seth." I walked past Declan without even looking back. He said a hurried goodbye to the pair and followed me. Not feeling like being confined in the elevator with him, I went left and took the stairs, jogging down the steps like I could outrun my stupidity. Declan's footsteps thudded behind me reminding me that I couldn't.

The faster I found the flash drive, the faster I wouldn't be ready to curl into a ball and cry until graduation. If I ever graduated. I clenched my jaw through my annoyance. People moved out of my way as I blazed a trail off campus to my apartment complex. Declan kept up with me like he was going for a Sunday stroll. Damn him and his ridiculously long legs.

Taking the steps to my apartment two at a time, I raced inside and into my bedroom, leaving him out in the living room, dropping my stuff and going through everything on my desk. Despair clawed at my chest like an angry animal looking to go straight through me.

There was no clutter. There weren't piles of clothes and other stuff for anything to get hidden under, so where the hell was it? I picked things up that I hadn't moved all semester except to vacuum.

"Hey, Books." Declan's voice came from the living room. I didn't have time for his teasing right now. I'd deal with him in a bit.

"Makenna." His voice was closer in the hallway. I pulled back my bedspread and searched under my bed. Not even a dust bunny.

"Makenna Halstead." His voice boomed from the hallway.

"What?" I snapped from my hands and knees on the floor.

"Were you looking for this?" He waved the navy and white thumb drive in front of him, and I let out a startled cry. Jumping to my feet, I held my breath not wanting to believe it until I had the drive in my hand. He dropped it into my hand.

"Oh my God! Where did you find it?" I clutched it to my chest with numb fingers. My heart hammered against my ribs as I wrapped my hands so tightly around it I was afraid I might crack it.

"It was out on the kitchen counter on a giant piece of neon green paper with a black circle around it." He led me out into the living room, and I spotted the oversize sticky note stuck on the counter with the circle with nothing in it.

Found this by the front door. Figured it was yours. Tried to call but couldn't get through. Hope you didn't freak out too much when you couldn't find it. -Fiona

The note was scrawled across the paper.

The lab also had terrible cell reception. I sagged against the counter, blinking back tears. For those few minutes everything had been spiraling out of control, and now that I had the drive in my hand, it was like everything was okay again. Such a small thing. I stared blankly at the counter when another piece of paper slid into view.

"I know you're still in freak-out mode, but I wanted to give you this. I know I've been a pain in the ass, so I made sure I did all the technical references and yes, I made sure to use the proper format." Blinking back my tears, I peered over at him and nodded. My throat was too tight to trust with words.

Without thinking, I threw my arms around him, squeezing him. I was a split second from kissing him full on the lips. It was our senior prom all over again. Pressing my face against his warm shoulder, I breathed in his soap-and-something-more smell. My lips were less than an inch from his skin, my face on his soft black Henley.

It wasn't until his arms wrapped around my back and we stood there for a second that I realized what I was doing. I jerked back and untangled my arms from around him. The back of my neck felt like someone was holding a heating lamp up to it.

"Thank you," I mumbled, glancing down at my sneakers. The cold sweat that had broken out all over my body made me shiver.

I flipped through the sheets of the small stack of neatly

stapled papers and checked over the first few pages. The references were always the piece I hated doing the most, and he'd plunked it down in my lap, looking like it had been done perfectly.

He peered over at me and opened his mouth like he wanted to say something. The butterflies were back, but they'd brought some friends. There was a stampede going on in my stomach from one look from Declan.

"No worries. I figured if you had a heart attack during the semester, then I'd have to do all this by myself, and I'd rather we shoulder the burden together."

I rolled my eyes and got my stuff from my room. We sat on the terrible sunken couch with my phone on the table, computer balanced on my lap. He emailed me a soft copy of the work he'd done, and we got down to it.

After a couple minutes my phone vibrated as notifications rolled in. They were texts. If something serious had happened, my mom would call. I ignored it and kept going through the paper.

Like a puppy, Declan was easily distracted. His gaze darted to the phone every time a message came in, and exactly like a puppy who gnawed on your favorite pair of shoes, he didn't know how to not touch things that weren't his. He picked up my phone.

"You know, you really should lock this. Got a hot date tonight?"

"Give me my phone." I grabbed for it, but he unlocked it and held it up high, scrolling through the messages.

"What's with the secrets? What do you have on here?" He stood up when I tried to swipe the phone from him.

"None of your business. I wouldn't go through your phone." Just when I thought he was okay, he had to pull something like this. I glanced at his legs. Maybe I could trip him, but with my luck he'd fall into the edge of the coffee table and die, and then I'd have to chop his body up and hide it all around campus.

"Here, go ahead." He tugged his phone out of his pocket and threw it at me. I caught it out of reflex.

"I don't want to go through your phone. Plus, it's locked."

"Wow, are these your parents?" He held the phone up and replayed their bungee jumping video.

"Yes, they are. Now give it back to me. And take your phone." I thrust it at him, but he took two steps back, scrolling through my parents' adventure thread.

"My password is 1-9-3-2."

For a split second I was tempted to unlock it, but the possible dick pics and who knows what else that was probably on there dissuaded me, and I held it by the corner. Irritation bubbled up and threatened to overflow.

"Looks like your parents are pretty freaking cool daredevils, Books." He handed my phone back to me, and I chucked his at him. He caught it against his hard-planed chest. "What happened to you?"

"Yeah, really easy to be a daredevil and start living your life again when you know you're going to die," I snapped. My eyes got wide with horror at what I'd just said. I sank back down onto the couch.

That little pill of bitterness had blindsided me. Tapping my phone against my hand, I tried not to let those old emotions boil over. But it was one of those days where it seemed like everything was hanging on by a thread.

"What do you mean, dying?" He gingerly sat on the couch next to me. Letting out a deep breath, I raked my hands through my hair. I hadn't meant to blurt that out. All this time they had, they could have been living.

"He's sick. He's got ALS. After finally going back to work

a couple years ago, in the spring he tripped a few times and then a few more. He used to hike mountains all the time. He was steady on his feet. Once he ended up in the ER needing stitches. That's when they found out."

There was a pause as my morbid life bomb detonated all over my apartment.

"That's why you moved back."

I peered over at him with a sad smile. The look on his face almost made me laugh.

"I'm sorry, Makenna. I shouldn't have said what I said about you leaving Stanford." He rested his hand on my knee and squeezed it.

"Sometimes life wants to kick you in the teeth when you're already down. This was their bucket list trip. They'd planned it before. Years ago, but then things happened, and they were both out of it for a...while. The doctors have him on some meds, so he's pretty much a hundred percent, but things can progress quickly. They wanted to do all this stuff while they still could."

"When will they finish the trip?"

"Just before Thanksgiving. We'll get to have that together, and then he goes to the doctor and who knows." I shrugged.

"Is that why you're pre-med?"

I jerked back and stared at him. "How did you know I was pre-med?"

"No one takes the course load you have unless they are. I might seem like a big buffoon sometimes, but I can be pretty observant." He nudged my shoulder with his.

"It's part of the reason." Not wanting to go down this path with him, I shook my head and picked up my computer off the couch. "Enough chitchat. Stop trying to distract me. Let's get down to business." I gave him a weak smile and pulled the paper back up.

He let out a sigh and grabbed some of the papers off the table.

"Yeah, let's do this."

I didn't like the warm fuzzies I got sitting beside Declan and how easy it would be to unload everything on him. I didn't like it at all because I wasn't supposed to feel this way about him. I wasn't supposed to want his arms wrapped around me and holding me close. I wasn't.

Well maybe a little...

13

DECLAN

The phone call came, and Heath and I dropped everything and headed into downtown Philly. Being spread out all over the country meant opportunities to see the other guys came few and far between, especially since Heath and I were the only ones who hadn't made it to the pros yet.

Ford and Colm left junior year and Emmett even earlier, during sophomore year. We were shocked he ended up in college at all; he'd been so secretive about what the hell he was doing after high school graduation. Well, other than his plans to marry Avery, but we all knew how that panned out. Everyone had their hang ups. Times when life was like, "haha you thought things were going to go your way."

Emmett had been traded, this time to LA, where he was enjoying his enforcer status full tilt. It was surreal watching the guys on TV out there with the rest of their teams living the dream we'd all talked about in high school. They'd done it. Heath and I were pulling up the rear and needed to nail this down. My Archer issues had gone on long enough. I was going to end this.

Walking into the stadium that dwarfed ours on campus, I got a chill down my back—and not from the Baltic temperatures inside. Getting out on the ice with Heath and Emmett would take some of the edge off not being a part of the team for now, but it wouldn't be for much longer.

In only a few months it would be me walking down this tunnel to the locker room with tens of thousands of fans in the stands. My heart hammered as we stared at the empty stands around us. This was the first time I'd been here when it was empty. Something caught my eye in the sea of seats, and it was a slamming gut punch as the vision of Archer looming over me from up there dissolved like a horror movie villain.

"Would you two hurry up? I don't have all day."

We whipped around at the booming voice before breaking out into a smile.

"I've been training with Heath, so we'll see who's slow out there." I dropped my bag and gave Em a hug, clapping him on the back.

"Damn, I feel bad for you. I'm surprised you can still feel your legs. I made the mistake of asking him to help me work out after senior year. I couldn't walk for a week after the first session." Em laughed, and Heath shrugged his shoulders.

"It's not my fault you two can't keep up. I mean, I make sure to only go at eighty percent when I'm working out with other people."

I totally believed it. Heath was a laid-back dude everywhere except on the ice, he was an unrelenting beast out there. If it were possible to stack a team with eight Heaths' you'd never even know what an opposing team scoring on you felt like. And it wasn't just the skill, it was his endurance. He could go for what seemed like hours without stopping.

Em guided us back into the locker room, and we got changed before stepping out onto the one place where everything made sense. Our playground. Our training ground. The ice was our refuge.

"I can't believe you're a King again." I pulled back my stick and released, sending the puck flying. The freezing air of the rink glided across my face as my blades sliced through the ice. Massive overhead lights lit up the whole area. A perk of being a star pro player.

"I thought once a King, always a King." Emmett skated toward me, showering me in a spray of ice as he changed directions.

"Fucker!" I shouted after him and gave chase, digging in and pushing ahead. Heath was in his own world, basking in the impressive pros stadium as he whipped around the rink, going faster and faster with a stick in one hand and trading the puck back between his skates and the stick.

I caught up to Emmett and managed to get the puck away from him by slamming him up against the boards.

"Have you played against the Dynamic Duo yet?"

"Of course." He grunted, pushing off the boards and going for the puck. "I played against them a few weeks ago. I went out to dinner with them and Liv. She and Grant are graduating from high school in a few weeks." He skated backward, taunting me.

"Damn, seriously? Little Olive Oil and Grant are going to be in college." Grant was Ford's little brother. He and Liv had gone to Rittenhouse Prep together before Colm moved Liv up to Boston to go to boarding school while he went to college and then went pro.

"Not so much Olive Oil anymore. Colm would murder me if he heard me say this, but she's actually a little hottie now."

I scrunched up my face at that. It was hard to imagine the little beanpole eighth grader as anything but that.

"I'll take your word for it." Heath whipped past us, giving me the distraction I needed. I slid my stick between Em's legs and grabbed the puck, racing toward my goal. Emmett's skates sliced across the ice in pursuit, and I made a sharp turn to throw him off, but he wasn't fooled and kept coming.

Changing tactics, I turned and threw my shoulder into him, smashing him against the glass. He pushed off the glass and darted after me as I dug deep and sank the puck into the back of the net.

"Looks like the college senior beat out the pro player." I pumped my hands overhead and simulated the roar of the crowd.

"Tell that to my bank account." Emmett grinned, resting his head on top of his hands on the stick.

"Like that wasn't always the case. No other high school senior I knew could drop thirty grand on an engagement ring," Heath called out from the edge of the rink. My chuckle died in my throat once I realized what Heath had said. Heath came to a stutter stop beside me as we waited for Emmett's reaction.

"Don't worry. I'm not going to freak out. That was years ago. Dodged a fucking bullet, right? You tried to warn me." The hard look in his eyes couldn't hide the hurt there. Emmett whipped around and skated to the bench.

I punched Heath in the shoulder, and he winced, rubbing the spot.

"Relax," he said, shooting me a look. Avery was a no-go when it came to any of us. I'd been the only one at the party where they broke up—no, that wasn't even the right word. *Imploded* seemed more fitting, but that didn't mean everyone else hadn't heard in excruciating detail how things went down.

The gut punch of finding out your girlfriend of three years was cheating on you when you had an engagement ring in your pocket was seriously fucked. I'd never heard someone make a sound like he did that night, and I'd been hit by a puck in the nuts with no cup. He'd shattered his front door when he bolted, and everyone else in the party stood there in stunned silence.

We'd learned not to talk about her. *Ever.* If we did, he'd walk away. Mid-conversation, mid–car ride, it didn't matter. Heath—it was always Heath and his loose lips—brought her up when we were driving back from Boston to see Colm and Ford play in their first pro game, and Emmett almost jumped out of the moving car. He pulled on the handle as we approached a stoplight and left, finding his own way home.

It seemed that after nearly four years the wound still hadn't fully healed. Who knew if it ever would. Memories of high school came back, and knowing Makenna now, some of her old annoying behavior changed in my mind. She wasn't the stuck-up rich girl who always had to be right. Like Colm, whose parents were killed in a car crash during our senior year of high school, having money didn't insulate you from the kinds of things some people didn't recover from.

All the money in the world hadn't kept her dad from getting sick, Colm's parents from dying, or Emmett's almost proposal from blowing up in his face. Growing up, I'd always thought the non-scholarship kids had it all, but I knew now that wasn't true.

Archer walking out on us was probably the best thing that ever happened now that I saw what a colossal asshole he was. Sure, I'd messed up sophomore year trying to work a job to help Mom with some extra money and not passed a class or two, but it paled in comparison to how things could have shaken out.

We pushed ourselves out there until someone blew a whistle letting us know our time on the ice was over. Of course Heath was only just getting warmed up, but my legs were wobbly after the big push with those two. And it had never felt better. Being out there brought back all those feelings from high school. The invincibility. The promise. It had all been so much easier back then.

"I don't know why you guys are even still here." Emmett popped his head up from unlacing his skates when we stepped into the box.

"My mom is really hung up on me graduating. She never got to, and she'd really like me to get my degree before I start playing." I shrugged and worked on my skates.

"You can come back later and play. There are seventeen- and eighteen-year-olds from Slovenia and stuff gliding right into those spots you two aren't filling."

Heath bent to get his skates off. "I'm working on my botany degree. Can't come back later. It would mean leaving my work behind."

"They're plants, Heath. I'm pretty sure plants will still be around in a few years."

"I like college. I have the rest of my life to play hockey, but this is a special time. Gotta soak that shit up." We both stared at him, but he gathered up his stuff and left the box. He didn't miss a step walking past us with our mouths hanging open. At this point he was used to everyone gawking at him when he dropped some weird-ass Heath wisdom on us.

Emmett and I burst out laughing as we followed behind him. I gave the ice one last look before turning to catch up with the guys. It would be me out there skating soon, under the lights with the roar of the crowd pushing me harder than ever before.

"Some things never change, huh?"

"I live with him; imagine how that is. You have no idea how many situations he walks into blindly and dodges every bullet like he's got a superpower or something. He turns around like, oh, was that building on fire? Shrugs. It makes me want to punch him in the face and stand up and clap all the time."

"I can imagine. I'll try to come to one of your games. I think I'm back in the city sometime in November."

"That would be awesome. Have a young upstart show you how it's done."

Emmett rolled his eyes and shook his head.

"How's LA?" I called out as he grabbed a towel.

"It's LA. Sunny. Warm. Hot women. Got an apartment. My dad's out there sometimes." He grimaced and pushed open the locker room door.

"Really? You see him?" Their relationship had always been distant at best. They didn't even come to his graduation. It was part of the reason he got away with murder back in high school. Boatloads of money, a family name, and absentee parents were more than enough to get most people in a lot of trouble. But he'd kept things in line. The craziest thing he did was practically have Avery move in with him when she wasn't watching her little sister.

He rolled his eyes. "I didn't even see him when we lived in the same house together. You think he would deign to drive across town to see me? *Hell no.* I only found out because my mother's assistant forwarded over their final divorce papers. Like I needed that shit. The only time I see him is when I have to deal with something with my trust we can't do through the mail or assistants."

"That sucks, man."

"It is what it is." He shrugged and grabbed a towel. I slid one off the tall stack of bleach white towels, and we headed into the shower. We each stepped into the frosted glass enclosed shower stalls. Talk about luxury surroundings.

We showered up and grabbed a cab to get some food.

A few people came up to say 'hi' and get a picture with Emmett or ask us about the upcoming season.

"You two have no idea what it's like once you're playing in the pros, man. You think this is fun? Wait until you are recognized everywhere, not just in your hometown." He stretched his arms over the top of the booth, soaking up all the attention.

"You only say that because you're a man whore." Heath laughed and took a sip of his beer.

"Man whore would imply I sleep around. I don't cheat. Not when I'm dating someone."

"You also don't date." I bit into my massive burger. Emmett used to be the most romantic guy ever. Sickeningly and to the point that we gave him shit about it all the time when he was with Avery. He was all bouquets of roses, limo rides, and nice dinners out. From what I'd heard from the other guys, things had changed a little.

"I date within the right perimeters. Under circumstances that keep things from getting too serious." Emmett stopped scanning the bar and grabbed his beer. "It's all about making sure everyone knows the deal up front. Then no one gets hurt."

"I'm sure that works out just fine. 'Listen, I'm not in this for anything long-term; will you let me bang you for a few months and then you're out? And here's a nice check to keep your mouth shut.' Yeah, that sounds like it would never go off the rails."

Emmett's head whipped around to Heath, who held up his hands in surrender.

"You know you can't tell him anything without him blabbing about it everywhere."

Emmett squeezed the bridge of his nose. "You know what, you're right. I don't know what I was thinking. Anyway, it's working out so far."

"For you."

He narrowed his gaze. "What the hell is that supposed to mean?"

"I'm just saying sometimes I'm sure people get their feelings hurt even if you don't mean that to happen." The look on Mak's face back in high school when I'd taunted her about her perfect life or even that first day at the diner when I got on her case about Stanford...I couldn't shake how shitty that made me.

"Look at you, Mr. Sensitive. I think I remember quite a few hearts broken in the McAvoy wake." He raised an eyebrow at me, and he wasn't wrong.

"It's probably because he's hanging out with Makenna from high school. She's keeping him in line."

Emmett's eyes got wide, and he choked on his drink. Heath chomped down on his fries with his eyes glued on the screen across from our booth. I shot him a glare he didn't even notice.

"You're hanging with the Ice Queen? Damn, things have changed. I thought you two hated each other."

"We never hated each other. We just liked to button push. And we're not hanging out really; we're partners in class together. Not that there would be anything wrong with us hanging out. She's cool." Both their heads swung in my direction with their mouths hanging open.

I mean, she was. Everyone was dealing with their own stuff. I didn't dread our sessions anymore. I liked them. When she stopped being so uptight about everything, she was actually pretty funny and—beautiful. I mean pretty—not pretty, nice. She was nice.

"We are friends. That's it."

Emmett and Heath exchanged looks and laughed. That did not bode well...

14

MAKENNA

"I think we've done more than enough." Declan laid back on my bed, staring up at the ceiling. We'd moved into my room when he complained last time that our couch was some kind of torture device.

"If we make it through these last few pages, think of how much less we'll have to do later." I turned back to my computer, my fingers flying over the keys. Declan let out a groan, and my mattress springs squeaked as he got up from the bed.

"Or we call it a night now." The screen started to close on my laptop, and I tilted my head, trying to type out the last couple lines before I had to yank my fingers out so they didn't get smooshed.

"Enough, Books. You can't give everything a hundred percent all the time. Have a little fun."

"What exactly do you think we're doing? This is fun." I smiled teasingly. He rolled his eyes and disappeared out of the bedroom. My stomach sank. *Did he just walk out on me?* I guess my joke didn't really land. Spinning in my seat, I was ready to go after him and yelped as he appeared in the darkened doorway.

He waltzed back into my room with a six-pack in his hand. His six-pack. Not like his abs—he had those with him all the time. His t-shirt always stretched tight over them. I shook my head. *Not that. Don't think about his abs.* It was a six-pack of beers.

"How did I know these would still be here untouched?" He stood in the middle of the room gently shaking the six-pack, staring at me like I'd been naughty for not drinking an entire six-pack on my own.

I'd forgotten all about those.

"Oh yeah."

"Oh yeah, is right. These things wouldn't last a night in my place. Maybe this is where I should start stashing my booze from now on." He picked up his wallet and slid a weird flat thing out of his wallet. He rested it on the edge of the bottle cap and popped it off. A bottle opener. Of course he'd be the MacGuyver of booze. He opened two beers and handed me one.

I stared at the cool bottle dangling out in front of me and reached my hand out tentatively. My fingers brushed against his and wrapped around the glass and the same sharp jolt shot through me. The kind that woke me in the morning when I'd knew I'd been thinking about him, even when I promised myself I wouldn't.

"Do you like Yuengling?" He clinked his bottle to mine and took a gulp of his.

"I don't really know." The heat crept into my cheeks as I thought about how few drinks I'd had in my life. I was twenty-one, and there wasn't much of an excuse for a college kid to not have at least a couple. "Don't they all taste the same?"

He stopped mid-drink and stared at me like I'd just said there was no difference between a 3.6 GPA and a 3.59.

"All the same? What kind of college is Stanford? They do have beer there? Or are you only allowed to have mixed drinks or something?"

"They have beer. I just never really liked the taste."

"You have to get used to it."

I rolled my eyes. "That's what everyone says."

I tested out the drink in my hand, taking a small sip. The bitterness had a hint of sweetness behind it as the slight carbonation rolled over my tongue. I grimaced and finished the swallow. The hopeful look on Declan's face fell. He looked like I'd just kicked a puppy.

"I'm sorry." I sat forward a bit. "I'm sure it's something I would get used to like everyone says."

He shook his head. "Never apologize for not liking something. If you don't like it, you don't." He tried to grab the bottle out of my hand, but I jerked it back and took another sip. The buzz of the beer traveled through my body. I wiggled my toes as the warmth reached down there.

"Let me at least finish this one." I needed to prove it to him and to myself.

He leaned back resting his elbows on my bed and tipped the bottle up. I kicked off my shoes and ran my toes along the chilly hardwood floor. Fall was quickly turning to winter.

We talked about the semester and hockey, naturally.

"I still can't believe all of you still have your teeth. Isn't that a big hockey thing? Gap-toothed smiles from getting bashed up against the Plexiglas?"

"I'll send you a picture when I lose my first one. Maybe I'll mail you the tooth." He gave me a dopey grin that made me squeeze my thighs together.

I glanced down at the beer like it had betrayed me, but I'd had feelings like this before when I was around him.

"Ew, gross." I winged one of the pillows on my desk at him. He caught it midair and lobbed it back at me. My attempt at a catch was thwarted by my beer, and I laughed as I spilled some on my hand.

Our talk drifted to our families, and he thought it was hilarious that my parents were roaming the country as we spoke. I was happy they were having their fun. There weren't any pain-tinged edges around it this time. They deserved this time. A chance to build those memories while they could.

Sitting in my room with Declan was the lightest I'd felt since before I could remember. He finished his beer and grabbed another. His Adam's apple bobbed up and down, and I did a double take at the surreal scene in front of me. Declan was sitting on my bed, relaxed, and hanging out. His muscled and lithe body sprawled out for me to soak in a little at a time.

Chuckling to myself, I took another sip of my beer.

"What's so funny?" He leaned forward with his elbows on his knees, rolling the beer bottle between his hands.

"If you'd told me senior year that I'd be hanging out with you and having a beer or two, I'd have said you were crazy."

He laughed and glanced down, picking at the label on his bottle.

"Definitely." There was a comfortable silence as we enjoyed our drinks. Well, he enjoyed his. I was mustering my way through mine. "Hey, Mak." He peered up at me with a worried look on his face. "I wanted to apologize about the whole party thing senior year."

And just like that I was transported back to a time I'd

hoped to forget. All the lightness didn't go away, but it wasn't ready to lift me off my feet like it had been before.

"I wouldn't have said what I said, if I thought it was going to be such a big deal for you. Who knows? Maybe I would have. I was trying to make a joke, and I came off as a dick. I was having a bad few weeks." He rambled and shifted on the bed like it was suddenly made of sandpaper and rocks. "It wasn't something I meant for you to take so personally. I was only trying to lighten the mood. You were so serious then. Still are." He tipped his bottle to me and drank some down.

I didn't like seeing him like that. As much as I was wrapped up in my own head, I didn't need to drag him down with me over it. I laughed, my buzz getting stronger with each sip. He glanced up at me, wide-eyed.

"I'm sorry too. I know you work hard at hockey and I'm sure you'll love playing in the pros. It was really admirable that you stuck with school the whole way through. I shouldn't have said what I said either. So, let's say we're even. Don't worry about it. I shouldn't have taken it so personally. There was a lot going on in my life. I...I was just under a lot of pressure back then." And now, I silently added. "You transferred into Rittenhouse Prep freshman year, right?"

He nodded. I took a deep breath. Way to kill the fun and lively mood. I was about to run it over with my car.

"You missed the Halstead family implosion that happened in seventh grade. I had a little brother. Daniel." I couldn't stop. The lump in my throat threatened to suffocate me, but I drank some more beer, hoping to loosen up the hold it had on me. I needed to power through this or I'd never get it out.

"He got sick when he was nine, and I was twelve.

Leukemia. And he died the summer between seventh and eighth grade." Our twin gurneys being pushed down the hallway. The smell of industrial antiseptic. It was like I could taste the sterile air just by thinking of it.

Declan made a small noise, and I glanced up. He'd leaned forward on the bed, perched on the edge.

"While he was sick, I tried to do the best I could with everything. I didn't want to be another problem for my parents to deal with. We were all in and out of the hospital so much, and things at home started to slip." I cleared my throat, trying to talk past the boulder lodged there.

"I wanted to help out and try to keep things clean. Started cooking or at least heating up the food people brought over to the house. After Daniel died, my parents were kind of a mess. It was like a part of them died because I guess it had. They weren't exactly...functional."

He reached out and tugged my chair forward. The wheels glided across the floor until my knees were between his opened legs. I stared down at the beer in my hands.

"I thought that if I was helpful enough and perfect enough that maybe it would help them come back from the dark place we all went to when he died. Maybe I could make them happy again. I could get them to smile at me without the sadness in their eyes. Maybe I could get them to see me again." My voice cracked, and I blinked furiously, trying to keep the tears at bay.

Taking a shuddering breath, I peeked up at him. His eyes had their own sheen of tears in them.

"I sure know how to kill a fun time, right? Sorry." I lifted my beer and took a gulp.

He slid his hands onto my legs, just above my knees, and squeezed gently.

"Never apologize for that. I'm glad you told me. I'm sorry

I never knew about your brother and about everything going on with your family. I was a self-absorbed asshole back then."

"Was?" I cracked a smile. The weight pushing down on me, and the sadness that settled over me lifted some the moment his hands touched me. There were a lot of things that felt different when I was around Declan McAvoy. I gazed into his eyes, and the fluttering was back in full force, but I knew it had nothing to do with the beer this time.

"Yeah, I know. I can be an asshole sometimes now too."

"No, you're really not. I'm just a bit high-strung some-times." I darted my gaze away.

"Sometimes! Come on, you're the entire string section of an orchestra."

I barked out a laugh and nodded, draining the rest of my beer. Shaking it at him as a testament that I wasn't high-strung all the time, I reached for another one at the same time he did, and our heads were an inch apart.

His freckles weren't as bright as they had been at the beginning of the semester. The fall weather meant the summer sun wasn't there to kiss them, to make them come alive, but this close I could see every one in vivid detail. We froze like that, bent over with an arm reached out to the six-pack on the floor.

My fingers brushed against his over the cool glass bottle, and I sucked in a sharp breath. The pupils of his eyes got bigger, the mossy green giving way to black as he lifted the bottle with my hand still on his. Setting the beer onto the bed, he reversed his hold and threaded his fingers through mine. My pulse pounded as the replay I'd kept going of the senior prom dance we'd had slammed right into me. How much I'd wanted to taste his lips. How good it felt to have his arms around my waist. He gazed into my eyes with his never leaving mine.

"Mak." His voice came out deeper than usual, and a shiver crept down my spine. He said my name like a prayer he hoped I'd answer. With our fingers intertwined, he pulled me closer until my knees hit the edge of the bed.

I hesitantly reached my hand out and slid it along his neck and up into his hair, letting his curly strands run through my fingers. He shuddered and closed his eyes for a second. When they popped open, the overwhelming desire in them made my body hum. Emotions running this high, I couldn't talk myself out of wanting him. My body and I were in full agreement this time. He was ours, at least for tonight.

"Declan." My voice came out, and it didn't sound like me at all. It was breathy and needy, like the ache I had could only be cured by him.

Like he was afraid I'd evaporate into thin air, he leaned in until our foreheads touched.

"Are you sure?"

My throat was tight. He sure as hell wasn't asking if I wanted another drink. I don't know what I was sure of, but whatever he had in mind, I needed. I needed him to help me get these feelings under control or get them out of my system.

The ones that slammed into me the second he walked into a room, or that ache when he left. Somehow I'd gotten to the point where Declan McAvoy threatened the careful equilibrium I'd struck in my life and I didn't know how to fix it. The long silence stretched between us, and I nodded.

It was the only warning I got before he lifted me out of the chair, pressed his lips to mine. He tasted like the beer, and it had never tasted so good.

I spread my legs and straddled his lap, our bodies fitting

together as he pushed his tongue into my mouth. Without thinking, I rocked my hips against him, closing my eyes as the little jolts of pleasure rolled through my body.

His hands roamed all over my back, pressing me in even closer. My heart hammered so hard, it was like I was playing my own drum solo in my chest. Every inch of me wanted to be around him. There wasn't enough air in the world to fill my lungs, and I couldn't think straight with his lips on mine. Wrapping my arms around his neck, I moaned as his fingers ran up my spine under my shirt. The bulge under my ass made my core throb. Every story from the locker rooms in high school rushed through my head

My pussy clenched as his hard length nudged me through my jeans, demanding his presence be known. Oh, I knew all right. Breaking our lip-lock, I tugged on his hair. His eyes darted to mine, green clashing with blue.

"What's a girl gotta do to get past first base?"

"Always so bossy." His chuckle turned into something deeper as I ground my hips against him. It came out like the groan of a starving man finally presented with a buffet. It made my breath catch as he cupped my ass and flipped me around. I bounced on the bed, and he stood at the end of the mattress.

Gripping the hem of my shirt, I whipped it off. I had to be one step ahead of myself or I'd chicken out. I'd never forgive myself for not going for it at least once.

"I'll show you exactly what you have to do." He ran his hands over my thighs, keeping his eyes on mine. My eyebrows scrunched together when he leaned in with a smirk on his face. I sucked in a sharp breath as he popped the button to my jeans open with his teeth. My clit throbbed, and I knew I was in for the ride of my life.

15

DECLAN

The look on her face when I popped her jeans open almost made me laugh. Almost, but the pounding of my cock and the overwhelming need to touch her pushed everything else aside. I had no other purpose in life other than touching Mak and making her want me as much as I wanted her. The tension building between us was ready to blow, and so was I if I didn't get inside her. She lifted her hips to help me drag the jeans and her thong down her legs.

One look at her glistening pussy and my chest got tight. It was hard to breathe. Like that anticipation before unwrapping a present you didn't even know you had coming. The small strip of hair she had right above her pussy was perfect. I wasn't a Brazilian kind of guy. I liked that she had something there, but my eyes were riveted to the shining spots on her thighs. Like she'd been thinking about doing this with me as much as I'd been thinking about it with her.

"Beautiful, Mak. Absolutely beautiful." I barely recognized my own voice. Things had never been like this before.

But she wasn't like anyone I'd met before. She challenged and frustrated me to no end. And I wouldn't have it any other way.

She pushed up on her elbows, smirking before crooking one of her fingers at me, beckoning me closer like a siren to the rocks of pleasure, ready to shred me. But I didn't want to change course now. I couldn't. She owned me. I wanted to see this bold side of her more often.

I slid my hands along her skin, working my way back up her body, peppering her with kisses as goose bumps broke out all over her.

I resisted the urge to go too quickly.

I wanted this to last.

I wanted her to crave me as much as I did her.

Her legs trembled, and she sucked in a sharp breath. I wasn't the only one anticipating how good this was going to be. She reached up for me. Her fingers touched my skin, sending fiery-hot tendrils of desire through my body like a gut punch. She ran her hands over my back, and my cock strained against the zipper of my jeans. I should have taken my jeans off, but I was in a daze when she was in front of me. I hadn't wanted to waste another second not touching her.

With her arms reaching out for me, she was spread out on the bed like an untouched pond after a fresh snowfall. I wanted to make my mark on her so she'd never forget. Those emotions welling inside of me scared the shit out of me. Pushing them aside, I settled my hips between her opened legs.

Dropping down on top of her, I brushed back her hair off her face. I wanted to look into her eyes and I wanted her looking into mine. Every second pulsed with the promise of sinking into her and taking us to the point of no return. The anticipation in the air was so thick between us I could taste it like I wanted to taste her. I ran my lips along her neck until she wrapped her legs around my hips, her heels digging into my ass with insistent, urgent need.

Tilting her head up, she moaned at my nips along her skin. Her smell, her touch, her taste, everything made me want this night to last as long as possible. Make it something she couldn't forget.

"Stop teasing me." She grabbed my hair and tightened her grip, making my scalp tingle.

"It wouldn't be as fun if I didn't." I caught her gaze. Equal parts playful and wanton, she stared at me with a crooked smile. Like she knew she was driving me wild. The bright blue of her eyes threatened to drown me as she licked her plump, pink lips.

I pushed up and kissed my way back down her body until I was off the bed. Winking at her, I unbuttoned my jeans.

She rolled her eyes and whipped off her bra. The light pink fabric went sailing across the room. Her pebbled nipples cried out for my touch, for my mouth. Seeing her this open and needy and demanding, all wrapped into one beautiful package, made my cock throb in anticipation of giving her everything she needed.

Her desire for me was on full display, and my dick bounced off my stomach. I couldn't focus on just one part of her. I wanted all of her. I'd done that to her, made her every bit as hot as she made me. My mouth watered as I smelled her, and while I wanted to be inside her, I needed to taste her even more. I knelt on the floor and dragged her down the bed, hooking her legs over my shoulders when she bolted up.

"What are you doing?"

I kept my hands on her thighs, kneading the flesh there. Her heated, supple skin glided under my grip.

"Thought it was pretty obvious." I inched my hands higher on her legs, and she sucked in a sharp breath.

"I can't come that way." She snapped fully up straight. Her eyes darted around the room like she'd rather look anywhere other than at me. I froze as I processed what she'd said.

"Never?"

"No. Never. I've only ever had it done a couple times and it was fast and awkward and I don't really like it." It came out like one long word as she rushed through it. Her cheeks were red now, but I knew it wasn't from my touch.

"I'm pretty much one hundred percent sure that it's because you did not have the right person doing it. I have never had any complaints before, and I can assure you, I will always make it so good you'll be demanding I go down on you on a regular basis."

"How generous of you." And like that the embarrassment evaporated, and she looked a second away from rolling her eyes.

"I aim to please." I lowered my head again, but she blocked me with her arm.

"Let's skip all that and get to the good stuff." She said it like she was trying to distract a yappy dog that was stuck on a bone. "Please." Her voice hitched, needy and clear, and her eyes softened, her uncertainty and desire clear to me. My heart pounded as she lifted her arm and threaded her fingers through my hair.

"I'd really like you to fuck me." The words fell from her lips like she was saying, *I'd really like you to walk me home.* So sweet. I was torn between sating my hunger and giving in to what we both needed. *Who am I to deny her?* She reached down between us and cupped my hard cock. I sucked in a sharp breath and fought to keep my eyes from drifting shut. I didn't want to miss a second of this.

"I think a jump-to-the-good-stuff one-time pass could be arranged this time around." She let out a throaty chuckle and let go of my hair. I crawled onto the bed, and she scooted back to give me space. Our foreheads almost touching, our eyes locked, I followed her up the bed like a predator stalking his prey. Coming down on top of her again, I ran my hands through her hair and laid another searing kiss on her lips.

Her knees came up and opened more, letting me get even closer to her and giving me even more access to her sweet pussy. Her hot, wet heat rested on my stomach just above my cock. I shuddered and counted in my head so this wasn't over before it even began.

Breaking our kiss, I stared down at her. She was the most beautiful thing I'd ever seen. Her pink lips were plump and wet from my kisses, her breasts rising and falling in anticipation of me finally making her mine. Lifting my hips, I ran my cock along her pussy, her wetness soaking my head.

We both moaned, but I reared back when she pushed her hand against my chest.

"Wait! Condom," she breathed out. And it hit me. I had been about to sink into her without protection. I'd never done that before. Never even thought about doing it before, but she had me out of my mind, and I'd wanted to without even thinking about it.

"In the drawer." She flung her hand toward the bedside table, and I reached out and opened it. A spark of jealousy shot through me thinking of another guy there with her doing the same thing. I got the box, and the green-eyed monster chilled out a bit when I saw it was unopened. I ripped into it like a bear after honey and dropped a strip of condoms onto the bed beside us, taking one out and rolling it on.

She touched herself while I got ready, her fingers pumping into herself as her back arched off the bed. The sounds of her desire sent a shiver down my spine as I lifted her legs.

I grabbed her hand and brought her fingers to my lips as I lined up my cock with her. Her musky flavor exploded in my mouth, and I knew I'd have to taste her soon.

Up on my knees, I pressed into her. The head of my cock more than making its presence known, I was demanding entrance. There was a hint of resistance, and her breaths came out faster before I jerked my hips and sank into her. For a split second it flashed into my mind that she might be a virgin, but there was no turning back at that point.

Her pussy wrapped around my cock like a fist, and I got light-headed. Thrusting my hips, I bit my lip. Watching her writhing under me had quickly become my new favorite sport. Every sound. Every taste made me a little bit more addicted.

Mak's back arched off the bed. My name on her lips sent a shiver down my spine. She cried out, and I was lost in her.

I'd felt like a king skating across the ice and slapping a goal into the net, but I'd never felt invincible until she stared into my eyes, crying out as I explored her body with mine.

Reaching down, I strummed her clit with my thumb, and her legs locked around me, keeping my thrusts short and fast. She bounced back against me as our rhythm synced up.

All that running sure paid off. She grabbed a pillow

and shoved it over her face as she screamed into it. It sounded a lot like my name. I tried not to let it go to my head—either one. My jaw clenched tight, I rode out the vise grip she had on my cock. Her pussy milked me for all I was worth, and I couldn't hold back anymore. Watching her come apart was my favorite sight in the world. I'd rather watch her than hockey. I roared out her name and followed her, shooting rope after rope of come into the latex between us.

My arms gave way, and I collapsed on top of her. My ears rang from all the blood that had rushed to my head when she squeezed me so tightly. That had to be the quickest I'd ever come. I took solace that I'd gotten her there first. We'd both been so ready and in tune with each other. This first one was just to take the edge off. There would be a lot more where that came from.

Rolling to the side, I panted as my heart hammered against my ribs. Her arm brushed along mine as we laid there in stunned silence, trying to recover from what had just exploded between us. My brain was mush, but I knew this was different. Scary as hell and like nothing I'd experienced before. Groaning, I stood and got rid of the condom.

"You totally thought I was a virgin, didn't you?" Her sexy voice was full of laughter as I slid back into bed.

"Why do you say that?" I rolled to my side and propped my head up on my arm. I wanted her again. Even while I was still catching my breath, I knew once wouldn't be enough. Hell, finishing her box of condoms wouldn't be enough.

"You definitely had a look when you were about to sink into me, like 'Oh shit! What if she's a virgin? She's totally a virgin!' You have a very expressive face during sex." Her mock fear face had me laughing. *Busted!* She ran her hand along the side of my head and trailed a finger down my neck, bringing the goose bumps back.

Her touch was everything I needed, and I had no idea how to hold on to. I had no illusions about what this was because I knew Mak. At twelve o'clock everything would turn back into a pumpkin, and she'd start freaking out. It was like she was a different person. Bolder, relaxed, even more beautiful than usual.

"So how was this nonvirgin during sex?"

I glanced up at her and saw the hints of worry creeping back in. It wasn't even midnight; I was going to keep her in this place as long as I could.

"I don't have enough empirical evidence to make that judgment yet." I ran my fingers along my chin in deep thought. "I think we're going to have to try this a few more times before I really know for sure."

"Is that your normal way of testing theories? Bang your way through them?" Her smiles and laughter were like a drug, and I wanted as much as I could get before she took them away from me.

"Sometimes I show extra dedication to research that really moves me." I nipped her bottom lip and tipped her over onto her back. She let out a gasp that turned into laughter. Each note that fell from her lips was like a precious gift wrapped up with a bow. Her hair fanned out across the bed and surrounded her.

"I think this research has definitely moved you."

She reached down between us and wrapped her fingers around my cock. The fiery tendrils of pleasure stole my breath away as she worked her hand up and down my shaft.

"It really has. Now let's get to work. There will be a full questionnaire after that I'll need you to fill out. You know, for research purposes."

"I think that can be arranged." She felt around for the strip of condoms and snagged one, handing it over to me. The edges of her lips curved up as she tried to keep a straight face. Her lips glistened in the dim light, nice and plump from my attention. "Get to work, intrepid researcher. I'm interested to see the firsthand results of this study."

16

MAKENNA

We both drifted into a dreamlike nap for a little bit. I don't know how long it was, but I woke with Declan's lips on my shoulder, kissing his way along my neck.

Letting down my walls even a little bit had been inevitable with him. He was always pushing my buttons and doing his best to get me to lighten up. Being free for a while...the feelings he brought out in me completely blind-sided me. It was like the air was being squeezed out of my lungs as the shaking, throbbing pleasure raced through my body.

There had never been a doubt in my mind that Declan would be good in bed. But this all-consuming, mind-shattering rapture threatened to consume me whole. It was too much, but at the same time I wanted more. So much more. It was beyond anything I'd experienced before and would probably experience again.

He had way too many women fawning over him not to be a sex god, but when he was with me, I couldn't even be jealous. I was thankful for all the practice he'd had because it meant I was ready to wake up everyone in the apartment complex when he changed angles and tempo and my orgasm crashed into me so hard I wished I could live in that space on the edge of a painful pleasure that exploded through every cell in my body.

Stars twinkled in front of my eyes. Actual stars as my vision blinked out, even though I knew I still had my eyes open. I sank my nails into his back and screamed, hoping I hadn't made him deaf. My body shuddered and trembled. I tried to catch my breath, but he kept going.

Like a machine determined to wring every last bit of pleasure out of me, Declan thrust his hips with such precision it was like he'd found the instructions to my vagina and was working his way through the manual so no step was missed. The trembling was back even stronger, and the lights were so much brighter even with my eyes closed. Like a dam bursting, I dug my fingers into his back and screamed into his shoulder with a voice I didn't even recognize. Holding on to him, I bit down on his shoulder, and my eyes rolled back in my head.

His pace never slowed, so hard and fast that he kept me suspended in a body-shuddering, can't-remember-my-name place, where his body was the only thing that existed, and my body tried to keep up with his ministrations.

"Declan." I breathed his name into his ear as I held on for dear life. And then all the muscles in his body tightened like that was what he'd been waiting for, and he groaned, called out my name, and collapsed on top of me. With my arms still wrapped around him, I breathed him in as his weight settled over me like a warm blanket in the middle of winter.

I ran my fingers through his hair as we both panted, trying to catch our breath. He lifted his head and kissed me on the tip of my nose. The black ebbed away and left behind his deep green eyes filled with tenderness. Staring up at him, I was lost in the emotions swirling in his gaze.

My chest tightened, but this time it wasn't out of worry or anxiety or pain; it was something else. Something I'd never felt before and never thought I'd feel with him.

"That was amazing, Books. Give me ten minutes, and I'll show you just how dedicated I am to your pleasure. I mean, our research." With a quick peck on the lips, he pushed off me and took care of the condom. Losing his body heat made me shiver as I lay completely bare on top of my bedspread.

He came back to me, dragged the sheets down the bed, and tucked us in together. Gathering me up in his arms facing him, he ran his fingers down the side of my face. These tender moments were not what this was supposed to be about.

I considered him a friend now. One of the few I'd had over the years. It was hard to open up to people when your life wasn't your own. I knew the hard realities of life. It was only a matter of time before he faded away like everything else, but I'd hold on as tightly as I could until then, even if it was just for tonight.

"I think I'm going to probably need a few more demonstrations of your prowess." My gaze dropped to his mouth as I traced my finger along his full bottom lip. *How would it have felt to have his mouth on me?* The temptation to let him try was strong, but my anxiety over being so exposed kept me quiet about it. "You know, continuing the research." I peered up at him.

"I think a repeat performance could be arranged." He felt around on top of the blanket until he hit the telltale crinkle of the foil package. His delicious grin made me nip his bottom lip and run my tongue along it to soothe the pain. He made me want to be wild and free, like the kind of girl I'd always wished I could be.

"I'll make you pay for that, Books. And the only payment I'm looking for is this spectacular body." He got onto his knees and rolled me onto my stomach and palmed my ass. His fingers sank into my flesh, and I arched my back.

My hair fell into my face, and I pushed it out of the way as his hands slid under my hips, lifting them.

The cool air hit my pussy, but it was quickly replaced by the heat and hard press of his body as he rubbed himself up and down my slit. I glanced over my shoulder to see him staring down at where our bodies were almost joined. I wished I could see it too, but all thoughts of anything except trying to breathe were pushed out of my head as he slammed into me in one long thrust. Reaching for a pillow, I buried my face into it as I screamed out my pleasure.

Running his hands along my back, Declan grabbed on to my shoulders and used them for leverage, changing the angle of his thrusts and dissolving the last thread of control I had over my body. In his arms I could just be. And right then I was a pool of raw sexual energy gasping for air so I didn't pass out.

He dropped one arm from my shoulder and reached under me, tapping on my clit twice, and it was enough to make me come apart. My toes curled, and I clawed at the sheets as I came so hard I could hear the blood pounding in my ears. Declan's arm tightened around me, and he groaned as he continued to slam into me. My arms couldn't hold me up anymore, and I collapsed with him following right behind me, his back covering mine.

We lay on our sides, melded together as one. His heart pounded against my back, and he brought his arm up between my breasts. I knew he could feel mine racing. Not wanting to move a muscle or even being sure we'd be able to, we laid there in each other's arms for a few minutes. He hopped up to throw out the condom and then slid right back into bed behind me.

His heavy leg settled over mine, and he wrapped me in his arms. I didn't feel stifled or caged in; I felt warm and safe. I could say or do anything with him, and he'd be right there beside me, ready to go.

"Give me twenty minutes, and we'll get to work on finishing that box." His voice was laced with sleep already.

"We don't have to finish them all tonight." I yawned and snuggled in deeper against him, wrapping my arm around his draped across my chest.

"I know we don't have to, but that doesn't mean I'm not going to try. Just give me a little bit." My yawn triggered his, and my eyes drooped. Just needed to close my eyes for a few minutes and rest up to see what he had in store for me later. I couldn't wait. I might even have a few tricks up my sleeve.

17

DECLAN

I woke up, running my hand across the bed beside me, and my eyes snapped open when my hand hit cold, empty sheets. I shielded my eyes against the morning sun pouring in through the open blinds in Mak's room. Sitting up in bed, I ran my hands over my face.

I glanced down at the nearly finished strip of condoms on the floor and broke out in a lazy grin. She'd absolutely worn me out, and I'd never fallen asleep more satisfied.

We'd had almost made it through the whole box. Waking up to Mak sitting on top of me, grinding her hips in circles with my cock firmly embedded inside her silky smoothness had to be the best all-time way to ever open my eyes in the dead of night. I would make it to eight a.m. classes no problem if she were my alarm.

Gazing up at her as she rode me, taking the pleasure that she didn't seem like she let herself enjoy much, made me want to never leave that bed. I'd cupped her breast, holding her pert and plump mounds in my hands, pinching and teasing her nipples.

Her short, sharp gasps and clenching core had sent a

shuddering shiver down my spine. I toyed with her clit while she threw her head back, calling out my name with her hair wild and sexy, flowing around her shoulders. It was an image burned into my brain. I sat in bed for a few minutes listening for any movement outside the room. *Where is she?*

Picking my boxers up off the floor, I slid them on and knocked on her bathroom door. No answer. Concern warred with disappointment that she wasn't there beside me in the bed.

I opened it, and there wasn't anyone in there. The bedroom door clicked and creaked as I swung it open and tiptoed out into the rest of the apartment, not wanting to wake her roommates—not that we'd been thinking about that last night. *Maybe she's out there?*

"Dude, I've got a bruise on my ass in the shape of a handprint."

Nope, only her startled roommate whose eyes got wide as saucers as she saw me pop out of the end of the hallway. She quickly shoved her skirt down that she'd had hiked up, craning her neck to see the handprint bruise.

"Hey." A little thrown by how aware I was of being a kind of exposed, I fought the urge to cross my arms over my chest. Not having a shirt on in front of someone had never even occurred to me, but for some reason in my boxers, with Mak's roommate there and Mak nowhere to be found, it felt weird.

"Hey. You're Declan McAvoy." Her roommate had her hand wrapped around a mug and took a sip of coffee. The life-giving smell called out to me, but I didn't have time for that.

"Yes, I am. Do you know where Mak is?"

"She went out. She said running and studying and stuff.

She had her backpack." She rubbed her eyes and yawned, still wearing her clothes from the night before.

"Right, thanks." I turned back down the hallway, running my hands over my face. This was not how the morning was supposed to go.

"Do you want some coffee?" her roommate called down the hall after me. My concern turned into something else.

She was gone. From her own apartment. I checked my phone and there were no messages or missed calls. After sending her a quick message, I searched around the room thinking maybe she'd left a note, but once again I came up empty. *What the hell?! Who sleeps with someone and just walks out on them in the morning like that?*

All the times I'd done that in the past came flooding back to me, but this was different. With us it was different. I snatched my shirt and jeans off the floor and got dressed. Grabbing the rest of my stuff, I triple checked the room, not believing she'd seriously ditched me.

I left the apartment with an audience of two. Her bleary-eyed roommates waved to me as I walked out the front door for my walk of shame. With each step away from her door, I felt like everything that had happened the night before was being erased. The cool fall air blew around me, and I crossed my arms over my chest, determined to get answers.

My mind raced as I rushed across campus. *Was it bad? Is that why she left?* I'd made sure to make her come even though she wouldn't let me go down on her. She'd been into it. We both were. More than I'd ever been into anyone before. *Did she freak herself out?* Hell, I was a little freaked out by those tender feelings and the comfortable way she felt with her hair tickling my chin, but I wouldn't have just run out on her.

Without meaning to, I ended up outside her study room.

My shoulders slumped as I peered through the small window beside the door. Empty. The rest of the floor was deserted.

When I finally got back to my place, I knew the pit in my stomach wasn't from the beers; it was because I had it bad for Makenna, and she didn't even want to stick around after we slept together. Maybe there was another reason. Maybe it was all a mistake. Hopeful, I sent her another text and waited for her to reply.

And waited...

18

MAKENNA

Waking up in stages, I cycled through about fifty different emotions before realizing exactly what I'd done. Declan McAvoy was passed out in my bed. Not from getting too drunk and sleeping off a bender, but from sex-haustion. Shooting up in bed, I tried to run my hand through my rat's nest of a hair horror on top of my head.

Flashes of the night before bombarded me. Him running his hands through my hair, my hair wrapped around his fist as he took me from behind. I dropped my head into my hands. I'd never been that out of control before. Wanton and ready and needy. He did that to me, and it scared the shit out of me.

I was sore in places I hadn't even realized could be sore. Sliding out of bed, my muscles screamed at me like they never had after a long run. I searched the floor and found my clothes from the night before. Intertwined with Declan's on my floor.

As gingerly as I could, I untangled them and got my pants on, wincing at the ache between my legs. For a split second I entertained brushing my teeth or something, but the risk of him waking up was too high. My breath hitched as a skin-tingling memory from last night had me gripping the edge of my desk.

I could still feel him everywhere. And he felt good, but this wasn't what I needed. Maybe I'd needed it last night. I must have because there wasn't anything other than a fire that could have kept me from wrapping my legs around his hips and demanding he fuck me.

Attributing it to a severe lack of sleep and way too much stress, I was totally over the hump now. *You know you're not* came a small voice at the back of my head. Even standing at the end of the bed, where he was sprawled out with his hard, muscled ass peeking out from the sheets, I wanted to climb back under the covers beside him.

I wanted to slide back into his arms and pretend running away had never crossed my mind, but I couldn't. Attachments were the last thing I needed, and definitely not with him.

Being as quiet as possible not to wake him up, I packed my bag and raced out of my room with my shoes in my hand. I stopped short when I spotted Fiona standing in the middle of the kitchen in her outfit from last night.

"Hey. Did I send you a text last night?" She glanced up over her soup bowl–sized mug of coffee. Her voice sounded like she'd been gargling shrapnel.

"Hey. And no, I don't think so. Why?"

"Because drunk me keeps fucking deleting all my texts and my contacts. So I'll start getting all these weird messages and I have no idea who is sending them and what they are talking about. It's really annoying." She glanced at me with bloodshot eyes.

"What are you doing up so early?" I'd pieced it together,

but maybe she hadn't just gotten home and passed out in her clothes instead.

"I just got in. Your auto coffee maker setting was running, so I grabbed some before I pass out for like an hour and then get to brunch with my parents." She rolled her eyes and choked down another gulp of the steaming-hot coffee.

I hadn't expected anyone to be up. Glancing back at my room, I debated telling her Declan was there, but that would have brought up a whole host of other questions.

"I had a friend over last night, but I need to get going. I'm going for a run and then studying, so I'll see you later."

Bolting from the apartment before she could ask any questions, I ran faster than I've ever run in my life until I hit the edge of campus. I'd thought about taking my car and driving somewhere, anywhere, maybe even going home, but doing that would almost be like admitting defeat.

Like I needed to separate myself to handle what had happened between me and Declan. I was fine. It was fine. We'd both blown off some steam, and everything would be okay. He had to do that kind of thing weekly. It wasn't a big deal.

That small voice was back, trying to tell me it was, and kept bombarding me with flashes of the night before that had me standing in the middle of the walkway with a shiver racing through my body and a tingling in my decimated vagina. It was going to need at least a week of bed rest after this. I was surprised no one asked where my spurs were, because I was pretty sure I was walking like a cowboy.

Walking across the grass on the quad, I felt like everyone knew what had happened. I'd had dirty, wild, nonstop sex with our very own hockey superstar.

How had I let things go that far with him? Was he hot? Yes.

Sexy? Absolutely! But to sleep with him? Not only once, but like five times or however many condoms were in that box. I'd had that box for over a year, and in one night we'd nearly demolished it.

It was definitely the most irresponsible thing I'd ever done. Sure, we'd finished the midterm and I'd turn it in a little later, but still...

Sitting in the deserted dining hall that smelled like a mix of barbecue sauce, chicken fingers, bacon, and cinnamon, I stared at the worn wooden table in front of me. I decided carbs were the way to keep that little voice at bay. Stuff my face with syrup, bacon, and other breakfast foods and the night before would melt away.

I resisted the urge to bang my head against the table. I'd slept with Declan last night. The hard planes and muscular bulges flashed in front of me. I squeezed my thighs together making me completely aware of the soreness and aching that warred for dominance.

All my belongings were piled on the table in front of me. It looked like I was a little kid getting ready to run away from home. I should have gone to my study room, but that would be the first place he looked for me. *Why was I running again?*

Oh yeah, because Declan was not the kind of guy to have warm, fuzzy, wake-up-in-your-arms-and-want-to-snuggle-in-deeper kinds of feelings. He was the wake-up-in-the-middle-of-the-night-so-we-can-bang-one-more-time-and-then-he-sneaks-out-at-the-break-of-dawn kind of guy. I figured I could beat him to the punch. Get out before he did.

My phone pinged, but I refused to look at it. There was only one person who'd be texting me this early, and avoiding him meant texts as well. Probably checking to make sure I wasn't going to screw him over for our class.

The dining hall staff loaded up the buffet, and I dragged myself out of my chair. I grabbed a damp tray from the stack of always-wet trays beside the breakfast foods. This time of day there weren't that many people around. A few freshmen who were still used to waking up at high school times and ate early, people who'd been out all night and needed solid dining hall food to help them sleep through their hangovers, and me.

My stomach was fine from the only beer I'd had the night before. My lightweight status was still firmly in place. Bacon and carbs wafted from the kitchen out to the food lined up under the heating lamps along the buffet line. I snagged French toast sticks, bacon, and orange juice and waited for eight a.m. That wasn't too early to call a college-aged person on a Saturday morning, right? *Wrong.*

"Who died?" Her groggy voice on the other end of the line told me maybe it was a hair too early.

"No one died, Avery. I just needed to talk."

"And you couldn't text like a normal person? What the hell, Mak? It's like five in the morning." Avery's bleary-eyed voice came through even over the phone.

"It's eight in the morning." I dipped one of my crunchy sticks into the syrup and took a bite.

"Eight, five, whatever. I worked last night and didn't get home until five."

I winced. I forgot about her crazy shifts while she was in community college. "Sorry."

"I'm up now. Spill to me what happened that warranted an eight-in-the-morning honest-to-God phone call, and then I can go back to bed."

"I had sex with Declan last night." I blurted it out louder than I'd intended, and a few people on the other side of the dining hall looked up.

"Declan who?"

"Declan McAvoy." I cringed, waiting for her response.

"Declan McAvoy?" She said his name like it was in a foreign language.

"Yes."

"The Declan McAvoy voted Biggest Flirt back in high school?"

The bits of shame grew by the minute. "Yes."

"Did he drug you or something?" Her voice got higher, and I could almost hear her going to battle stations. All hands on deck for ball removal!

"What? No, of course not. We were both into it." I had been into it. Probably way too into it.

"Really?" The confusion in her voice mirrored the confusion swimming around my head.

"Absolutely. It was a hundred percent consensual." Even more if that were possible. I'd even said please. *Ugh!*

"In that case, fuck yeah! I'm glad. That's so awesome." She yawned big and loud.

"What do you mean, awesome? It was a huge freaking mistake. You know him."

"I mean, I knew him back in high school, and while he could be a bit full of himself, he was never a bad guy. You two just loved to fight. Both of you were button pushers."

"I was not." I dropped some of my syrup on the table. Declan was the button pusher. Ice Queen, Mak the Knife, Books, Specs, all his names for me back then. Needling me. But I had to admit they didn't bother me as much as they had before.

"You totally were. I saw it even back then. He'd get all worked up about the stuff you'd say, and Em would have to tell him to calm down." Her voice caught when she said

Emmett's name. It was the first time I'd heard her say it in a long time.

"I forget you used to hang out with them all the time."

"It was a lifetime ago, wasn't it?" She had a far-off sound in her voice. I'd been there when everything went down. When the couple of the decade, Avery and Emmett, broke up at the end-of-the-year party. Emmett had shattered his front door, and Avery had looked like she'd had her heart carved out of her chest. It took her almost a year to tell me what really happened that night, and I still wasn't sure I knew all of it.

"It feels like it." I'd seen her over the summer, but not enough. She'd been shuttling Alyson to her various summer enrichment camps and working.

"I, more than anyone, know how different things can be and how much a person changes after high school. Things back then seemed simple, but they weren't always." She got that faraway sound in her voice before clearing her throat. I still didn't know why she'd let him believe she cheated, but whenever I brought it up, she said to leave it alone.

"Now on to the most important question...how was it?" I could almost hear her rubbing her hands together, eager to get the dirt.

"That's the most important question?"

"Of course. The stories about Declan were legendary."

And there was part of the problem. His reputation had preceded him ever since freshman year of high school, but that didn't mean I couldn't enjoy the memories. And that's all there would be from now on, the memories from that night.

"It was mind-blowingly good. I can barely walk." I laughed at the soreness in my muscles as I mopped up some of the syrup with my bacon.

"Hell yeah! That's what I want to hear. Nothing worse than a hot guy who doesn't deliver."

"You're glad? Declan may have done permanent damage to my lady bits."

Avery's bark of a laugh shot out of my phone so loudly I had to pull it away from my ear.

"I'm sure you'll be fine. No, I'm glad you got to do something a little crazy for once. And no, leaving Stanford doesn't count. Are you going to see him again?"

"We're study partners for the rest of the semester, so I don't really have a choice." That reality came crashing down onto my chest like a heart attack waiting to happen.

"I don't mean like that. I mean like last night. You going to let him show you all the tricks he has up his sleeve?" I knew she was waggling her eyebrows even though I couldn't see her.

"The best course of action will be to pretend it didn't happen." I finished my breakfast and dumped my stuff, stashing the tray on the conveyor belt next to the kitchen.

"Come on, Mak, don't be like that."

"Like what?" I held my phone in one hand as I slung my pack onto my back.

"Running away from your life."

"I'm not. I'm protecting it."

"You're not. You're hiding. You can't always live for other people. Sometimes you need to live for you."

"I'm living. I'm studying. I'm going to get into med school, and I'll be a doctor just like—" The word caught in my throat.

"Just like Daniel wanted to be," she finished as it felt like the air had been sucked out of my lungs. "I can't even know what it was like to go through what you did, but you can't do everything for him. You have to do some things for you."

Her soft voice had tears building in my eyes before I could stop them. "I do."

"Not enough. I want to come up and visit sometime soon. They cut hours at my cleaning, so I should be able to find a day to come visit. Alyson has been having a lot more sleepovers with friends to get out of the house. I can't blame her. Does me coming up in a couple weeks work you?"

"Whenever you want to come, I'd love to see you. You can stay over at my place. It will be fun!" I wanted to squeeze her and be silly and relax.

"I'll let you know."

We ended our call, and I wandered aimlessly around campus for a while with everything on my back like a hermit crab. Finally, my shoulders screamed *enough,* and I parked myself in an out-of-the-way coffee shop on campus. It was busy but not packed like the others. Camping out at one of the tables, I tried to focus, but my mind kept drifting back to Declan.

How do I fix this? How did I keep it from being an awkward clusterfuck of the rest of a semester? And how did I keep myself from wanting him so much it hurt? It was like in one night he'd woven himself in as a part of my DNA, and I didn't know how to extract him, but I knew it would be painful, if it were even possible...

19

DECLAN

"What do you mean, she left?"

"I mean I woke up, and she was gone." That gut punch still hadn't worn off. Not only was she gone, but she refused to answer any of my messages —for nearly a week. It seemed always working ahead and a gap in our assignments worked out to her advantage. We didn't have anything due until next week, but she'd crack. She had to talk to me.

Heath laughed, crowing like it was the funniest thing he'd ever heard. I was so close to punching him, but knowing him, he'd think that made it even more hilarious.

I couldn't wait until he found someone who got under his skin so deep that his easygoing, everything-will-always-work-out mantra was really put to the test.

I hated feeling like a needy chick waiting for the phone to ring, but damn it, I wanted that phone to ring and I wanted Mak on the other end.

"Karma is a bitch, isn't it? How many times have I had to escort your morning-after visitors out?"

He gulped down his water. His hair was still soaked from

his after-practice shower. I'd tried not to think about how this was what it must feel like when someone just ghosts you after sex. Not exactly a great feeling.

"And the fact that she disappeared on you has nothing to do with the fact that we are here at the exact same time that her shift starts?"

"This is the perfect time to get dinner." I shrugged and stared at the front door. It had taken nearly a week, but I finally caved and came here. "It doesn't have anything to do with her."

"And that's why we've been holding off on ordering food when the server already came over twice and asked for it."

"I wasn't hungry yet, but I know I'll be hungry soon." My stomach was shouting at me that it needed food now, but I'd hold off a little longer.

"And that's also why you gave her twenty bucks just to let us sit here."

I ripped my gaze from the front door to his smug, smirking face. He crossed his arms over his chest in self-satisfaction.

"I see all, man. I see all." He waved his hands around his head like he was some mystic seer. The door to the bar swung open, and my head whipped up. Heath laughed, smacking his hand on the table. I'd been hopeful it was her, but Preston and a few other guys from the team came in. I was about to go back to nursing my water when a streak of reddish-blonde caught my eye.

There she was, right behind them. Mak came in looking a bit flustered. She caught my eye across the bar and stopped short. Someone barreled into her back and nearly knocked her over. I half stood in the booth my muscles tense, ready to go to her, when she caught herself and rushed back into the kitchen before I could take two steps.

All the tables and booths were full, so Preston and the guys scooted into our booth.

"You didn't even order yet? Perfect." Preston slid in beside me and grabbed the menu off the table. Mak came out of the kitchen, and I dropped my gaze to the table. No need to be a stalker. Well, any more of a stalker than I already was.

She came over to the table, and everyone placed their orders.

"You're like our regular server now, Makenna." Preston handed her his menu.

"It seems that way, huh? I'll have your drinks out in a bit." She tapped her pen on her notepad, and her shoes squeaked as she spun away from our table. I was suddenly incredibly interested in the nicks and dents in the table in front of me.

"Dec got ghosted by Makenna." My head shot up, and I winged a spoon straight at Heath's forehead.

"You and Mak? Seriously, dude. Don't fuck things up with her. I know I said before maybe it was a good idea, but maybe not." The worried-older-brother look settled over Preston's face.

"It's fine. There's nothing to worry about; we're cool." I slid the container of sugar packets in front of me and took great interest in organizing and aligning them. It was best I wasn't practicing with the whole team; they'd never let me live this down. Preston took a deep breath like it pained him and leaned in closer to me.

"What happened? Did she shut you down?" I tilted my head to the side with the corners of my mouth drawn down.

"Of course she didn't shoot me down."

Heath and the other guys leaned in closer.

"Two Cokes, two Sprites, and a ginger ale." We all shot

up straight as Mak stood at the end of the table putting down five napkins and sliding our drinks in front of us. Everyone did an embarrassingly terrible job of trying to look natural. "Right, I'll leave you to your conversation." She held the tray against her chest and walked off.

"If she didn't say no, what's the problem?"

"She ghosted him. Totally left her own apartment to get away from him the morning after." Heath chuckled into his soda, and the guys stared at me wide-eyed before they burst into laughter like a bunch of women out on a bachelorette party.

Table-slapping, napkins-wiping-away-tears kind of laughter. And I wanted to strangle each of them. The guys really wanted to make sure I felt like shit about the whole situation. Really drive it home. I took a deep breath so I didn't climb over the table and wrap my fingers around Heath's neck.

Mak was back this time with a tray of burgers and fries balanced on her hip. She doled them out to the guys, who once again went stock silent the minute she appeared. She wasn't deaf or blind, so she knew something was going on. The cordial look on her face, the same one she had for everyone else in the bar, made me want to crawl out of my skin. I wasn't just some random person, and I wasn't going to let her pretend what happened last week hadn't happened.

"So, what's your plan?" One of the guys shoveled fries into his mouth.

I ran my hands over my face and up through my hair.

"No idea. I'm in new territory with her. Anyone have any bright ideas?" I glanced around the table, and everyone looked equally unsure. This was what I got for hanging out with guys who'd sworn off dating and girlfriends. Except for Preston, of course.

"What about you? You have a girlfriend."

Preston shrugged. "We've been together since sophomore year of high school. Not like I have any experience with whatever the hell you have going on. What I'm more worried about right now is your class. How did the midterm go?"

"It felt good. We worked hard on it. Turned it in early. Still waiting to hear back."

"Grades came out a few hours ago; at least that's what Becca told me." I kept forgetting Preston's little sister was at our school now. She wasn't in my class, but she would be in a Sophomore Seminar just like me. I froze, and everything around me got quiet. This grade could make or break me.

Snapping out of it, I whipped my phone out of my pocket. Logging in to the online course system, my eyes got wide as the notification icon blinked on my screen. A new grade had been added.

I tapped on the class and held my breath as I waited for the screen to load. My heart nearly leaped out of my chest as the image appeared what felt like one pixel at a time, and there it was. Our grade for the midterm: *98!*

Running a quick calculation of the assignments we'd done so far and the fact that the midterm was worth 35 percent of the final grade, it meant there was no way for me to fail the class. Even if we bombed the final, I'd still come out with a B-. Not that I'd do that, but fuck yeah!

I scanned the bar looking for Mak. She hadn't said anything, which meant she didn't know. There was no way she wouldn't be freaking out about this. Pushing against Preston, I tried to slide out of the booth.

"Dude, move. I need to get out."

"Calm down!" Preston shoveled a few more fries into his mouth before sliding out of the booth like a geriatric turtle. I spotted Mak heading back toward the bathrooms and rushed after her. She ducked into the women's bathroom, and I debated actually going in after her but decided that would probably freak her out.

After a couple minutes she came out wiping her hands with a paper towel and stopped short when she saw me.

"Hey, Declan...I'm—" Her full, pink lips were parted like she didn't know what to say, but I knew the thing to fix that. I thrust my phone in front of her face, unable to contain my excitement. She scrunched her eyebrows together, and then the realization hit her as her eyes scanned the screen. Peering up at me with the widest smile, she practically vibrated with happiness.

"We got a ninety-eight!" She covered her mouth with her hands and then threw her arms around my neck. I wrapped my arms around her, closing my eyes and letting myself just feel her for a moment before I lifted her up in the air, spinning us around.

Her bright laughter bounced off the walls of the small hallway. We'd worked so hard on it together and hit it out of the park. Breathing her in, my heart hammered against my chest. Moving my head back, I stared into the eyes I'd been waiting to see all week. Our mouths were less than an inch apart. Without thinking, I leaned in, capturing her lips in mine.

She didn't jerk away or push me off. Her lips were hungry. They parted and let me in like a welcome mat rolled out with a tall pitcher of lemonade. They were lips I hadn't been able to get out of my mind in days. She tasted like a long sip of water after crossing the desert. Her body pressed tightly against mine, and my body responded like she'd programmed it to after only one night.

"We did it." She breathed against my lips as I set her

down with her back against the wall. We stared into each other's eyes.

A churning well of emotion shot through me as she reached up and gently put her hand on my chest, not to push me away, just to rest it there like she wanted to be sure my heart was pounding as hard as hers was. She ran her hand through my hair, raking her nails over my scalp, sending shocks through my body.

"I'm sorry I ran. I'm sorry I didn't return your messages. I had a lot to think about."

I stared into her eyes and fell into her crystal-clear blueness. Someone stepped into the hallway, and she ducked her head. Her cheeks got all rosy and glowing. The guy walked past us into the bathroom, and the clattering of the bar rushed back into the little bubble we'd created around ourselves.

I leaned my forehead against hers.

"Just don't do it again."

She held my gaze and nodded. Relief washed over me, and we had two things to celebrate.

"We did it. I'll meet you after your shift." I dragged my knuckles along her jaw.

She shuddered and opened her mouth. I put my finger over her lips. Their soft fullness had me making promises to myself for later that I was determined to keep. "I'll see you after. I think this calls for a celebration."

Her tongue darted out, and she licked the tip of my finger, shocking the shit out of me.

"I'm going to be pretty tired after my shift. If you're going to be keeping me up late, you'd better make it worth my while."

Yes! She could deny a lot, but I knew why she'd been avoiding me. We were inevitable once we saw each other.

Touched each other. This wasn't a one-time thing, and I'd prove it to her.

I chuckled and rested my hands on the brick wall, caging her in against my body. With my lips barely touching hers, I let the heat pulse between us. Dropping my hand, I trailed it along the bottom of her shirt. Her breath caught as she kept her eyes on me like she couldn't look away, which was good because neither could I. I wanted to imprint this feeling on my soul and never let it leave. Snaking my hand along the waistband of her pants, I skimmed my finger across her skin.

"Don't you worry, Mak. I'll make sure every second is a memory you won't soon forget." I nipped at her neck, and she let out a shuddering breath as I stepped back and headed down the hallway, smiling as she pressed her hand against the wall before following behind me and going straight into the kitchen.

I loved seeing her laugh and smile and relax. In only a couple of hours I'd have her again. The building pressure and electricity between us meant it was only a matter of time. There was no way I was the only one who felt it. She could deny it for a week, but she couldn't deny it for long, and I wasn't going to let her forget how I made her feel. Because she made me forget anything else existed when we were together. I'd stop at nothing short of giving her everything she needed and more.

20

MAKENNA

The seconds ticked by like hours as I waited for my shift to finish. My body hummed in anticipation after one kiss. All my time away from him, vowing to fortify myself against anything he might say or do to get a repeat of our night together, flew out the window once I'd seen him in person. Once I felt him pressed against me and breathed in his clean, soapy smell.

His scent clung to my skin; not even running in and out of the kitchen erased that. He'd left the bar not too long after he left me in the hallway, practically panting. His presence drove me to distraction, and my customers preferred to eat their food off a plate, not be showered in it when their preoccupied server nearly toppled an entire plate of pasta into their lap.

I untied the apron from around my waist and waved to an overwhelmed squadron of bartenders under the crush of the Friday night crowd. The butterflies flapping in my stomach were ready to escape from my mouth when I stepped into the crisp evening air, headed to my car. We hadn't said where we'd meet, so I took out my phone. *No messages.* I bit my bottom lip which still tasted like him. Glanced up, I spotted my car and another treat.

Leaned against the side of my Honda like a Christmas morning under the dim lights of the parking lot, he stood with his arms folded across his broad chest. The lot was deserted. The music, laughter, and shouts from the bar were drowned out by the pounding in my chest.

Despite myself I picked up my pace, wiping my sweaty palms on my jeans. Every excuse I'd come up with and every reason I'd stayed away melted when I saw him. I hadn't even been able to talk myself out of this during my shift. He had an uneasy look on his face like he wasn't one hundred percent sure I wouldn't come out of the bar and tell him to stay away from me.

After a week of beating myself up and getting grades back on all my midterms, I realized maybe we could do this. It was As and A-s across the board. Maybe he wouldn't be too much for me to handle. Having fun with him didn't mean I couldn't keep my eye on the prize.

That's why, while the first word out of his mouth was *hi*, I went for it. Slamming into his chest, I pressed my lips to his full, soft ones and let myself melt into him. Not so much melt, but mount with Chernobyl-level ferocity that had him lifting me as I fumbled with my keys to unlock the door.

If he was shocked, he didn't show it. His hands were all over me as I turned the key. The *thunk* of the locks clicking open was all he needed.

Grabbing the handle behind him, I mauled him to within an inch of his life. We fell into the back seat of my Honda Fit. *Ha!* Appropriate. He slid back across the seat, dragging me with him.

"Eager much, Mak?"

I shut him up with a pinch to his nipple through his

shirt. He winced and laughed, covering my hand with his. His deep laugh made my body sway. I straddled his hips, soaking in his solid body beneath me. He grabbed on to my waist, his fingers tracing small circles on my skin.

My body hummed as sexual energy and naughty thoughts flowed through my head. *Are we really going to have sex in my car behind the bar?* I didn't think I could wait until we got to my apartment.

The cool evening air and a few shouts from outside filtered into the car. I glanced behind me at the mostly deserted parking lot. The thrill of being a bit dangerous had a small laugh bursting free from my lips as I slammed the door behind me. There weren't any sounds other than our panting breaths in my car. I had a feeling I'd never look at it the same after tonight.

The back seat was roomy. Part of the reason I'd bought it for my cross-country trips to school. But screw the mileage per gallon and the sensible steering; right now, it was the stage for the next time Declan was inside me. I wasn't even fooling myself anymore with calling it the last time. It wouldn't be.

His massive frame still filled the back seat as part of him hung off the edge. The dim interior lights of my car gave me the perfect view of him spread out in front of me, like a delicious treat I thought I'd never get to have or thought I didn't want.

His hands snaked farther under my shirt, and he unfastened my bra. I couldn't keep my hands off him, and I shoved his shirt up, getting a better look at all the hard work he'd put into his body as the last flicker of the light faded.

The second it went black, it was like a caged beast was unleashed, or maybe there were two of them because we were both clawing at each other's clothes. In unison, I whipped my top off, and he dragged his up, tugging it over his head. And then our hands were fumbling at each other's pants, unbuttoning and unzipping our way to the prize we both couldn't get enough of.

I managed to shimmy out of mine, and Declan got his pants over his ass. They were still on about halfway down his thighs. Sticking my hand along the side of the driver's seat, I pushed it forward as far as it went. There was something I'd wanted to do and in the darkness of the car I felt bold enough to do it.

My pussy clenched as I wrapped my hands around his cock. I wanted him inside me now, but I was patient enough to wait. Licking my lips in anticipation, I sank to the floor. His head popped up off the seat.

"What are you doing?" The dim lights from the lot cast him in shadow, but I could feel the fire of his gaze on me.

"Just lay back and relax." I wrapped my hands around the big, swollen crown of his cock and he groaned, throwing his head back against the seat.

Without another word I closed my lips around his huge mushroom tip. My lips strained to get him all inside. He sucked in a sharp breath, and I swore I heard his teeth clench. Using my hands to make up for the fact that he was practically choking me on the head alone, I worked my grip up and down his shaft.

"Fuck, Mak," he bit out and slammed his hand against the seat as I let my teeth gently graze him. "Your mouth is heaven, honey. Fucking heaven."

His fingers sank into my hair, tugging it up, piling it on top of my head. I ran my tongue along the crown of his head, savoring his musky flavor mixed with soap smell. I could feel the wetness coating my inner thighs as the muscles his legs tightened against my arms resting on him. I increased my speed, bobbing my head.

With his hand he helped me find the right rhythm that had him writhing under my touch. The stiff peaks of my nipples rubbed against his thighs, and my core throbbed, ready for him to sink inside of me.

Tightening his grip, he lifted me off him by my hair. My scalp smarted a little until I let him lead. My mouth came off his cock with a *pop*.

"Hey." I reached up into my hair, and he dragged me to him.

"Too good. Your mouth is too fucking good. I don't want to come in your mouth. I need to come in your pussy," he growled. He slammed his lips into mine, kissing me but not just kissing. He was trying to breathe me in, burn this kiss deep into my soul so I'd never forget the night.

My shaky breath matched my heart hammering against my ribs. Tracing his lips with my fingers, I yelped as he nipped the tip of my thumb.

"Sit on my face, Mak." His hands were still tangled in my hair, and our faces were less than an inch apart. His words caught me off guard and I faltered.

"What? No."

"I want you to get up here and sit your sweet little pussy on my mouth, so I can eat you until you can barely stand it, and then I'm going to eat you some more."

My body tingled at the hunger in his voice. But there were some things that were too far for me. I wanted to, but I didn't know if I could.

"Declan, I told you. I'm not into that." I tried to turn my head away, but he grabbed my chin, keeping me there.

"You think you're not into it. And maybe you aren't; maybe it's not your thing. Give me one try, and I'll do everything I can to show you how much you'll like it." He tugged me closer so our noses touched. My gaze locked on to his, and my clit cried out for attention.

"I want you bucking on my face so hard I don't know if I'll ever be able to breathe again. I want every drop of your sweetness, sweetness." He tilted my head and nipped my neck. Thank god, I was already sitting on top of him because my knees would have given out as he whispered in my ear.

"I want you writhing and trying to get off because it hurts so good that you think you're going to pass out. I want you to know how it feels to let me give you that and more." His deep, dark voice made me long for something I'd written off long ago. My pussy cried out for it. Raw. Primal. Fierce. That's what he was offering me, but I still didn't think I could do it.

I leaned my forehead against his.

"I promise that I'll let you go down on me, but not right now. *Right now,* I need you inside me. It's your fault. You got me all worked up by letting me blow you."

He chuckled. "That's one you don't hear too often. I'm holding you to this, Mak. Now get up here." He lifted me and slid me closer, the insistent nudge of his cock throbbed against my ass.

Digging in the pocket of his jeans, he grabbed a condom, but the shift made his head rub against the molten heat of my pussy. The temptation to slide him inside was dizzying.

The rip of the wrapper snapped me back to my senses. That was *insane.* Steamy windows insulated us from the outside world. It was just the two of us in this car and the primal need to get him inside.

All thoughts not centered around his cock splitting me open, fled my mind as he grabbed my hips and shifted me, setting me over his latex-covered shaft. The pressure was immense, and every inch of me screamed to slam down and take him in one solid thrust, but he was drawing it out, letting us savor the way my slick pussy struggled to take him in. Canting his hips, he pushed in more, and it stole my breath away.

"Declan!" It came out like I was battling a case of laryngitis, and I dug my fingers into his chest, trying not to pass out.

Running my hands down the hard plane of his chest, I relished his smooth skin. His eyebrows were pinched, and the look of determination would have made me laugh if I weren't being impaled on the instrument of my torturous desire.

"Jesus, so fucking tight." His voice came out strangled, and a low moan broke out from my chest as he slid inside. The pressure edged on pain, and I threw my head back.

I groaned as he let me lower myself the rest of the way down. The rough zipper of his jeans scraped against my ass with each grind of my hips in time with his as he hit spots I hadn't even known I'd had. A sheen of sweat covered my body even though it was chilly outside. The close confines meant our movements were smaller, quicker, more desperate. The wet sounds of our craving need for each other echoed in the car.

"More. More, Declan. I need it all." There was a keening edge to my voice.

His grip was so tight on my hips I couldn't even move up and down anymore. There would probably be bruises there in the morning, and I couldn't wait for that shuddery feeling every time I saw them.

The grind got more frantic as he lifted his hips. As if he knew exactly what I needed, he slid a hand off my hip and, spreading our combined slickness around, toyed with my clit in expert ministrations.

In less than ten seconds, I threw my head back, grabbed on to the headrest, my fingers sinking in deep, and screamed out his name like my body couldn't contain the ferocity of the pleasure coursing through me. I'd entered a different plane where a guy like Declan stood waiting for me outside work like an 80s movie version of a prince.

"Mak!" His voice was as desperate as mine.

His hands returned to my hips in a crushing grip as he shot me up so high I hit my head on the roof of the car. His cock expanded as he filled the condom, and another shudder raced through my body.

Collapsing onto his chest, my breaths came out fast and shaky. *Wrecked.* That's what I was. Our hearts slammed against our ribs as we drifted down from our sex high. I'd never felt more alive. Like every inch of me was in tune with something else in the universe. Someone else. He'd sexed me into a different dimension.

I laughed, bouncing on his chest. Nuzzling my head into his warmth like I was looking for a place to nest for the winter, I waited for the feeling to return to my limbs. I was content for it to never happen. To live out the rest of my days collapsed and satisfied on top of Declan.

His fingers brushed through my hair as he twirled it around my finger. I let out a sigh. And not one tinged with displeasure like I usually did. This was one filled with more contentment than I'd felt in a long time. The kind that scared you because it was so deep and complete. Our breathing slowed, and we slid out of the post-sex haze.

I peered up at him, and he had one arm tucked behind his head, propping it up some. Darkness enveloped us, and his eyes were in shadow. I traced my fingers along his chest, toying with his nipples, and he stroked my hair.

"That was fun. Should we do it again? Back at my place or yours?" I bit my bottom lip, and I made out the smile on his face in the nearly dark backseat.

"Someone's insatiable, huh?" He tapped a finger on my nose. I guess I was.

"It's your fault." I nipped his nipple, and he laughed. Whenever I was around him, I felt like there were possibilities for my life I'd never seen before. It was crazy and amazing at the same time.

He winced as I slid off his chest.

"What's wrong?"

"I have a cramp in my ass." He sucked in a pained breath.

"I think I might have a few ways we could work that out."

Grabbing my pants off the floor, I slid them on as he sat up, resting his head against the seat back.

"I think I've created a monster." He chuckled, trying to pull his jeans up over his butt. I was ready for a very long night, and I swore wasn't going to let any of my creeping doubts ruin it this time.

The slicing of skates across the ice and sticks whacking pucks into the net settled me after my antsy feelings from the second I ended the call with Preston. He'd told me to come down to the rink but hadn't said why.

Showing up, I checked with the guys. He wasn't there yet. I'd brought all my gear just in case. Leaving Mak early that morning had sucked. We were still working out what we were, and I knew it freaked her out a hell of a lot more than it did me.

I had been at least a little afraid I'd wake up and she wouldn't be there again, but she was. My arms were wrapped around her, and I nuzzled my nose into her neck breathing her in. She broke out into goosebumps even under the blankets and in the circle of my arms. Her body knew, and I needed her mind to catch up. Kissing her awake, I'd let her know about my practice.

She grumbled and pushed my face away, sticking her head under the pillow. I liked that I could make her lazy in the morning. So tired she couldn't even think of jumping up at dawn to go out for a run or to study. She wanted nothing more than a few more hours of sleep, and I couldn't blame her.

Sitting on the bench and lacing up my skates, I squeezed my shaking hands into a fist. Get it together. Nerves were not something that hit me most of the time, the Archer situation excluded, but damn if I wasn't freaking out a little. Not practicing with the guys had messed me up more than I'd let myself believe.

Preston called me out onto the ice. "Get your ass out here, McAvoy."

My skates hitting the ice with the team whipping around the rink was like settling into your favorite chair. Familiar. Comfortable. Right.

"Looks like the slacker is finally ready to rejoin the land of the living," Heath said, pulling off his best figure skating moves. If he wasn't one of my best friends, I'd be tempted to trip him on his skates.

I gripped the stick in my hand and took off across the rink, my skates slicing through the ice as I ran through some practice drills. Puck after puck hit the back of the net, no matter where I was on the rink. It was like I had a homing beacon installed and I couldn't miss. Seeing my freakish precision, some of the guys started to try to block me, stop my golden stick streak.

The game of "break Declan's run" was born. Heath couldn't even get in front of me, which had everyone's heads turning, even his. Feeling like I'd never been so clear on the ice, I skated around the back of the net and out front and slapped the puck into the goal. Sweat poured off me as it was almost two versus one, and it had never felt better.

I was alive on the ice like I'd never been before. My focus and determination had always been there, but that clarity was all about Mak. There were a few people in the stands watching us practice, even this early in the morning, but I wanted her there cheering me on, wrapped up in a scarf and probably with a book balanced on her lap.

Our game of two on one broke up, and Preston called out the drills for us to run. Heath's insanity workouts helped because I was blinded by sweat, wiping it out of my eyes, but I wasn't winded at all and ran through the drills, keeping up my precision. As my body took over the memorized routine, my mind drifted back to Mak.

She was probably still tucked under the blankets. If Preston hadn't called me, I'd had it all worked out on how I'd give her an early morning wake-up call. The disappointment the night before when she'd blocked me again from going down on her had transformed into a challenge.

I had no doubt she'd had a not so great experience before, probably from an asshat who didn't know how to do anything right. I didn't want that to be what her mind went to when she thought of someone going down on her. I wanted her to think of me with my head buried between her thighs. Her legs wrapped squeezing me tight as I savored all the sweetness she had to give.

She was so nervous and uptight about it, but that seemed par for the course.

All that pressure wasn't easy. I knew about pressure. I'd cracked under it too. Every damn time I stepped onto the ice with my development team, but I never let what happened with the team let me stop enjoying my life. When we were together, she let that other side of her out. The snarky, playful, sexy side that not many people got to see.

As much as I wanted to keep that side of her my little secret, I wanted her to be that way all the time, even if it was just to stop how down she got on herself. Every single mistake was not a reason to lock yourself away in the library forever.

My new goal was to get her to relax. Whatever I needed to do to get her there, I'd do. There wasn't that much time left in senior year, and then the real world came crashing down on all of us. If she didn't get a little messy now, it would only be harder later. Get her to relax and make her feel something she'd never felt before. I zeroed in on those goals with as much laser like precision as I did weaving my way across the ice.

I skated harder and faster; everything around me was a blur. Grades were good, I was out on the ice with my team and I had got my girl. She might not know it yet, but Makenna was mine. She'd fight me tooth and nail, but that was kind of our thing at this point. I wouldn't have it any other way.

My legs were like jello, and my heart pounded after nearly an hour of nonstop drills and scrimmages. Skating to the bench, I grabbed my water bottle and sprayed the water into my mouth. It spilled out of the sides and dripped down my chin. I leaned over as my breath came out choppy and fast.

"Maybe we need to have everyone sit out the first part of the practice season," Coach said, stepping into the bench box.

"Hey, Coach." I stepped off the ice and into the box.

"Shower up and meet me in my office." He jabbed his finger in my direction and took off down the tunnel leading to the locker rooms. The gnawing pit was back in my stomach, and I was torn between staying on the ice and soaking up the last of my time with the guys and facing my fate.

Preston clapped me on the back.

"Come on, let's go." I followed Preston back to the locker

room, balancing on my skates as we walked into the sweat-, antiseptic- and heat balm–soaked room. I didn't even bother getting changed. Taking off my skates and my jersey, I left my pads on and barely put on shoes. Looking like he had the same idea, Preston popped up in front of me.

"Ready?" The grim set of his lips didn't instill me with much confidence. Was this one last skate with the team before I was officially booted? I walked the long walk to the coach's office beside Preston on numb legs, and it wasn't from the workout.

The deans were notorious for not playing favorites when it came to student athletes. One of the football team's star running backs had been caught cheating, and unlike other schools where they would have covered it up, they booted him. The team ended up with a 10-6 record, but the deans didn't care.

My leg bounced up and down in the chair across from the coach's desk. Preston sat in the chair beside me with the same grim look on his face. Our first game was only a few days away. I'd been completely ready to make my case to the coach to let me back on the team bright and early Monday morning, but the text came in before six a.m., and they beat me to it.

"I was in with your dean this morning. Made him come in on the weekend." He flipped the folder on his desk closed.

I sat up a little straighter in my seat.

"Preston let me know you got an A on your midterm. He's been very insistent that we reevaluate your situation."

"Yes, sir."

"Your professor finally put those grades in, so I arranged a meeting to see what we might be able to do about your suspension from the team."

I held my breath, afraid to even move as he picked up the folder, stood and rounded the front of his desk. He tapped the folder against his palm.

"They don't generally make concessions during the middle of the semester. I don't want to set a bad example for the rest of the team." He squeezed his forehead, shaking his head.

"Coach, it's not possible for him to fail the course at this point. His grades have been high enough and in his other classes he's doing well enough that he's not in danger of getting anything other than a B- all semester."

I peered over at Preston. Someone had been checking up on me. As much as I didn't like that, he was going to bat for me. He always gave me a hard time, but to see him sitting there, not backing down to the coach, I had even more respect for him than I had before.

"I know. I made the same case to the deans. They looked at the rest of your grades, and you're not just passing those classes too, you're doing well. A real shift in attitude, even if it comes a bit late, but beggars can't be choosers." He dropped the folder into my lap, and I stared down at it, almost afraid to look. "And that's why Declan's back on the team.

"You looked good out there, kid. We need you out there and going strong like that. Keep that up and the championship is a lock. Go grab a shower. See you on the ice bright and early tomorrow. Bring your A game like you did today." He clapped me on the shoulder, and I glanced over at Preston with a smile so wide my cheeks hurt. We both shot up from our chairs and hustled out of the room before he changed his mind.

Swinging the office door open, I was tackled to the wall by an overly large, sweaty as hell blond asshole.

"I told you it would all work out!" He lifted me off the ground, which was not easy to do for anyone who didn't have the excitement level of a Labrador retriever and the ability to bench press 350 pounds.

"I take it you heard," I wheezed, walking back toward the locker room.

"Yes! I knew it. See, things always work out, man. You've just got to believe in the universe."

"Looks like you were right this time." We barreled into the locker room with smiles so big the entire team already knew what had happened. Heath also clued them in by screaming, "Declan the Demolisher is back," at the top of his lungs the minute the door opened. Everyone stared at him like he'd grown a second head because no one had ever in their life called me "Declan the Demolisher."

Piecing it together, everyone dropped what they were doing and came up to throw out back-thumping hugs and slick handshakes. Finally, I'd be able to skate beside them every day we took the ice and I had one person to thank. After peeling off my sweaty gear, I headed for the shower. What I wouldn't give to crawl back into bed with her and deliver the good news the best way I knew how.

She had me all twisted up in knots, smiling when I shouldn't be and never more certain that she was the one for me than I was in that moment. I should be ready to go out and party it up with the guys. Drinking my face off—well, the hockey season version of that—to celebrate.

All I wanted to do was run back to her apartment and lay in bed with her, showing her just how much I appreciated all her hard work throughout the semester, whipping me into shape.

22

MAKENNA

The insistent buzz vibrated somewhere almost nonstop for five minutes. Groggy, I rubbed my eyes, trying to find my phone. Last night we'd gotten a little bit adventurous, and it had ended up on the floor. My head cleared, and I dropped over the edge of my mattress, groaning at my sore muscles. Declan had been better than any workout I'd ever tried.

Spotting it under the bed, I reached out and snatched it up off the floor. My heart pounded. *Was it my mom?* The screen flashed *SEX GOD*, and I let out a sigh and tapped on 'Accept'. He'd changed it at some point, and it had taken me forever to notice. I really should lock that damn phone.

"Books, where you been? Answer your door!"

"You were just here like two hours ago. Did you forget something?" I slid out of bed and glanced around the room, looking for what it might be. His shirt was flung over the back of my desk chair. A pair of his shoes sat in the corner.

"I think I did, but I'm going to have to help you look for it." His voice went all growly like it always did when he was trying to get under my skin in the very best of ways. I tiptoed to the front door, not wanting to wake up Tracy and Fiona, who'd rolled in, in the wee hours of the morning. Turning the handle, I opened the door. I crossed my arms over my chest as a cold gust of air swept in around him.

"What did you forget?" I bounced from foot to foot, trying to protect my body with the door.

"This." He crossed the threshold and wrapped his arms around me and lifted me off my feet. The chill from his coat made me break out into goosebumps.

Kicking the door shut behind him, he stared into my eyes before ducking his head. His lips were cold from being outside, but we quickly warmed them back up. My body tingled in anticipation of his touch. Not through his coat, but back under the covers. He laughed with his lips still pressed to mine, and joy and excitement radiated off him. His smile showed off his eagerness and anticipation.

"Would you two get a room?" Fiona joked behind us.

We both turned our heads, watching her as she poured a giant mug of coffee. I ran my hand along Declan's face, warming him up. He peered down at me, and I could tell he was almost giddy.

"What is it?"

"I'm back on the team!"

I yelped and wrapped my arms tighter around him. His happiness was infectious, and I couldn't help grinning.

"Thank God." Our heads turned at the same time as Fiona stared at us over the brim of her mug before holding up her hand. "Right, sorry. Private moment." She headed back down the hall to her room.

"I couldn't have done it without you." He ran his hands up and down my arms.

"You could have." And I meant it. Everything I'd thought about him when the semester started had been all wrong.

"Maybe, but I know it wouldn't have been half as fun." He stepped backward, doing a tango of sorts as he corralled me back into my bedroom and closed the door behind us.

The glint in his eye told me everything I needed to know about his plans for celebration. My achy and sore muscles seemed ready to rally for some celebratory nooky.

"You're seriously going to break my vagina if you keep this up." I cupped my hands over the front of my boxer pajamas.

"I know one way to help soothe you." He bit his bottom lip.

My eyes got wide, and I shook my head. "Oh no, mister. Don't get any funny ideas. I don't know what kind of girl you think I am. We are strictly sticking to sex for the next two hours. No more, no less and then I need to go to work."

"That's just the kind of girl I thought you were, Books."

My knees hit the edge of my bed and I sat. My stomach flipped as he got closer, popping open the buttons to his coat.

He slipped his hands under the waistband of my shorts. "Just the kind of girl I need."

Our arms were loaded down with what seemed like a hundred books. Of course Alcott would want us to pick a topic that wasn't easily researchable online. There were some resources but not a lot. There weren't many places that kept his PhD thesis information on hand, which meant we'd been stuck in the library every chance we got. We couldn't even check these books out; they had to stay on premises.

Glancing over at him, I had to admit Declan looked pretty hot with his muscles bulging around a giant stack of books. Rippling biceps and musty old books walking through the stacks to my study room. It was almost obscene.

He leaned down, his hot breath tickling the shell of my ear.

"I can see what you're thinking, Books. Who knew you had such a dirty, dirty mind. Heath's out tonight. Let's go back to my place and we can work through another item on *the list*."

My gaze darted around to the few study carrels with people in them. *Had they heard?*

I blushed as my mind cycled through the ones we'd already tried. He'd managed to tease the sexploration list out of me after a night of sexual torture until I fessed up. Thirty-seven positions and locations. Over the past two weeks we'd made it through almost fifteen.

Opening the door to my study room, I laughed at how full it already was. Maybe I'd gone a little overboard. We dropped the books onto the desk. The second the door slammed shut behind us, his arms caged me in with his chest pressed against my back as I arranged them by the section in our paper. Warm, soft lips trailed their way along the curve of my neck as I tilted my head to give him better access. It was like this every time we were anywhere alone. Even in a room with a small window beside the door like this one.

"We're supposed to be working." My stomach fluttered, and my breath hitched as he gently sank his teeth into the spot just below my ear that he'd discovered turned me into a puddle of writhing sexual need. He'd weaponized that knowledge.

"Then maybe a certain someone shouldn't have been

looking at me that way when I carried all those books." He growled and nudged my ass with what I guessed was a very large banana.

"Are we going to have to switch to the sexual reward system to keep you on task?" I stopped stacking because I couldn't keep track of what I was doing.

"I'm not going to say no to that, but this isn't why I came here." He stopped his full court press and let up a little. I glanced at him over my shoulder. Mischief and desire danced in his eyes.

"It's not?" I poked my tongue out to wet my suddenly dry lips.

"Don't tease me, Books, or I'm going to have you screaming this place down, and you'll lose your study room privileges," he taunted with a big grin.

"Fine. Fine, you win. Why did you come?" I spun around, and he lifted me up so I sat on the desk. His hips wedged between my open legs.

"Since I'm back on the team..." Excitement and pride ran through his voice. He was so adorable.

"Yes?" I sucked in a sharp breath as his fingers danced along my spine, making the hairs on the back of my neck stand up.

"I figured I should probably ask." His hand moved in slow circles across my skin.

My breath hitched as I looped my arms around his neck.

"Ask what? And you should have seen people losing their minds after your last game. Now I see why they needed more people specifically on those after shifts." I'd beamed as I wove my way through the crowds. They talked about him and the rest of the guys after their games with so much awe.

There were play-by-plays and reenactments throughout

the bar for the nights of their first and second games. It was such a weird feeling, but good. It made my shifts go a lot quicker, and people were extra generous with their tips.

"So, you've been keeping track of me?"

"Maybe... The team won the first game by four goals, and you scored two of them."

I ran my fingers along the curls above his ears. His dark strands slid through my fingers as he smiled down at me.

"What?" I asked because he was looking at me so slyly.

"Nothing." He kept his grin plastered on. I still couldn't wrap my mind around the transition we'd made. From high school enemies to begrudging class partners to whatever we were. Almost two months ago we'd been ready to murder each other, but today that was all different.

Things had progressed a little with each hour we spent together, and those old hostile feelings fell away. While it had happened over almost two months, I still felt like I had whiplash from it all.

I still had no idea what I was to him, and there was no way in hell I was having the talk with him. There hadn't been a talk, and I didn't want there to be. I was enjoying living in the moment with him.

For some reason defining what this was felt scarier because then it was real. Like something I'd have to think about and evaluate and make a decision on. I was enjoying just *being* for a bit.

"Will you come to one of my games?" He tugged on the end of my braid.

"I don't think Larry would appreciate me missing a shift since he hired me especially for those shifts."

"I think if there was a special request from some members of the team, he might give you a break just once."

"I'm not really a hockey person. I don't know anything

about the rules. I'll be sitting in the stands on my phone the whole time, trying to figure out what's going on." I trailed my fingers along his forearms on either side of me.

"I'm sure you can study up between now and then and figure out the basics." His hand inched higher along my back, toying with the bottom of my bra. He was always a temptation. I'd watched a few hockey games before, and the ferocity of the players out on the ice and the violence had been a quick way to make sure I didn't come back.

"I'm not big into sports—"

"Please, I want you there. You helped me get back onto the ice, and I want you there to see the fruits of your labors at least once." Sincerity and uncertainty shone in his eyes. A small pang hit my heart, and I knew I couldn't say no to him. Letting out a deep sigh, I tilted my head to the side.

"When?"

"We're away this weekend for our games in Ohio, but we'll have a game here in two weeks."

"That's close to finals prep week." My mind raced through all the lab work, papers, and exams that all bunched together around Thanksgiving.

"You're the most prepared and capable person I know. I'm sure you're already weeks ahead in everything you have to get done. One game. That's all I'm asking. Three hours of your time to watch me out on the ice trying not to get my teeth knocked out."

I winced. That was part of the reason I hadn't wanted to go when I found out he was back on the team.

"I don't think I could handle watching you out on the ice getting hit." My fingers skimmed across the soft fabric of his t-shirt.

"Look at you, Ms. Softie."

Peering up at his big, goofy grin, I couldn't help but laugh.

"I'm not the one you have to worry about. I'm one of the best players out there, and it's everyone else who needs to watch out for me. I'm not partial to getting my bell rung; I prefer to ring other people's, and I promise you I'll do my best to ensure all my teeth stay firmly in my head for whatever game you watch."

"I still don't know anything about hockey."

"Not to worry. I can solve that right now." He grabbed my hand and tugged me off the desk. Picking up my bag and his off the floor, he smirked at me. It was one I'd seen hundreds of times. Back in high school it made me want to wipe it right off his face, even a few weeks ago it got under my skin, but now it was different. I lived for those moments. The little looks that made me forget to breathe or the smile that was only for me. He'd rewritten our story and I didn't know how many more pages were left. He hustled me out of the study room, down the steps and out of the library.

"Where are we going? We didn't even finish what we had to get done."

"We're going to your car. I will stay with you every night all week to make sure we finish the work. But I couldn't pass up this chance." He pulled out his phone, tapping away on the screen as we headed to my car.

With some prodding and repeated questions, I needled him for information, but he wouldn't say anything until we pulled up outside the stadium. I leaned forward on the steering wheel and peered up at the building looming in front of us through the windshield. Pushing my glasses up my nose, I glanced over at him.

"What are we doing here?"

"I'm going to teach you the rules." He tapped on his phone and slid it into his pocket. "Let's go." Jogging around the back of the car, he smiled at me in the rearview mirror. My body hummed as he opened my door and held out his hand. I hesitated before sliding my hand into his hold. Keeping my eyes on the building, I tightened my fingers threaded through his. He guided me toward a set of steel doors. There was an older man standing at one of the entrances.

"You have one hour, and you'd better not screw anything up." His voice was deep and gruff, and he tugged the door open, slapping a set of keys into Declan's hand and closing the door behind us.

The chill outside did nothing to prepare me for the frigid temperatures inside, even with my coat on.

"Come on, let's get you ready." Rushing like a kid in a candy store, he hustled us to the rink. Opening a door I hadn't even noticed, he popped onto the bench along the side of the ice. Sitting neatly arranged on the nicked and scuffed wood were a couple pairs of gloves, a hat, and a few pairs of skates on the floor.

Patting his hand on the spot beside him, he beckoned me over. The nervous energy had me all wrapped up in knots, but his wide smile calmed me. He had the annoying habit of being able to do that. With my lips tight, I sat on the bench with my legs rubbing alongside his.

"You arranged all this?" I glanced around the rink, which was lit up with small spotlights. The massive overhead lights weren't on, but there was a soft, gentle glow to the rink.

"I figured the best way to teach you was to show you." He grinned up at me as he lifted the skates and compared them to my feet. Lifting my foot, he slid my shoe off.

"You want me to get on the ice?" I squeaked.

"No, I brought you to the rink to check out my diving technique. Yes, we are going out onto the ice once I find the skates that will work for you."

The cold air of the building sank into my sock-covered toes. I wiggled them to try to warm them a little.

"These." He grabbed the last pair of skates and slid one onto my foot. "I never noticed you had such big feet."

I punched him in the arm as he laughed and laced up my skates. "I do not have big feet!"

"I mean, they aren't exactly dainty. I'm sure they come in handy when you need to put your foot down on someone's throat and show them who's boss."

"Yeah, there's a certain someone who's about to know exactly how it feels to have a size ten skate shoved right up their ass." I leaned back, holding on to the bench as he grabbed my other foot and got me ready.

I fixed my fingers in the gloves while he got into his skates in a blink. Picking up the two sticks leaning against the Plexiglas behind us and tucking a bag of pucks under his arm, Declan opened the half door leading to the ice.

Holding out his hand, he grinned back at me. I'd never seen him this excited before. Well, that was a lie. Outside of the bedroom or study room or any other place where we were alone where he thought he might get some, I'd never seen him this excited.

I eyed his hand warily before clearing my throat and standing on wobbly ankles. My steps were more like shuffles, but I made it to the edge of the bench box. Sliding my gloved hand into his, my stomach didn't just flip, it was doing a gymnastics routine to score a gold at the Olympics.

He moved backward so I could step out onto the ice.

Taking a deep breath, I wrapped my hand tightly around the half wall beside me and tightened my fingers on around his. The strong, steady hold he had on me calmed me a little. My skate hit the ice, and I pitched forward. The sticks and pucks clattered to the ice as Declan wrapped his arms around me. I pressed my face against his chest and clung to him. My heart pounded, and his gentle chuckle made me pinch his back.

"Hey, what was that for?"

"For trying to kill me out here."

"I'm not trying to kill you. It will be fun." Peeling my face off his chest, he took my hands in his and helped me stand. Slowly, like a foal trying to walk for the first time, I locked my knees. The skates glided across the ice, which wasn't as smooth as I'd imagined it would be, with small bumps and nicks along the way.

"You got this. Keep your knees bent a little, and I've got you. We're going to take a few laps." His voice was soft and gentle, like he was afraid any sudden noise would topple me over—and he was probably right. My body was like jello, and I tried not to run through every compound injury I could think of by being out there. The cool air off the ice had every muscle in my body bunched tight.

"Eyes on me. Keep your eyes on me, and you'll see there's nothing to be worried about." His smile and touch helped calm me a little bit.

He skated backward, keeping his eyes locked on mine, and his hands never left my grip, not that he'd have been able to shake me if he tried. After a few laps I was steadier on the skates, not bent over like a grandma with a walker. Switching his grip, he skated beside me only holding on to one hand.

"I told you, you'd get it." As we did a few more laps like

that, Declan pointed out the different spots on the ice and worked through the rules of the game. His steady voice kept me distracted from the possibly icy death that awaited me with one false move.

"Stop worrying about it. The ice isn't going to shoot up and sever an artery. You ready for a stick?" He skated away, abandoning me on the ice, and I scrambled to get my fingers on the small ledge where the half wall met the Plexiglas. His skates sliced through the ice, the distinctive sound filling the air.

"Declan, I don't think that's a good idea."

He was back lightning fast with a puck and two sticks. Dropping the puck, he handed me a stick.

"I think I'll stick to the wall. I think that needs my full attention right now." It was a wonder I hadn't reverted to scooting my ass across the ice to get out of this place.

"You're using it as a crutch. You had it before. Let go of the wall."

"I'm good here."

"Makenna, let go of the wall."

I held my breath and gingerly turned so I was facing him. My skates slid, but I managed to flail my arms and catch myself. Declan's hand pressed against my back to steady me.

"You're really not into this, are you?"

I thought about pasting on a smile and soldiering on, but I couldn't even hear what he was saying, the blood was thumping in my ears so loudly.

"Maybe we work up to sticks and pucks eventually. Like in a few months." I offered.

"In a few months." He said it like he was testing it out, and the bright smile he beamed at me meant he must have liked the way it sounded. And then it hit me. The future. I was making plans with him beyond right now or even this semester. Eventually had a much more in-the-future feel to it than next week or month.

Helping me back to the bench, he grabbed a stick and a puck and put on a one-man show that had me up, leaning on the half wall, watching him in his element.

I knew he was good. Declan wouldn't have been a King back in high school if he weren't, but seeing him up close and personal was different. He ran through all the positions, talked me through some plays and flew through some tricks that had me clapping my gloved hands as he skated by.

Tugging the gloves off, I stuck two fingers in my mouth and let out a high whistle when he did a drill and sank every puck in the back of the net. My whistle ricocheted off the rafters. He raced over to me with little bits of ice flying up in the air.

"I haven't heard that one in a long time. Looks like you approve?" He leaned in close, his breath coming out in quick pants.

"I definitely approve. You're amazing out there."

"You should see me with the rest of the team. This means you're coming, right? Coming to my game?"

"After that impressive display, how could I pass it up? I'll be there. You going to win for me?" I grinned so hard my cheeks hurt. He chucked his glove off, and it landed on the bench.

"What do I get if I do?"

He ran his hand along the back of my neck and threaded his fingers up into my hair, the warmth of his touch a sharp contrast to the freezing air. I sank into his hold as he leaned in closer.

"I'm sure we could come up with something."

He nipped my lip before running his tongue over the

sore spot and pushing it into my mouth. He tasted like hot cocoa on a cold night curled up in front of the fire. We were both panting by the time he finished, and he rested his forehead against mine.

"I'm sure we can."

23

MAKENNA

S winging by the train station, I waved out my window as Avery's head of light brown curls bobbed above the other people pushing out the doors.

"Avery!" I yelled and opened my door. She waved back and hustled across the street, wrapping her arms around me, nearly picking me up off the ground. Her telltale ripped jeans and hoodie were securely in place as always, but the bag slung over her arm made me smile.

"Can you stay over?" I leaned on the hood of my car as she walked around the other side.

"Alyson's staying at a friend's house tonight, so I can if it's cool with you. I have to be at an interview early tomorrow morning, and I figured this would be easier." She jerked the door open and climbed inside.

"Of course. I told you that. How's she doing?" I pulled out of the lot and drove to my apartment.

"She's great. She's a senior at Rittenhouse. I'm freaking out."

"Wow, a senior already?!" Her chubby, fresh faced little

sister was going to be walking across a campus like UPhil in no time.

"You're telling me. I'm trying not to lose my mind, but she'd already in at UPenn, so at least she'll be close."

"That's awesome." Her comment from before came back to me. "What's the interview for?"

She glanced down at her nails like she was actually thinking about not telling me. I had a way of making people talk.

"It's a college thing." She peered over at me.

"Really? Awesome. An admissions interview?" It had to be hard seeing her little sister go off to college when she hadn't had the same chance.

She nodded. "It's for a transfer spot. I finally finished all my associate's degree credits after nearly four years and I put in some applications and I have an interview."

I reached over and squeezed her hand.

"That's amazing, Avery. I know you're going to kill that interview. You've worked so hard, and I know you'll get in."

"At least one of us is confident." She picked at the shredded jeans around her knee.

"Don't forget, I was your study partner back in high school."

"And if it hadn't been for you, I would have failed everything." She glanced out the window.

"No, if you hadn't been working while you were in high school like thirty hours a week and taking care of Alyson, then maybe it wouldn't have turned out that way."

"You worked too. You were in the coffee shop all the time."

I dismissed her attempt to compare our situations.

"I worked to get the hell out of my house. I always felt like I was suffocating there. You worked to pay bills, keep the lights on, and make sure your sister never wanted for anything. Two completely different situations."

"If you say so." She was always so hard on herself. Sleep deprivation had a hell of an impact on your life, and I didn't think Avery had had a full night's sleep in a decade.

"You got the material in high school. You're smart, Avery." Going to Rittenhouse Prep on a scholarship because her dad worked as a janitor there couldn't have been easy. I'm sure some of the people were real assholes about it. It sucked always feeling like you were never good enough, even though she was amazing, and anyone who thought otherwise was an asshole.

"I don't know how many times it will take me saying it before you believe it."

She glanced over at me and gave me a small smile. "Maybe one more time."

"I'll say it until I'm blue in the face."

We dropped Avery's bag off at my apartment, and I introduced her to Fiona and Tracy who were actually staying in for the night. *Shocker!* After grabbing something to eat, we got to the stadium. There were cars everywhere. People dressed in hockey jerseys with their faces painted by the hundreds. I'd seen Three Streets after games, but this was completely different. Finally finding a spot, we parked and hopped out, joining the flow of people.

"I haven't been to a game in a long time." Avery bent back, looking at the lights on the side of the stadium as we handed over our tickets. She'd been to every one back in high school because of Emmett. I'd stayed well clear of anything resembling a sporting event back in high school, which made it even weirder that I was here. And who I was here to see.

The cold air inside matched the blustery temperatures

outside, and I was glad I'd worn my coat and sweater. Had I known it would be this cold, I would have worn my gloves and a hat. Last time I hadn't remembered it being that cold, probably because a hockey player heated things up with his skating prowess and sexy body.

I shook my head as I followed Avery to our seats. That was not a sentence I ever thought I'd think, but even when I'd thought I hated him, I'd had to admit he had a hot body. Now it was one I knew intimately. The tips of my ears burned, and Avery turned around to quirk her eyebrow at me.

"What?" I felt like she could see what I was thinking.

"You made a weird noise. And the tips of your ears are all red. What the hell are you thinking about?" She scooted along the row.

"Nothing," I mumbled and kept my head down. We found our seats smack-dab in the center of the ice. While we waited for the game to start and everyone took their seats, she filled me in on some of the finer points of the game that Declan hadn't already gone over with me.

People had on team scarves and hats. Families were there with little pennants. It amazed me that people were so excited for the team, even though there was a professional team not too far away.

"Some people just love hockey." Avery bit into her hot dog and clamped her soda between her legs. My teeth were chattering just looking at it. The team stepped out onto the ice, warming up, and I spotted Declan immediately.

"There he is." I grabbed onto Avery's jacket and pointed him out. Peering back at her, I hadn't realized I'd scooted to the edge of my seat. She smirked at me and laughed.

"Looks like someone's a bit excited to see her man out on the ice." I opened my mouth to dispute it, then snapped it shut. The reflex to deny it was there, but deep down I knew it was true. I'd never felt like this before. Like I needed him. Needed to see him and touch him. When he traveled for away games my phone was practically attached to my hand because I didn't want to miss a message from him.

He whipped around the ice and spotted me. Lifting his stick up, he motioned in my direction. My chest got tight, and I resisted the urge to raise my arm in the air, wave back like a complete idiot, and instead, I lifted my hand and gave him a small wave. A few people around us glanced over at me, and my cheeks heated at the attention.

He and Heath skated around the ice together, loosening up and taking some practice shots. At one point he stopped at the glass like he saw someone, and then he kept going. I checked out who it might have been. There was one guy with a scowl on his face and an expensive coat, but that was it. The stadium-shaking horn bellowed, and the guys left the ice.

"Could that thing get any louder?" I felt like someone had held an air horn right up to my ear.

"Oh yeah." Avery took a sip of her drink and then a wave of cold soda splashed on my legs and covered her.

"Shit." I shook the drink off my hands. She grabbed some napkins and tried to clean the droplets of soda on me, looking like she'd seen a ghost.

"Avery, what the hell?"

"I'm sorry. It slipped." She tried to clean it up, but her eyes weren't on me. They were on in the ice—well, close to the ice. I glanced up, following her gaze, and grimaced when I saw why she was freaking out. All dark and gloomy like a black-haired harbinger of doom, Emmett stood in the aisle down by the ice. He might have shaved the beard from back in high school, but I'd recognize him anywhere. People flocked to him in his impeccably tailored wool calf-length coat asking for autographs, but his gaze kept darting to Avery.

"I'm going to go." She stood, her seat bouncing up.

I grabbed her arm.

"Don't let him run you out of here. There is no reason you two can't be in the same building together." This thing with them was ridiculous, and I could see that nothing had changed in the years since we left school.

"It's fine. I shouldn't be out late anyway because of my interview tomorrow. I'm just going to go. I'll head back to your place and grab my bag and go."

"Avery..."

She shimmied by me and gave me a weak smile before chancing another look at Emmett, who was glowering just as much as before.

"Really, it's fine. I'll go. You stay and enjoy the game. Tell Declan I said hi." She rushed up the steps just as the buzzer rang again and both teams skated onto the ice. Torn, I glanced back at her one more time and she motioned with both hands for me to sit. Reluctantly I sat in my seat, not ready to be completely lost in whatever the hell was happening, but I'd told Declan I'd watch, so I did.

24

DECLAN

S tanding in the locker room, I shifted from leg to leg, waiting to head out onto the ice. It was the same smell of sweat, ice, concessions, and victory. Those mingled together to settle over everyone as we got ourselves pumped up to put another game in the W column.

Coach had already given us his give-them-hell-and-don't-get-stuck-in-the-Sin-Bin speech. I was never nervous before games, but my stomach was a giant ball of 'don't fuck this up'.

Makenna was out there. Sitting in the stands waiting for me to show her everything I'd worked hard at since I was little. My mom had done everything she could to keep me in hockey. Early morning practices, expensive equipment—she'd done a lot to make it happen, and I'd worked my ass off so I could give her everything she'd missed out on making sure I had enough.

The stadium vibrated with the energy of the crowd. We were undefeated so far this season, and they were expecting a win. Who were we to let them down?

"She's out there, right?" Heath said, standing beside me

looking like he was about to enter a bubble-blowing championship, infuriatingly chill about everything.

"Yeah. She asked for two tickets."

"Maybe she's bringing her boyfriend."

I glared at Heath, and he laughed in that way that made his whole body shake.

"Relax."

If he weren't wearing his helmet, I'd have punched him.

"There are these things people tell sometimes and they're called jokes. You might have missed the memo." He pushed against my shoulder, pointing out that the guys were walking out to the rink. The people in the stands roared when we came out of the tunnel and onto the ice. My body vibrated with barely contained intensity. I was back and ready to get in the wins we'd worked our asses off for. It was a feeling that never got old, basking in their energy out on the ice with my teammates.

I skated along the edge of the rink until I spotted her. In her bright red sweater, looking straight at me. I lifted my stick, and she went all red waving back, but I almost stumbled when I saw who was next to her.

"Is that Avery?" Heath asked like we were sitting in study hall.

"Yeah, that's Avery." A bad feeling rushed over me.

"Didn't Emmett say he might be coming to this game tonight?"

And the small gathering of people on the other side of the glass let me know he had decided to show. But it was another scowling face that caught my eye. Archer stood on the other side of the glass looking like he owned the place. Those old feelings I always got when he was there tried to bubble up, but one glance over at Mak pushed it all away.

I wasn't going to let him get in my head. I wasn't going to

fall into the same trap he wanted me to. *Screw him.* With one last look I pushed off the ice and blocked him from my mind.

Trying to keep my head in the game, I went back to warming up with Heath. I'd have to figure how to sort through the lingering animosity between them out later, but it looked like I didn't have to. Avery was walking up and out of the stadium.

Worried Mak had gone with her, I found her spot in the stands again where she was worriedly staring back at Avery but still in her seat. I breathed a sigh of relief. The last thing I needed was to be worried about what happened to her while I was out on the ice trying not to let my team down. I needed her there. I needed her to ward off the shitty glare Archer tried to shoot me.

She was my good luck charm.

And then Emmett was up the other set of steps and out. I shook my head. When the hell were those two ever going to just hash it out? Fight. Fuck and forgive. Probably never, but this wasn't the time to get wrapped up in their drama.

Digging extra deep and with Heath on during the game like never before, we sailed to three goals in the first period. I scored two of them. Sitting on the bench, I sprayed the cold water into my mouth. A wave of satisfaction rolled over me as Archer got up from his seat and left with his hands shoved deep down in his pockets. *Hell yeah!* Someone held out a stick for him to sign, and he pushed them out of the way like the asshole he was. I could feel Mak's eyes on me as I traded onto the bench and back out on the ice.

Gulping down some water, my gaze darted up to her before they were right back to the guys giving it everything they had out there. The action was fast, and our skates were faster. Sweat poured off me, and I glanced up from the bench, watching her nibble on her lips. While Heath and I were on the bench, the other team managed to score two goals in the second period, nearly equalizing. It was time for us to head back in and make sure they knew winning was not an option for them. It was time for me to win this game once and for all for my girl.

25

MAKENNA

The crowd buzzed with an electricity I'd never experienced before. Everyone held their breath, got out of their seats, and cheered until their voices were hoarse all at the same time. It was like being a part of one giant genetic organism that grew with each goal. It amazed me how quiet so much of the play was.

The puck was so small and it flew so fast, sometimes it seemed like people didn't even know a goal had been scored until the buzzer and the lights went off. Then everyone was on their feet. My ears rang as the final buzzer blared in the stadium.

"That's quite a set of lungs you have there, young lady." One of the older guys who'd been sitting behind me clapped me on the shoulder as everyone filed out of their seats. I may have gotten a little carried away with the whistling.

"Thanks." I gave them a small smile.

"Declan's lucky to have someone like you in his corner cheering so hard for him," he said, disappearing into the rushing crowd. His words bounced around my head as I moved with the flow of people down the few concrete steps.

Walking around to where the team would exit the ice, there were a lot of people crowded around the door on the side of the rink leading to the tunnel. The guys celebrated on the ice, and I couldn't wipe the smile off my face.

He'd worked hard to make sure he could be there for his team. The second I'd found out he was back on the team, I was elated for him. For some reason, I'd thought it wouldn't matter much to me. But I knew how much it meant to him, so it mattered a hell of a lot to me.

He flew across the ice, and it was like nothing I'd experienced before. I was equal parts raving lunatic, busting out my two-finger whistle, and cringing weenie who held her breath every time he ended up slammed against the boards. It wasn't too often because he was fast and Heath was by his side, helping him out when he needed it, but it was enough to make me worry about a full-on panic attack in the stadium.

They piled out of a small door at the side of the rink, and it was so weird to see them off the ice. On the ice they were all precision and power, but watching them lumber around still on their skates, hauling those sticks and hockey pads, had me laughing. It was like seeing a fish out of water.

People crushed in, trying to get autographs and pictures with the guys still in their uniforms. Hanging back, I let the team pass. Declan scanned the crowd when he stomped through the door. Our eyes met, and I gave him a small wave.

"I'll meet you outside." I cupped my hand around my mouth, hoping he could hear me over the noise. Pointing behind me, I smiled and turned, happy to wait to congratulate him.

I hadn't made it more than three steps when I was lifted up off the ground and spun around. My hair whipped around into my eyes, and I was face-to-face with a sweaty, smiling, and unreasonably sexy Declan.

"Hey, Books." The overpowering smell of sweat and his hockey gear hit me, but on him it wasn't terrible. It was a display of his raw power and talent.

"Hey, I was going to meet you outside." He set me down, so I was standing on the toes of his skates. I glanced down at the ground and back up at him.

"I know, but I wanted to see you in here. You came." His eyes searched my face like he thought I might disappear at any moment.

"I told you I would."

"You even broke out the whistle."

My cheeks flamed, and I dropped my gaze. "You heard that, huh?"

"I think everyone did. Quite impressive. And Mak, one more thing—"

I gazed into his eyes, and his lips came crashing down on mine. The salty taste of his sweat mingled with the mints I'd been stress eating throughout the whole game. It was a heady mixture, and he rested his forehead against mine when we both came up for breath.

"Wait right here. I'll hurry up and get changed."

I opened my mouth to protest, but he ran his fingers along my back and a shudder raced through me. Not trusting my voice, I nodded. He smiled back at me like I'd handed him a championship trophy. Helping me step down from his skates, he grabbed his gear and took off down the tunnel to the locker room.

Sitting in the front row of stadium seats near where the team came off the ice, I grabbed my phone and sent a text.

Me: He left right after he saw you.

Avery: I figured, but I wasn't taking any chances.

Me: Why not?

Avery: It's a long story. But I thought it was best to stay away.

Me: You guys broke up four years ago. Why don't you tell him the truth?

Avery: Let's not go there.

Me: Do you really think you coming with me to the game and watching Declan would cause problems?

Avery: Yes.

Me: I barely got to see you. Maybe you could come back again soon.

Avery: Maybe, if I can get time off.

Me: Hopefully you'll have tons of it once you get accepted into college.

Avery: Maybe...

My alert pinged, letting me know there was less than eighteen hours until our final paper was due. I had no idea why Alcott had us turning it in so early, but it was fine by me. It meant I'd have more room to study for the finals for my pre-med courses.

A small pit of sadness hit me in the stomach. The weekly study sessions with Declan were coming to an end. We still hadn't had the talk about what it was we were doing together. He'd head off to the pros after graduation, and medical school didn't exactly give tons of time outside school to have any type of life. He'd be traveling, and the spotlight he'd lived in since high school would be even bigger with even more attention on a professional team. And women. He had them fawning all over him now, what would it be like when he was in the pros?

"Stop thinking so hard. You're going to break something."

I jumped as his voice sliced through my heavy concentration.

He strolled past my chair in a t-shirt and low-slung jeans, loaded with some of his gear, and sank into the folding stadium seat next to me. I breathed in the icy smell of the place now that it was almost empty. The Zamboni glided across the ice, smoothing it out for later.

"Did you like the game?" He peered over at me, his dark green eyes shining with equal parts exhaustion and elation, like he was the happiest guy in the world. It was a lazy contentment brought on after serious exertion, and it made me slam my thighs together against the growing throb between them. It was the same look he gave me every night we passed out wrapped up in each other.

My heart squeezed, and my fingers ached to touch him, but I held myself back.

"Did you drive?" He trailed his finger down my arm, dragging it along my sweater. The hairs on the back of my neck rose.

"Yeah, I didn't want to walk back to my apartment at night, and I knew the campus transport would be packed with people going out for the night." My voice came out huskier and hungrier than I meant it to.

"You're not driving back. You're coming to my place." Not a question. A statement. Practically a foregone conclusion by the sound of his voice.

My gaze snapped up to his, and he had a lazy, cocksure smile on his face. A few months ago I'd have wanted to hit him, but now I wanted to crawl into his lap and nibble on his lip until he flipped me around and pressed me up against the Plexiglas surrounding the rink and took me from behind. A tremble shuddered through me, and my nipples pebbled. Resisting the urge to slide my hands between my thighs to alleviate the ache, I bit my lip.

"Now you're definitely coming home with me. You can't look at me like that and bite your lip like you do when I've got my fingers inside you and think you're getting away from me. Not until I wring at least three orgasms out of you." He growled and buried his head in my neck, snaking a hand under my sweater as I glanced around, making sure no one saw.

I breathed in his clean soap smell as the goosebumps rose on my arms. Watching him out on the ice, skating with such ferocity and power, made me appreciate every bulging muscle and his incredible endurance even more. Breaking off his attack on my body, he peered up at me.

"You'll come back with me, right? Come to the party at my house."

The heady haze I slipped into whenever he touched me cleared a little.

"A party?" Being surrounded by a huge crowd of people I didn't know wasn't exactly what I'd had in mind for our evening. And then there was our final paper.

"I still need to proofread our final and turn it in, and I have work tomorrow night."

"It's not due until noon tomorrow. I'm sure you've already proofread it three times, and I know I did it twice. It's perfect. Come to the party."

Running through the list in my head of why I couldn't come died on my lips when he traced his thumb along the sensitive skin on the inside of my wrist.

"I want to introduce you to the guys. Not as our server but as my girlfriend."

A light, bubbly feeling like the one time I had two

glasses of champagne at an honors brunch at Stanford made a sharp laugh burst out of my mouth.

Declan's forehead creased, and he dropped my wrist from his hand, hurt shining in his eyes. I snatched his hand back and rested it in my lap, tracing the deep grooves in his palm and the calluses on his fingers.

"I didn't mean to laugh like a *laugh* laugh. It was a you-caught-me-off-guard laugh. Are you serious? Am I really your girlfriend?" I tilted my head up at him, halfway nervous it would be something I'd imagined in my head and it would be his turn to laugh.

"I've never been more serious about anything in my life, Books. Come to the party with me so I can show you off and then take you upstairs and do every dirty thing I've thought about doing since I saw you sitting up in the stands in this sweater. It's practically obscene." He ran his finger along the high scoop neck of my red cable-knit sweater. I glanced down at my completely covered body and quirked my eyebrow up at him.

"Obscene?" I laughed. "I'm a nun in this thing."

"I know, but I also know everything you're hiding under there. More than a handful of the most mouthwatering breasts that I could bite and suck on all night, and don't get me started on what's under those jeans. Why didn't you just walk in here naked?"

"You're insane." I pushed against his shoulder. He stood and lifted me out of my seat, pressing his muscled chest against my body.

"I'm insane for you, Mak. Let's go." His warm breath fanned across my face. I glanced out at the ice behind him and nodded my head.

"Okay, let's go." I grinned at him, ready to do a little damage, get a little drunk and have some toe-curling, walking-like-a-cowboy, dirty sex. "But promise me we go to bed early so I can give the paper one more read through before I submit it."

"You're driving me crazy, Books!" He plucked my glasses from my face.

"Hey!" I grabbed for them.

He dipped his shoulder, and I looked down at the floor to see if he dropped something when his shoulder nudged into my stomach. I yelped as he lifted me off my feet, slung over his shoulder. He wrapped his arms around my legs, and his fingers dug into my ass, squeezed and the *crack* from his smack echoed in the rink. The sting was sharp and fast and sent a line zinging straight to my pussy.

"Ow, what was that for?" I rubbed my ass and gave his a smack with my perfect vantage point hung over his back.

"That was for looking at me like that. Don't think I didn't see your nipples get hard. Like they were ready to cut through glass. You think I don't know how your mind works yet? Plus, we still have ten more positions and places to try on your list."

His hands kneaded my butt through my jeans, and I ran my fingers down his back. With my hair flopping in my face, my broad-shouldered boyfriend—*holy shit*, I had a boyfriend—carried me out to my car caveman style.

I ran my hands over my hair again as we climbed the steps to Declan's house. It was like a different place as people spilled out of it and music thumped its way down the street. I had to park almost five blocks away because everyone seemed to have the same idea about celebrating.

His fingers interlaced with mine, and I peered up at him.

The streetlights made his eyes sparkly, and the tension in my stomach eased a little.

"It will be fine. I want to introduce you to the guys."

People streamed down the street. Some headed into Declan's house while others headed to other parties along the street. It was a different world from our relatively quiet apartment complex on the far side of campus. People came up and high-fived him, shouted congratulations and seemed ready to burst with happiness over being in his presence. The entire time kept his fingers interlaced with mine.

Some people glanced down, usually other women, and saw our hands intertwined. The looks they shot us made me laugh. I could see them trying to work it out in their heads. *Good luck.* Their guess was as good as mine on how I ended up as Declan McAvoy's girlfriend.

Stepping through his front door was like going from a freezer into a sauna. The house was jam-packed with people, and within seconds I was regretting my sweater. It was blazing in here. The second he stepped through the door, a huge cheer broke out from the crowd. People were all over him, but the more people crowded in, the tighter his hold got on me, like he didn't want me to freak out and run away.

I'd have thought I would feel that way too, but I watched him smile wide, soak in the accolades and I was proud of him. He introduced me to everyone who came up to him as his girlfriend, and again the surprised looks and a few catty glares from some of the women. I just shrugged my shoulders, as if to say, *What can I do? He gets what he wants.*

A head popped up above the crowd back in the bathroom, and it was Heath standing on their kitchen table, staring up out the skylight in their kitchen.

"He's going to break the freaking table." Declan shook his head and grabbed us both a beer.

"What is he looking at?" I craned my neck to get a better look.

Heath held out his hand, when someone nearly took a header off the table and helped them stand beside him.

"I think she's one of the TAs for my biochemistry course. I'm pretty sure she's a bio master's student."

"Figures." Declan laughed into his beer and walked us around the party. Sweat trickled down my back, and I tugged at the front of my sweater, trying to cool myself off as I sipped my beer.

"Guys, I want you to meet Makenna." Declan held on to my shoulder and walked me down the line of his teammates standing beside the beer pong table set up in the back room. Preston came up and squeezed me so tightly I could barely breathe.

"Thank you, Makenna. I would kiss you full on the lips for keeping him in line this semester, if I didn't think Dec would try to knock my teeth down my throat. He's already glaring." I peered over at Declan, and he wore a not amused expression on his face, which transformed the second Preston let me go.

"He's exaggerating. I wouldn't knock his teeth down his throat; that would be a choking hazard, and we don't need our fearless leader being sent to the hospital. I'd be sure to knock them clean out his mouth. Safety first." The guys burst out laughing.

"What did I miss?" Heath popped his head into the room, his blond mop sticking up every which way.

"Nothing. We were just offering Makenna and Dec next game."

"Ohh, can I play?" Heath chugged his beer and turned around, refilling all the cups on the table.

"You up for it?" Declan tucked some of my hair behind my ear. The sweat gathered at the base of my neck. What I wouldn't give for a hair tie so I could put my hair up. The one time I wear it down and I'm in the middle of an inferno. The warm fuzzies I'd gotten from my beer weren't helping. "I'll drink your beers for you," he whispered in my ear. I nodded and he laid a hot, hard wet one on me. My eyelids fluttered as I steadied myself on him.

"We're first up." Declan picked up the Ping-Pong ball and stood at the end of the table. Bending his elbow and cocking his wrist, he let go of the ball, and it sailed through the air, landing without a bounce in the cup in front of Heath.

"And that is how it's done." He gloated as Heath downed the cup. Throughout the night people kept coming up to the guys and bringing them even more beers, wanting to toast to their victory. They'd been undefeated so far this season, and it looked like the trend from previous years was going to power through without a hitch.

A buzz of energy flowed through the party, and it wasn't only the booze. The team had too many people they made incredibly happy just by doing what they loved. That was a true gift, and I couldn't even imagine what that was like. To make the people around you practically burst out into song by seeing your face.

I slid my hand into Declan's back pocket as he let go of the Ping-Pong ball, trying to win our game. It went way off course and bounced off Heaths' forehead.

"Hey, we almost won."

I licked my lips and leaned in close to him, almost pressing my lips against his ear.

"Take me to bed." His eyes turned into liquid desire, and I was ready to ride the wave all night long.

"You only have to tell me once." He grabbed my hand and practically dragged me up the steps to his bedroom, not giving a second look to anyone trying to high-five him or congratulate him along the way. I couldn't blame him. My body hummed in anticipation of his touch.

The door slammed shut behind him with the throbbing of the bass vibrating the floor. And it was like we were both wearing clothes made of asbestos. We needed them off. *Now.*

Stripping each other, I ran my hands along his face. Our tongues danced, and our lips smashed together. It was a tipsy, teeth-clinking, sweaty-body-groping, moaning, and writhing kind of foreplay.

The wet sounds of our mouth and the frustrated groans of us getting caught up in our clothes as we tried to rip them off were the only ones in the room. He backed me up, using his body just like he did on the ice, to control a situation.

With a gentle push he tipped me over onto the bed and climbed on top of me. I craved his touch like an addict, and I didn't care how I'd handle withdrawal. But I needed him pressed against me and inside me now.

26

DECLAN

The plaintive and naked way Mak asked me to take her to bed nearly made me cause a scene right there on the beer pong table. The couple beers had loosened her up, but it was more than that. I don't know why it took me so long to tell her she was my girlfriend.

In my head that's what we were doing all along. It had been inevitable from that first night her lips touched mine. Hell, it had probably been inevitable since that first night in her study room. I'd never even thought about being with anyone else. There was never enough time, and hockey always came first, but with Mak it was right. Even seeing Archer on the other side of the glass with his eyes boring into mine hadn't made a dent when I knew she was out in the stands for me. She unlocked something in me I hadn't been able to unlock myself. I could skate for her, and nothing else mattered. She was everything.

The dim light from my desk gave the room a subtle glow. I was tempted to turn on all the lights so I could see every inch of her, not miss a thing.

The way her voice got husky but honeyed at the same

time when she wanted me made the hairs on the back of my neck stand up. She was the one I'd never counted on. All our bickering and snarky comments, the way the energy between us hummed—it had always been leading to this.

Every time my hands were on her, I discovered a new way to love her. My body jolted as it dawned on me. Staring at her in the bed on her knees, waiting for me, I loved her. Not just there, but everywhere and in any way she'd have me.

"Do I have to come over there and get you, or are you going to give us what we both want?" Her chest rose and fell, those dusky nipples tight and calling out for my mouth. Drinking her in, I wanted everything all at once. Have my cake and eat it too.

"Are you sure you want this, babe?" I stroked my cock, and her eyes zeroed in on my hand moving up and down my shaft. She licked her lips, and I groaned. "Are you wet for me?"

She slid her hands down her stomach and dipped her fingers inside herself, moaning as she did. My knees nearly buckled as I watched my girl touching herself. Letting go of my cock before I exploded, I stepped to the end of the bed. The driving need to get inside her hot little pussy made me light-headed.

Crawling on top of her, I stared down at her afraid to blink. Like this would all be some fever dream and I wasn't back on the team, she still hated my guts, and I'd never actually felt her wrapped around me. She was more beautiful than anything I'd experienced before. Our hands roamed all over each other. It was second to no other feeling, not even slapping in another goal at the buzzer to win another game that season. Not even that.

Rolling her nipple between my fingers, I dipped my

head, trailing my tongue along the curve of her neck as her back arched off the bed.

"Declan..." Her raspy, needy cry made a drop of precum leak out of my head. She reached down between us and stroked my hard-on, sending a shudder down my spine. Things were going to be short and sweet this time. Her moans made me want to bury my head between her legs until she screamed so loud we were both deaf, but that would have to wait.

"I've got you." Fumbling around in the drawer beside my bed, I grabbed the condoms. Sliding one on, I lifted her legs and rested them against my chest. "Are you sure you're ready? Is that pussy ready for me?" Dropping a hand, I slid my two fingers inside, and she let out a strangled cry, lifting her hips off the bed.

"Fuck, you're soaking wet, Books." Her liquid heat coated my fingers as her pussy clenched like she never wanted them to leave. I pumped them into her, and her breath caught. She made a mewling sound as her head thrashed from side to side. Her hair clung to her forehead and was plastered to her neck.

"More." She opened her eyes and stared into mine, her desire building and connecting us as the thin line of restraint I had finally snapped. "Declan, I need you."

Kissing her sleek, smooth calves, I lined myself up with her. Spreading her wetness around, I pressed into her. The fit was always tight almost painful. Every time. The kind of pain you got when something was too good. So overwhelming you wanted to bask in the feeling forever. That was her. She was it for me.

I sucked in a sharp breath as I leaned back. She urged me forward, trying to angle her hips to get me inside. Grabbing my cock, I pushed my head in, gritting my teeth. Her body went rigid before she cried out for more. I slammed into her, driving my cock in to the hilt and giving us both exactly what we wanted.

Her fist-like grip on me made me clench my jaw tight. I groaned as I basked in the intense pleasure so good I could barely breathe. Her legs shook against my chest, and my name became a chant falling from her lips.

I kept my arm wrapped around her legs, and she used her body to try pushing me in deeper. Leaning forward, I sat up on my knees, and she screamed my name. The thumping beats of the music downstairs drowned it out. But I didn't care if it didn't, hearing my name on her lips was the sweetest sound I'd ever heard. I wanted it daily. Fuck that, every hour on the hour.

"I've got just what you want." Spreading her legs, I dropped down on top of her and ground my body against her. Our hips worked in unison to bring us to the place where we both forgot our names and nothing else mattered but how good everything felt.

She grabbed the side of my face, pushing her hot, wet tongue into my mouth. Her taste made me wild. Her mouth was sin, her pussy was bliss, and her body was everything I should have been warned about. Addiction was real when it came to her. I slammed my hips down as she lifted hers. Our bodies moved in frantic unison, trying to see who could make the other come first. I was determined to win. To watch her come apart in front of me as I lost myself in her one more time.

The hot, wet slapping of our bodies trying to meld together filled the air over the driving music downstairs. Our movement was in time to the beat, getting closer to the bass drop and our explosion. Her moans and cries matched mine.

The headboard slammed against the wall, and I held onto it for extra leverage, leaning forward and pushing her hips higher.

Her eyes were pools of need and a fine sheen of sweat on her skin that matched my own. The vise grip she had on my cock made me grit my teeth. Her pussy clenched around me and nearly sent me over the edge. With the new angle her cries changed, and I glanced down to make sure she was okay.

"Don't you dare stop! Touch—" A gasp broke free from her, and she cried out before licking her lips. "Rub my clit."

So open in bed. Ready to tell me what she needed. I reveled in the fact that I got her to drop her walls and be free when we were like this. Never one to let my girl down, I reached between us and gave her soft, tight nub a stroke with my thumb.

Like she was trying to throw me off, her muscles tightened, and her back arched off the bed. I held on and kept going as she screamed my name louder than I'd ever heard.

A rush of wetness coated my cock and thighs and her pussy got even tighter, the silky prison threatening to milk the come out of me as she shuddered and moaned, riding out the wave of her orgasm. I'd never seen or felt anything hotter in my life.

She trembled under me and wrapped her arms around my back, pressing her full breasts against me. Picking up my pace, I drove into her with abandon and pressed my lips to hers as every muscle in my legs seized up.

I yelled her name, the tightness in my back overwhelmed my whole body as she turned me inside out. Grinding myself against her like I was trying to leave a permanent impression of my dick inside her, I shook and came into the condom. The muscles in my body slowly uncoiled, and I tried to catch my breath. She wrecked me.

My arms collapsed, and I fell to the side to keep most of my weight off her. My chest rose and fell, and I felt like I'd been doing drills out on the ice for the past hour.

Her hand stroked a lazy path down my back as we both tried to get our breathing under control. Hopping up, I got rid of the condom. I climbed back into bed and trailed my fingers along her hips. Small circular scars I hadn't noticed before were dotted there.

I ran my hands over the spot, the extra smooth skin even softer than the rest of her. She snuggled in closer against my chest. That swell of emotions at having her in my arms, of her being my girlfriend made my head swim, and it wasn't just the booze.

"What time is it?" Her warm breath fanned across the sweat on my chest, giving me goose bumps. I leaned over and dragged the blanket over top of us, tucking it in behind her. The heat pouring off our bodies cooled, and the chilly temperature from the November air crept into the room.

I squinted to get a good look at my clock on the desk across the room, but I couldn't see it. Exhaustion, drunkenness, and a sexual coma had apparently stolen my vision.

"I don't know. Not too late. It's fine." We lay wrapped in one another, content and worn-out. I'd never felt this way after sex before with anyone other than Mak. Every time I learned something new about her body. A new thing she liked and something else I couldn't wait to try next time. I'd never get tired of showing her how good things would be between us and how much better they'd be the next time.

I trailed my fingers down her spine, sliding along the slight sheen of sweat covering her. She shivered and tucked in tighter against me. Breathing her in, I sunk deeper into the bed and buried my nose in her neck. She smelled like the library and a field full of strawberries. Like sitting out on the lawn reading a book under a tree with a tall glass of lemonade on a warm spring afternoon.

The party downstairs was winding down, so the bass wasn't shaking the floor as much. Some laughter punched through the quiet cocoon we'd created for ourselves snuggled up in my bed. Her head dipped, and her body relaxed, and then her eyes shot open, gazing up into mine.

"Can you set an alarm? I want to make sure I'm up early." She yawned, and I tapped the tip of her nose.

"Don't worry. I'll wake you up."

Nodding and snuggling in tighter, her hands slid under my arms and wrapped around me. I smiled at her gentle snores and the way her body wrapped around mine like I was a vine she was trying to climb. She threw her legs over mine in her sleep, and I ran my hand down over her hair. My fingers glided through her strands as I cradled her to my chest.

Her heart beat soft and steady as she slept. Craning my neck, I searched for my phone. I knew I should get up and grab some water for Mak and for me, but I didn't want to leave her warm embrace. I gave up looking for the phone when I couldn't see it from the bed.

It would be fine. It couldn't be that late. We'd wake up and turn in the paper together in the morning. My eyelids were heavy, and I savored her body against mine.

This was how it should always be...

27

MAKENNA

A groggy fog in my head made it hard to get my bearings, not to mention the massive arm across my chest. I tensed for a second before everything came rushing back to me from the night before. A flutter in my stomach and a smile spread across my face as I retraced my steps from the day before.

Declan winning his game. The party and the way I'd asked him to take me to bed. My cheeks heated, and I hoped no one had heard me, but from the way he nearly bowled people over to get us upstairs, I don't think there was any question about what was said. Then there was the sex, although somehow that felt like an inadequate word for how we'd attacked each other's bodies only a few hours ago.

The room was still almost pitch-black with his heavy curtains drawn, but there was a peek of light streaming under his bedroom door. The night's drinks caught up to me, and I slid out of the bed. Grabbing his boxers and a t-shirt off the floor, I cracked open his bedroom door.

Squeezing my eyes shut against the blinding light out in the hall, I peered outside. The house was quiet, and the coast was clear. I tiptoed to the bathroom. I'd take a morning-after face-off with Heath in the hallway over peeing myself in the middle of Declan's room.

Finishing up the morning business, I dragged my fingers through my hair. Well, I tried to. It was a nest on top of my head. Any second two birds would fly in through the window and begin feeding worms to their little hatchlings nestled safely in my hair. Running some cool water over my face, I tried to get ahold of the throbbing as my brain punished me for last night's fun.

Glancing out the bathroom window, my stomach plummeted, and my fingers wrapped tightly around the porcelain sink. It was way brighter than it should be for early morning.

The long streaks of sun streamed through the glass. I got that watery mouth feeling, but it didn't have anything to do with the drinks from last night—well, maybe a little.

Like everything was moving in slow motion, I raced into Declan's room. The door slammed against the wall as I scoured the floor, looking for my phone. He groaned and rolled over.

It was halfway kicked under the bed. Snatching it up off the floor, my hands trembled as I turned it on. The battery was almost dead, and the time flashed on the screen. A strangled sound burst out of my chest, and I covered my mouth, trying not to hyperventilate: 12:05 p.m.

"No!" I shouted without meaning to. Declan shot up in bed and pressed his hands into his temples.

"Mak, what's going on?" His voice was sleepy and pained.

"It's after noon, Declan. What are we going to do?" My heart thumped against my ribs, and the bile churned in my stomach. I searched the floor for my clothes. *Why had I stayed out? Why hadn't I just gone home?*

I grabbed my jeans from under his desk chair as my world spiraled out of control. If we didn't turn in the final, the best grade we could get was a B-. I wouldn't get into the program. I wasn't going to get into the med school program. The room tilted, and I held on to the edge of the desk as my world ripped apart. So many plans I'd had and promises I'd made myself and Daniel, and in one careless night I'd thrown it all away.

"Why didn't your alarm go off?"

"I forgot to set it." He groaned.

I whipped around, the sick feeling in my stomach morphing into something scarier.

"You did what?" If I could have breathed fire, I would have.

"I couldn't find my phone, and you were already asleep. I didn't think we'd sleep so late." He sat on the edge of the bed and squeezed his head. "It's fine. We're still going to pass."

"Pass? Pass! Did you just say pass, Declan? I didn't need to pass. I needed at least a B+."

"One B- is not going to ruin your whole life." He stood from the bed, completely naked, the heavy instrument of my temporary insanity swinging between his legs. I'd *failed*. I'd let myself get sucked in and I failed. Bile raced up my throat and threatened to make this the perfect morning by puking everywhere.

"This isn't about my whole life. It's about my future. A future that is now in jeopardy because you didn't set an alarm, had me drinking the whole night, and let me oversleep."

He angrily shoved his legs into his boxers.

"So this is all my fault, huh? I held your mouth open and made you drink last night? I tied you to the bed so you couldn't escape from my idiot caveman grip." He pointed at the bed, and the shame curled in my gut. I'd failed. All because I couldn't keep it together. I tugged my shirt on over my head and looked for my shoes.

"I should have never come here. I shouldn't have done this with you." I spotted my shoes and slid my feet in. Anger, shame, sadness warred for dominance, and I tried to blink back the tears building in my eyes.

"Why are you doing this?" He crossed the room and grabbed my arms to keep me from dashing out the room.

"I'm not doing anything." I released the fire churning in my stomach. "This is over."

He dropped his hands and jerked back like I'd slapped him.

"This isn't anyone's fault. It was a mistake. I'm sure we could go to Alcott and plead our case."

I slid my nearly dead phone into my pocket. "There is no 'we,' Declan." I jabbed an angry finger at the center of his chest. "There is no 'we'; there never was and there never will be." I blinked to keep the tears pooling in my eyes from spilling over. "I was stupid to get involved with you. I should have known better. This is who you are, right? Mr. 'It Will All Work Out.' Only you know what?" My eyes burned, and my chest heaved as I tried and failed to get my emotions under control.

"Sometimes it doesn't work out. Sometimes life comes up and kicks you in the fucking teeth. Sometimes it takes people who never should have been taken, and you're left holding the pieces, trying to glue shit back together that's never going to fit again. Sometimes real life is hard, and there are actual consequences to things you do!" The tears I couldn't hold at bay anymore spilled over, and I raced from his bedroom.

"Mak! Stop!" His heavy footballs thudded behind me as I flew down the stairs and out the front door. But I didn't stop. My name carried on the wind as he called after me.

I took off down the street and kept going. My legs screamed as I pushed myself harder, trying to get to my apartment as quickly as I could. Cutting through campus was easier than waiting for a taxi, and I wasn't going to stand outside his house, waiting for one to arrive. I hadn't even remembered until I was halfway across campus that my car and keys were at his place. My mind was a mess.

Sliding on the frosty grass, I skidded across the lawn. Running over the syllabus for the class in my mind, I tried to figure out the percentages. Maybe I was wrong. But the longer I ran, the clearer it became. There was no way. There was nothing I could do to get a B+ in the class.

I'd be kicked out of the joint program because I let myself get sucked into this college crap. *Have fun! Don't worry so much! Make mistakes!* Well, I had, and they'd led me here. My heart was hammering against my ribs like I'd run a marathon. The panic overwhelmed me. *How would I tell my parents?*

What would I do now? I could apply to a med school not in the program in a year. It meant losing that time and the extra money. How could I let Daniel down like this? I was supposed to be looking out for him. I was supposed to be able to give him this dream. I'd failed so many times before. I had to stop in front of the library and fell onto a bench, my tears blinding me.

Sticking my head between my knees, I let the sobs overcome me. They broke free of my chest like everything inside me was cracking in two. I shouldn't have come. I shouldn't have left Stanford. I shouldn't have gotten involved with Declan in the first place. Every warning arrow and signal all pointed to stay away, but he had been too irresistible.

"Hey, are you okay?" Someone walked up to the bench. I wiped my eyes with the backs of my hands and nodded. A sharp gust of wind shot across the open area, and I tried to keep the tremors running through me at bay.

Mom and Dad were home now. I'd have to tell them I'd let them down. Let them and Daniel down. Picking myself up, I made my way to the apartment. I was pretty sure there were multiple reports of a sobbing woman racing across campus made to the campus police.

Bursting into my apartment, I startled Fiona and Tracy, who sat on the couch.

"Hey, Declan came looking for you," Fiona called out as I strode into my room and gathered up some stuff. I uploaded the paper and clicked submit on the webportal, even though the giant red warnings said that the paper was late. Slamming my computer closed, I squeezed my eyes shut. I needed to pack a bag. I'd take a taxi to my parents if I needed to. The bus also got close enough.

He would be back. I needed to leave and go home. See Mom and Dad, let them know everything that had happened. The only thing worse than facing them was having any conversation with Declan. I couldn't do that now.

With my bag over my shoulder I hurried to the parking lot, stopping short when a tall, green-eyed monolith stood in my way, leaning against my car. He pushed off the black metal and stalked toward me.

I dropped my eyes and charged forward. He'd driven it back, so he had my keys.

"Mak, where are you going?"

"Away. I'm going away. Can I have my keys?" I held out my hand.

"Why are you running away?" He followed me back to my car.

"I'm not running away. I'm going somewhere I can focus. Somewhere where I'm not distracted. Can I have my keys please?" I couldn't look at him. He set the keys gingerly into my hand. I jammed them into the lock.

"Somewhere without me."

"Somewhere without you," I parroted back to him.

"You can't just leave, Mak. Don't run out on me."

There was a tremble in his voice, but I didn't turn around to look at him. I squeezed my eyes shut against the pain in his words. Each pained inhale like a razor to my heart.

"I'm sorry about the alarm. I didn't think we'd sleep so late."

"Neither did I." I shook my head and tugged the door open. "I'm sorry I blew up at you back there. It was my mistake. I shouldn't have gone out last night. You didn't make me drink and you didn't make me oversleep." I wasn't going to touch on the land mine of the other thing he hadn't made me do the night before.

Declan's hand wrapped around the top of my door.

"Let me help you fix this."

I peered up at him, and my heart squeezed at the crestfallen expression on his face.

"There's nothing you can do. I...I'm not going to be around as much and I know you're busy with the team and stuff now, traveling all over the place, so I think it's best if we just focus on our futures and don't let ourselves get distracted."

I stared into my car, shifting my bag on my back.

"I'm not going to let you run away like this. We can figure something out."

I dumped my bag into the passenger seat. "Don't worry, Declan. I already turned the paper in, not that it matters." A weight settled on me that made it hard to breath.

"You think I care about the paper? Mak, look at me." The pain in his voice made me slam my eyes shut.

I couldn't look at him. If I did, I'd break again. I wanted to throw my arms around his neck and let him tell me it would be okay. When I was in his arms, it felt like that might actually be true, but I knew it was a lie. It was a mirage, and I'd fallen straight into it headfirst. "It's not your fault. You're not responsible for fixing my life."

"And you're not responsible for fixing other people's. You can't think that if you can be that perfect girl, you're going to fix all the broken things in the lives of the people around you. You still think you have that kind of power and you don't. All you can do is hold onto anything you need to be happy." He stared down at me, his gaze searing the side of my face, but I kept my eyes straight forward, sticking my key in the ignition.

"Thank you for the advice." My voice cracked, and I jerked my door. His hands dropped away from the top of it as I slammed it shut. Throwing my car into drive, I sped out of the parking lot, unable to keep myself from looking. I glanced back in my rearview mirror. Declan stood in the middle of the lot, staring after me. He stayed there watching me go until he disappeared from view.

The sharp sounds of my sobs punctuated the crisp, silent air in the car. I had to pull over after fifteen minutes. Squeezing my hands around the steering wheel, I punched it as tears flowed down my face.

Why can't I just be normal? Why can't my mistakes be no big deal? It seemed when I screwed things up, I had to be as thorough as I was with everything. And I'd managed to implode two of the best things in my life, but it seemed like they couldn't coexist together. Declan McAvoy wasn't compatible with my life plan because he made me think I deserved to be happy, and I knew that was a lie.

28

DECLAN

S tanding in the middle of the parking lot watching Mak leave was like watching a part of my soul run away from me. The best part. My vision dimmed, and it was hard to breathe, like someone had sucked all the air out of my world. The temptation to chase after the car warred with what little pride I had left when it came to her.

I don't know how long I stood there, but it was long enough that the midday sun didn't sting my eyes anymore. Long enough for at least two people to come up to me and ask if I was okay. No, I wasn't okay, not even a little bit.

My heart just drove off in a Honda Fit.

I'd fucked up, and she shut me out.

Like she could snap her fingers and everything that had passed between us melted away.

Like she could wipe away the feeling I couldn't stop having for her.

Every mile she put between us was like another barb sunk into my heart.

I walked back across campus in a fog. She'd left me. I'd asked her not to go, and she had.

Grades were important to Mak. Anyone who met her knew that as a fact, but she acted like every missed mark was a reason to hate herself. Like if she enjoyed life too much, it was wrong.

It wasn't until my fifth missed goal during practice that the looks shot my way. I gritted my teeth, ready to tell them both to fuck off, but the look in Preston's eyes shut me up.

Mak left. The way she drove off...once the numbness wore off, it left behind a raw, angry spot. One I kept needling by staring at my phone.

By the time the two of them flanked me on the ice, I didn't even fight it. I was playing like shit. Not even with the worst hangover in my life had I ever been this screwed up on the ice.

We had a game in a few days, and I couldn't get my head on straight. I swore Heath must have gotten me geared up and on the ice, because I didn't even remember doing it.

When they dragged me to the bench, I didn't even try to pretend to be okay. I shook my gloves off.

"What happened with Mak?" Preston shoved my shoulder, so I dropped down onto the bench. I jerked my head back and stared at him.

"How did you know it had something to do with Mak?"

"Only she could have you pouring off waves of sadness, frustration, and anger to the point that your game play is shit. Do you need to hit something?"

My hands were balled up in fists, and I unclenched them, running them along my padded legs.

"No, he doesn't need to hit something. He needs to get this shit out in the open so he can feel like he can breathe again." Preston and I peered over at Heath. He shrugged. "You do. You came home like a freaking zombie after racing out of the house and screaming Mak's name down the street this morning. Seems to me that you probably need to talk it out."

Why does he have to be so infuriatingly right so much of the time?

I dragged my hands through my hair, tugging on the strands. Giving them the CliffsNotes version of our wake-up call from hell, I ran my hand over my forehead.

"I don't understand her. You saw her last night. She almost never lets herself have fun like that. She's never that relaxed and smiling and laughing, at least not as long as I've known her. And now with this, she'll never let herself go again. It's like she thinks every time she laughs or is happy, a puppy gets murdered or something."

"Maybe she likes being that way. She likes trying to do her best and doing well," Preston said, resting his head on the top of his hands, propped up on his stick.

I shook my head. "It's not like that. She doesn't enjoy it. How can you have a life where you're never allowed a few hours, even a few minutes to enjoy the things around you?" The tight-chest feeling was back, and it had nothing to do with the sweat pouring off me from the drills on the ice.

"Like she doesn't think she deserves to have fun and go a little crazy. She's the only one holding herself to a standard that high. She's the only one thinking everything she does is never good enough. It hurts for me to see her punishing herself for living."

"What can you do about it?" Heath leaned against the boards inside the box. The rest of the team whipped around the ice behind him.

"What do you mean?"

"Can you change her? Can you make her do anything?"

I squeezed the back of my neck and came to the heart-breaking conclusion, shaking my head.

"No. I can't. But I can try to make her see that there isn't a way for her to fail. It's not in her DNA, but that doesn't mean she should shut everyone else out."

"Shut you out," Preston added. I shot him a look, and my shoulders slumped.

"Yeah. She shouldn't shut me out."

"This thing with Mak is the real deal, huh?" Preston sat on the bench beside me. "I mean, she's got you knuckling down to wrap up school. You don't even go out and party after away games." Preston sounded impressed.

"No interest, man. Not even a little bit. Those away games suck because I don't get to crawl into bed with her after. I don't get to wake up beside her."

Heath laughed and pushed off the wall, sitting on the other side of me. "I never thought I'd see the day." He clapped me on the shoulder.

"Shoe's on the other foot, huh?" Preston knocked his shoulder against mine.

"It is." Only this angry burning in my chest wasn't how I wanted it to be. It helped push down the fear. The fear of what would happen if she didn't come back to me.

We always gave him shit for not going out to party, but he had his girl back home. He told us we didn't get it. Now I did. More than I ever thought possible, I completely understood what it felt like to have no interest in anyone but the person who walked around brightening up every room they walked into.

As much as I loved her. The words, even in my head, were like a boot to my heart. I loved her. Those feelings that bubbled up at night when I watched her sleep or when I sat beside her studying were exactly what scared the shit out of me. I loved Makenna Halstead, and she'd left me.

As much as I loved her, she might not love me back. Not

like I loved her. Maybe I was a playful distraction, but I wasn't ready to give up. I finished practice only moderately terribly. The coach was ready to intercept me on the way off the ice when Heath and Preston intercepted him. I owed them both a beer.

"Should have known it was a fluke." Archer's gruff voice bounced off the walls in the tunnel as I almost made it to the locker room.

As if my fucking day couldn't get any worse. My hand clenched into a fist as I whipped around to face him.

"What the hell do you want?"

"You thought you were hot shit after that game, but I knew you'd find a way to screw things up again."

The fire in my gut that had been burning since that long walk across campus dissolved. Poof, just like that it was gone. I looked at him with new eyes. He was a sad shell of the all-star he'd once been.

"You know what? Part of me was doing all this so I could stick it to you. Show you that I didn't need you and that I could be a better player than you." I jabbed my stick in his direction. "But you know what I just realized?" A calm settled over me, even though Mak had ripped out my still-beating heart. She'd also shown me that I could win even with him watching. If I didn't care about him one bit, he didn't matter.

His chin jutted out. "What?"

"I don't give a shit about you. I'm not doing any of this for with you. I'm doing this for me." I jabbed my finger into the center of my chest. "I'm doing this because I love being out on the ice and I love being with my team and I am a hell of a player. I'm done trying to prove anything by comparing myself to you. You're nothing. A sperm donor who fucked his career and is hoping and praying that he can relive those glory days forever. Have at it, but I'm not going to let you rule any part of my life ever again."

As the words fell from my lips, a weight lifted off my shoulders, and I knew Archer's cloud wasn't going to follow me over my career. Whether I got his number or not, it didn't matter. Because he didn't matter. This was about me. I was doing this for me.

He opened his mouth to say something, but I didn't even care what it was. I backed into the locker room and let the door slam right in his face. Because fuck him, that's why.

By Monday the calm I'd felt walking away from Archer outside the locker room was long gone. I didn't care that she'd walked out on me. She was hurting, and I needed to help her fix it. She'd helped me figure something out in more ways than one. I couldn't do what I did for anyone else but me. I needed to do it or I'd always be wrapped up in what happened in someone else's head. But just because I was doing it for me didn't mean I didn't want her by my side every step of the way.

I was ready to go out of my head. Even Heath snapped at me to just call her or see her because I was driving him up the wall. Like I was walking into the fiery pits of a volcanic eruption, I crossed campus to the library.

The old musty smell wasn't one I'd appreciated before, but now it reminded me of her. Jabbing my finger into the button out of muscle memory, I pushed back the nerves that almost forced me to turn around. The only thing worse than not finding her there would be finding her there. The distance in her eyes the last time I saw her still clawed at my heart.

The ancient elevator groaned and shook until it dinged, the doors sliding open to her study room floor.

It wasn't as quiet as it usually was. Every table and chair was covered with books, notebooks, and laptops. This was why Mak had freaked out about getting a study room. Being stuck outside with so many distractions would have driven her crazy.

My shoulders slumped as I peered into the small glass window beside the door to her room. It had been a long shot. I'd missed her after every one of her Monday classes because of my exam times. Her roommates hadn't seen her either. Leaning against her door, I banged my head back, trying to think of a way to see her. The dull *thud* reverberated through the wood.

The door beside hers popped open, and a bright head of hair poked out, followed by a big smile. Anna? *No.* Angela? No. Angel. Yes, maybe she'd seen her.

"Angel, right?"

I swore her smile reached all the way to her ears. All teeth. I felt like I should be practicing for a dental exam.

"Yes." She nodded and took the two steps between us in a rush, nearly colliding with me. I stepped back.

"Have you seen Mak around in the past few days?"

"Why? Has she disappeared on you?" Her face morphed into mock sadness, and she rested her hand on my forearm.

Her flirting had been fine before because I liked it when it pissed Mak off, but I wasn't even a little interested in her. Pointedly staring at her hand, I took a step farther away.

"Have you seen her?"

"No, I haven't. But you're more than welcome to hang out in my room and wait for her if you'd like." She bit her bottom lip. On Mak I always loved that. The way she'd nibble her lips when she was nervous or when she was working her way through our sex list, trying to figure out which number she wanted to tackle next. Like it needed serious consideration to get the best results.

But on Angel it looked exactly as it was. A bad attempt to draw my attention to her mouth, and she probably hoped that would get me thinking of other things. Well, it was. It got me thinking of how much her lips weren't like Mak's and how I didn't want anything to do with her.

I'd backed up so much that when the door on the other side of Mak's study room opened, I was right there when the guy rushed out. Seth.

"Hey, Seth, have you seen Mak?"

He glanced between me and Angel, and I prayed he wasn't thinking anything was going on. That was the last thing I needed.

"No, I haven't. She hasn't been here too much over the past few weeks." I couldn't tell if that was a dig or not.

"If you could let me know if you see her, I'd really appreciate it. We have a final project we need to get finished, and I know she's probably freaking out over it." A little white lie, but desperate times called for desperate measures. Seth's eyebrows knit together as he stared at me like he was trying to burn a hole through me. Maybe it was that I kept inching a little bit away every time Angel advanced toward me.

"Sure." He held out his phone, and I put my number in, glad I didn't have to say it out loud.

"I can call you too," Angel volunteered a little too loudly, and a few heads turned our way.

"I think we're good." I handed the phone back to Seth. "Thanks, man."

"No problem."

I left the library with the sinking pit still firmly in place in my stomach. A week was the longest I'd gone without talking to Mak since we were paired up in class together. Initially it had annoyed the crap out of me that she'd check in almost every day with an email or text asking about my progress on our papers like I was a kindergartener who couldn't be trusted with a pair of sharp scissors.

Now I'd do a backflip in the middle of the frost-covered quad for a check-in message. I'd told myself I'd give her some time to sort things out and then I'd make my move, but I didn't know how much longer I could hold out. I wanted to find out where she lived and go there.

It wasn't that far from campus, close to our high school. That wouldn't be completely insane, right? Riding up and down the streets of our Philly suburb shouting out the window, asking if anyone knew Makenna Halstead. Because my girl had left me behind, but I needed her. I needed to hear her voice and feel her touch. Any longer without her and I might lose my mind.

29

MAKENNA

My hands trembled as I reached for the knob to the front door. After speaking with my dean, I'd finally gotten confirmation that they wouldn't be able to accept me into the joint BA/MD program. It was the day before Thanksgiving, and I'd gotten the last appointment before everyone left campus for the holiday.

Breaking down in sobs in my car, the tears pouring down my face, threatening to choke me. It seemed like I was doing a lot of that lately. Now I had to face my parents. I'd put off their questions about why I was there and not at school, chalking it up to missing them after them being away for nearly three months. It was partially true, but it was because I hadn't wanted to face Declan.

Showing up to campus just before my classes and driving home after each wasn't ideal, but I'd made it work. The one saving grace was that after the final paper Sophomore Seminar didn't meet anymore. My abandoned study room only had the barest bones' books in there that I didn't need until after the break. With classes winding down and a lot of people leaving for the break, the shifts at Threes had been light, so I hadn't been in to work since the night before the game.

Seth and Angel informed me the couple times I'd stopped by to grab something that Declan had in fact been hanging around a lot. I made sure to go only when I knew he had practice or he was out of town for a game.

Nothing made sense anymore. My life's plan was a mess, and I didn't know how to fix it. I didn't even know if I wanted to. With a weariness I hadn't realized settled so heavy on me, I took my key out of the lock and turned around, sitting on the front steps. My breath came out in small white puffs in front of my face.

Wrapping my arms around my legs, I rested my head on my knees. Tilting my head to the side, I stared at the small drawings on the column beside the steps. The old crudely drawn representation of our front yard jumped out at me. It was a pain so deep and biting I sucked in a sharp breath. Tracing my fingers over the badly drawn pictures of our family that my parents had painted over with clear gloss to preserve, I squeezed myself tighter and tried to breathe through the ache.

The warm spot on my leg where my breath seeped into the fabric was quickly replaced by the sharp, freezing temperatures. Each breath was a warm shot to the spot that was quickly eclipsed by the stinging cold. It was like my life. Every time I felt like I was walking into the sun, maybe getting a small taste of normalcy, it was like someone set me in a slingshot to send me right back into the freezing rain. The memories of the sun faded, and it was like they had never existed.

Declan sent messages almost daily now. They ran the gamut from apologies to rational statements about being happy to anger that I wasn't responding. I couldn't respond. I was seconds away from cracking. Of shattering into a million pieces and ceasing to exist. I couldn't face him. I didn't want to face anyone.

A blast of warm air hit my back as the front door opened, and I wiped away the tears on my face and the ones that dripped down into my jeans.

"I thought I heard you out here." Dad stepped out of the front door. Already his movements were less smooth than they had been before. The meds laid out across the kitchen counter were the first step to keeping him at home as long as we could, but he and Mom had already made the arrangements for things once he couldn't stay anymore.

"Sorry. I was just coming in." I unfolded myself, pushing against brick steps to stand. His warm fingers dropped around my shoulder, and he held me still. Taking his time, he lowered himself down beside me. He smelled like shaving cream and freshly cut grass even though he hadn't mowed the lawn in months.

"It's okay. Why don't we sit out here for a little?" He stared out in front of him at the leafless trees lining the front of the house. "I know this has all been hard on you."

"I'm fine, really—"

"What are you two doing out here? Come inside." Mom stood in the doorway, concern heavy in her voice. Dad glanced over at me and let out a deep sigh before nodding toward the open door. I got up, and Mom and I helped Dad stand before we all went inside. Climbing the stairs to my room, I glanced back down at them.

Mom and Dad sat in the living room holding hands. I tried not to think about how I'd let them down. How I'd let everyone down.

Finishing my work at my desk, I slammed my book

closed. Everything was taking me so much longer than it should. I couldn't focus. Rereading a passage or an equation three times was the norm for me since I'd left campus.

Smells of allspice, onion, and honey drifted upstairs. Lured by the promise of food for my rumbling stomach, I left my den of solitude and padded my way downstairs. My feet sank into the carpet runner on the steps.

In the kitchen, the two of them were in deep discussion. Huddled together with their arms draped over each other's shoulders, Mom and Dad watched the pots on the stove. Mundane things like that seemed to take on a whole different color to them these days. Not wanting to break up their moment, I stepped back, ready to stop my hunger pangs with an energy bar or something from my room when Mom's head popped up.

"Hey, sweetie. Where are you going? Come sit down."

"It's okay. I was going to get some water, but I'm okay now."

"Makenna, come sit." She patted the seat beside her, and I slowly made my way across the floor to the chair. Worry churned my stomach as I sat down. They'd given me my space since I got home, but from the looks on their faces that space was about to end.

"Are you ready to tell us?" Mom squeezed my shoulder.

"I'm fine." I put a smile on my face and gently rested my hands on the table.

"We're your parents." Dad glanced over at me with the knowing-dad look. "You're not fine, but we can't help if you don't tell us what's going on. Let us help."

I saw it for what it was. After years of not being there for me, this was their chance. In some ways I wished they were back in their zombie days. Less observant. Less present so I wouldn't have to hide. Taking a deep, shaky breath, I felt the tears prickling the backs of my eyes before I even spoke.

"I'm—" The sound caught in my throat. "I'm not going to make it into the joint MD program. I know I made you promises when I transferred that I'd be able to do it, and this means another year of school and another year of loans and with my grades I might not even make it in through the regular admissions process." Everything poured out of my mouth like word vomit I couldn't hold back. I slid my hands off the table into my lap, staring down at them.

"And I know you have so much to deal with right now, and I know I'm letting you down and myself down and Daniel down." My voice broke on his name.

The chairs screeched against the floor as Mom and Dad got out of their seats. Their warm arms wrapped around me, and it broke me.

"I made a mistake. I messed up and I'm sorry. I'm so sorry." Like a torrential flood of emotions so strong they stole every bit of air I'd ever breathed, and I couldn't catch my breath. Being wheeled down the long hallway in the hospital side by side with Daniel. Those bright fluorescent lights leading us into another surgery.

"I'm sorry. I'm so sorry. I couldn't save him." The tears choked me as I was back in that gurney with Mom and Dad beside the two of us.

"You're a perfect match, big sis. If there's anyone who can do it, it's you." Daniel's eyes were worried, but he grabbed on to my hand, and I squeezed his back. *A perfect match.*

I was the perfect match to be a bone marrow donor. Everyone was so relieved when they tested me. The searing pain from the biopsies and donation were worth it to give him what he needed. It was like I'd been put on the Earth to save him when he needed me most, and in the days and weeks after his surgery he got better. I'd make my way to the hospital every day after school with new sealed comics, coloring books, or anything else I could find to keep his boredom away.

Until the day it wasn't better. Until the day I showed up on the floor, and Dad was holding Mom out in the hallway as she made a sound so terrible I slapped my hands to my ears to try and block it out. No one had called me. No one came to get me. No one told me, but I knew.

I'd stood frozen at the end of the hallway thinking maybe if I didn't take those final steps, it wouldn't be real. If I could push back on reality a little longer, maybe it wasn't really happening, But it was. I'd failed him. It hadn't been perfect. If it had been perfect, he would have still been there. If I'd been perfect, he would still be there. I wasn't, and neither was he.

He died, and I lived. His dreams and his life were gone, and I was still there.

"It's not your fault, Makenna. It's not your fault."

I hadn't realized I'd said it all out loud until I heard her words against the side of my head.

Mom's hot tears trailed down my face as she brushed her hand through my hair. Dad had his arms wrapped around the two of us. All three of us were a mess with tears. All my fears and emotions I'd kept pent up for so long had come pouring out of me without meaning to.

The choking sobs turned into pained hiccups in my chest as their words flowed over me, their arms wrapped around me and giving me the comfort I hadn't gotten all those years ago. We'd all been destroyed for a while, but I'd put myself together faster than they had, at least on the outside.

"I know your mother and I haven't done the best job

when it came to making sure you were okay over the years. There were so many things we didn't do right by you, Mak, but never, ever think for a second we have ever blamed you for anything that happened. Never."

"I—"

He gave me a look and took a deep breath. I needed to let him get this out.

"When Daniel died, it was like we did too. It isn't something anyone should ever have to go through. It's the most horrible feeling in the world, and nothing makes sense anymore, but what we did to you... how we left you to shoulder the burden that should have been ours... I'll never be more sorry, Mak." He slid his hand into mine and squeezed it.

My blurry gaze never left his face. We didn't have much time left. Soon all this would be memories, and he'd be gone too.

"You held us together. Carried us when that should never be the job of a child. Never." Tears glittered in his eyes, and he lifted my hand, kissing the back of it. "I'm so sorry for that. And I'm sorry it had to take this diagnosis for us to realize how much we screwed up."

"Dad, you didn't." I shook my head.

"We did." He peered over at Mom. They stared into my eyes with their own filled with conviction and remorse.

"What's worse is we made you think you had the power to fix any of it. The power and the responsibility to make things better that only someone can fix for themselves or sometimes no one can fix at all." His hand shook as he squeezed mine tighter.

"What happened with Daniel was not your fault. It wasn't anyone's fault. Just like what's happening to your father isn't anyone's fault." My mom ran her hands over the side of my face.

"So, we had two choices when we found out. We could fall back into that place we'd only just climbed out of and die before we were dead and buried, or we could get out into the world and wring every last drop out of what time we had left together. None of us have much time, but having that reminder helped us remember how much there is to live for, including you."

"We don't want you living your life for anyone except for you. You can't fix what happened to Daniel or make it make any sense by living your life for him or up to whatever standard you think we're holding you to. All we want you to do is be happy. We want you to do something you love and be happy." She squeezed me and another of round of tears threatened to drown me there at the table.

I'd made this life for myself in my mind where if I did everything I should, things would be okay. I had control over those things. The life I'd built made sense, and I could always get the right answer. Things were in order and fell in line where they were supposed to except for one place.

There was one time I'd let myself feel and not follow my plan. Declan. He was the monkey wrench in the order of my life. Derailed everything I'd known for sure and who I wanted to be. When I was with him, it was the only time I felt like the real version of me. The one that wasn't afraid of never measuring up.

We sat in the kitchen for a long time talking through tears, tea, and turkey. By nightfall we were all exhausted, emotionally and physically. After being shooed out of the kitchen by Mom and Dad, I dragged myself upstairs into my room.

Turning on the light, I grabbed my phone out of my bag

and turned it on for the first time in days. Even more messages rolled in than before, and I sat on the floor with my back against my bed and scrolled through each one.

I didn't know what to do about Declan. I loved him. I tested those words out in my head before I said them out loud. It was so unexpected. I hadn't planned on him at all, but sometimes life had a way of interfering with the best laid plans.

30

DECLAN

er text came in when I was on my way back to campus the day after Thanksgiving. No break for us; we had a game to play.

Mak: Can I see you?

The car rumbled through the narrow streets to my house. I was glad Mom was driving or I'd have had to pull the car over to the side of the road. My hands shook as I tapped out my reply.

Me: Yes. When?

Mak: Soon. Are you on campus?

It was like she was a frightened bunny I'd managed to coax into my lair, and I didn't want to rush in too quickly and scare her off. I was afraid to say more. Between away games and classes, Mak had managed to evade me for almost a full two weeks. That little bit of pride I'd talked about having? Yeah, that went away after day three.

I had called and texted her, but no response. Over the last few days I'd stopped. I figured giving her some space was probably the best thing to do. Plus, each unanswered text was like another little slice to my heart. My trip to Alcott had been a bust. He couldn't understand why I cared that we were getting less than an A. Made a snide remark about Makenna rubbing off on me and her high-strung tendencies must have been contagious. *Asshole.*

It meant something to her, so it meant something to me, which made it worse that I'd fucked it up for her. I said bye to my mom as she drove off to yet another job. Only a few more months and that would be all over for her. She wanted me to get this degree, but once I did and I started playing, all bets were off. I'd drag her out of those shifts if I had to.

Dumping my laundry from home on the couch, I joined Heath in the kitchen. Giant foil-wrapped containers covered the counters.

He glanced up, his hair partially covering his eyes.

"My mom might have gone a bit overboard." He opened the fridge already half-full of trays. My mouth hung open.

"Man, I love your mom." I peeled back the foil on one of the still-warm trays, and my mouth watered. Onion, parsley, sage, rosemary mixed in with some awesome-looking bread. It smelled like the stuffing of the gods.

"I told her we'd be able to take it off her hands." He grinned at me. His mom's food was the stuff of legends.

I grabbed a plate from beside the sink and loaded it up with some turkey, stuffing, green beans, and every other treat the saint who was Heath's mom had made for us. And then I sat at the table and I couldn't even eat it. My mouth and my stomach were not in agreement.

Mak would be here soon, and my gut churned with equal parts anticipation and worry. Heath finished up in the kitchen, wolfing down his food while we went over what had happened over our two days away from campus. *Nothing.*

He got up and headed into the living room and up the

stairs. Poking his head down over the banister, he called out, "Did you know Mak is standing out on the porch?"

I pushed my chair back, and it scraped against the floor.

"What?" Peering out the small pane of glass beside the front door, my heart sped up. Mak stood in a cream coat that hit her just above the knee. A navy skirt peeked out from under the coat. She had her gloved hands clasped in front of her as she fidgeted with them. And her hair was out just the way I liked it, falling in gentle waves around her face. It was topped off with a cute little hat I wanted to drag off her head so I could bury my face in her hair.

Glancing up at her lips, I couldn't take my eyes off her. She alternated between nibbling on them and talking, like she was rehearsing what she was going to say. I probably watched her a lot longer than I should, but I couldn't help myself. If this was the end, I really didn't want to speed things up.

Heath came rumbling down the stairs with his coat on and a backpack slung over his shoulder.

"Why don't I give you two some privacy?"

Before I could stop him, he wrenched the door open as she stood there wide-eyed with her hand raised midknock.

"Hi, Mak. Bye, Mak," he said cheerily as he hustled down the steps. We watched him go because it was easier to do that than to look at each other. The nervous coil in my chest made it hard to breathe. And then like a rubber-band snap, our gazes flew to each other.

"Can I come in?" She broke away from my gaze and stared down at her gloves. I soaked her in. Only when she glanced up did I realize I was still standing in the doorway and I hadn't in fact said, *Please, why don't you come in? May I take your coat?*

I stumbled back on numb legs, letting her in. She skirted past me, careful not to touch me as she stepped into the living room. *That hurt.*

Closing the door behind her, I took a deep breath and followed after her. She stood in the middle of the room like a vision of composure and restraint. My body hummed being so close to her. Wiping my sweaty palms on my jeans, I motioned for her to sit.

She dragged the hat off her head and held it in her lap. I sat and tried not to blurt out the first thing that came to mind. The silence stretched on between us, going from slightly awkward to someone-walking-in-on-you-in-the-bathroom levels of awkward. She sucked in a deep breath and glanced up at me with tears in her eyes. The moment I saw them, everything around us transformed. All I wanted to do was make it better.

"I'm sorry," I blurted out.

"I'm really sorry," she said at the same time. Her voice was shaky, and she pursed her lips together like she was trying to hold back the tears.

She took another breath. "No, I'm sorry. I shouldn't have run out on you like that, and I shouldn't have ignored your calls and texts. I was scared. I was really scared, Declan." She peered up at me, pinning me with eyes filled with so many emotions I couldn't catch on to one long enough. I was stunned. Frozen and unable to move as she poured it all out.

"I'm not exactly the best with being open about things." She made a cute little noise like *understatement of the year*. "And I freak out, as you saw." Her eyes lifted to the ceiling, blinking rapidly.

"I'm sorry about the paper. I should have made sure we

were up and we turned it in together. I know you didn't want to go to the party, and you didn't want to be out late, but I got so wrapped up in the win and being out with you that I fucked it up."

She tentatively put her hand over mine.

"No, you have nothing to be sorry for. It was me. If I didn't want to go, I wouldn't have gone. If I didn't want to drink, I wouldn't have. I should have made sure I was up to turn in the paper. Actually, I should have turned it in five days before it was due once we'd each proofread it once. I freaked out because anything less than a B+ in the class meant I wouldn't be able to get into the BA/MD joint degree program."

My stomach plummeted. I'd stopped her from getting into med school. She squeezed my hand and gave me a small smile that kept me from wanting to jump out a window. I put my other hand on top of hers, rubbing my thumb along her warm, smooth skin.

"It's okay. I've been doing a lot of thinking, and it ended up being a good thing."

I lifted an eyebrow, not seeing how her not getting into med school was a good thing.

"This gives me more time. Being a doctor was always Daniel's dream. He'd wanted to be a doctor since he was five, and I kind of took that on as my own dream. I was doing it for the two of us. When we missed the deadline, I freaked out not just because of the program, but because I was letting him down."

"You can't live your life for him, Mak. I have no idea what it was like for you and your family to go through what you went through and are going through right now." Her dad being sick was another blow. "But you can't hold yourself to impossible standards I'm sure your brother wouldn't have wanted you to have for yourself." The standards she had for herself were higher than any coach I'd had. Hell, they were probably higher than Heath's, and everyone knew he was insane.

"I know." Her voice was quiet, and she stared at our hands wrapped up in each other on my lap. "I know I can't. I'm slowly figuring that out. I'll start talking to someone about my guilt and anxiety over everything that happened before, but you helped me see that the way I was living wasn't really living."

"I'm glad I could help, but don't crap all over old Mak. She kept me in line this semester. It's on track to be my best semester ever, even with the B- from Alcott. You got me to knuckle down and get my stuff done. You rubbed off on me."

"You're good at keeping me from going overboard, and I keep you in line. I think that's a good combination." She peered up at me with a small smile. Unable to hold back anymore, I lifted my hand and cupped it along the side of her face. When she closed her eyes and leaned into my touch, the tightness in my chest ebbed away. This was it for me. She was it for me, and the thought that I might never be able to touch her like this again had almost eaten me alive.

Dragging her onto my lap, I stared into her sky-blue eyes and pressed my lips to hers. It was gentle at first, but she wrapped her arms around my neck and all bets were off.

"I know you don't think you are, but you're perfect."

Her mouth opened with a sigh, and I pushed my tongue in, needing to taste her. Two weeks had been too long. I slid my hand into her hair, the smell of citrus filling my nose even on a cold winter's day. "You're perfect for me, Mak."

"And you're perfect for me." She stared into my eyes and

nipped my bottom lip. My growl made her jump, and she squirmed. My shaft sprung to attention at her little dance of contentment on my lap. Palming her ass, I squeezed her even tighter, pressing her against my chest.

"We're perfect for each other." Coming up for air, I rested my forehead against hers. Our chests rose and fell in sync as we panted after breaking a lip-lock that had me threatening to burst through my jeans.

"I missed you." I stared deeply into her eyes. I wanted her to know there wasn't a minute we were apart that I hadn't been thinking about her. Dreaming about her.

"I missed you too. I'm sorry."

I pushed my finger to her lips. "We've said our sorries, but I think it's time for you to make it up to me for not talking to me for two weeks." I put on a pout, and she laughed. The hairs on the back of my neck stood up as that tingle shot down my spine. I wanted more of that.

"And how exactly do you propose that I make it up to you?"

Without another word I lifted her up off the couch and stalked toward the stairs.

"Declan, put me down! You're going to drop me." She wrapped her arms around my neck and clung to me.

"I won't drop you as long as you stop fidgeting."

She went stark stiff, and I laughed as I climbed the steps two at a time. Kicking the door to my bedroom shut, I set her on her feet, letting her slide down the front of me.

"All is forgiven on two conditions."

She nodded before she even heard my terms.

"One. Never do that again. If you're mad or you're upset, I need you to talk to me."

She nodded again. "I promise I won't do that again. What's the other condition?"

"You have to do one thing for me..." The corners of my mouth turned up, and I was sure I looked like a sneaky, villainous character out of a cartoon. Only I could assure her that both of us were going to love this devious little treat...

31

MAKENNA

"You have to do one thing for me..." The mischievous smile on his lips should have clued me in to the fact that I was in trouble. My body hummed in anticipation of what he wanted from me. It was written all over his Cheshire cat face.

"Can't I take a shower first?" I glanced at his bedroom door. Maybe I could make a quick break for the bathroom.

Using his chest to corral me, he backed me up until my knees hit the edge of the mattress and I plopped down on the bed. My eyes got wide as he sank to his knees in front of me.

"No." One word, laced with so much hunger and desire I could already feel the wetness pooling between my legs. My choice to wear a skirt seemed appropriate.

"Let go, Mak. Stop thinking and just feel. Not worrying about anything else. Not worrying about me or any other thoughts in your head other than how this feels. The only words out of your mouth should be telling me how you like it, my name, and I'll even let you throw in a few 'oh Gods.'"

My breath caught as he slid his hands along my thighs,

pushing my skirt up my legs. The fabric scraping across my skin made me hyperaware of every inch of me he exposed.

"So bossy." I meant it to come out jokingly, but it came out all breathy and hungry.

"I learned from the best."

He slid his hands under my ass, lifted me, and tugged my underwear down. Keeping his gaze on me like he was afraid to break the trance, he slid them down my legs. Goosebumps rose all over my body as he crumbled them up in his hand and lifted them to his nose.

"You smell gorgeous. But I'm ready to sample straight from the source. Are you ready?" He stared into my eyes, searching for my decision.

I nibbled my lip and nodded as a broad smile spread across his lips. It lit me up like a Christmas tree.

"I don't think I'm convinced yet. But don't worry. I will be." His hands were back on me, the rough skin traveling up my thighs. I parted them without any urging. My pussy was on fire, screaming out for his touch, but he seemed determined to draw this out.

Using his thumb, he traced the seam of my pussy, and my fingers dug into the bedspread under me. My hips jerked up, and he clamped his other hand down on my thigh so I couldn't go anywhere. Pressing his thumb into me, he kneaded my thigh as an electric jolt shot up my spine.

"Declan." I moaned his name and pleaded with my eyes for him to do it. Taking his thumb out, he replaced it with two fingers, getting in close between my legs, his chest between my knees. The fullness from his fingers had the crest of my orgasm close already.

"How does it feel, Mak?" He pumped his fingers in and out, and my pussy fluttered and clenched around them. The pleasure rolling through me stole my breath away. I might have made a noise that kind of sounded like *good*. I couldn't even form words.

He pulled his fingers out of me, and I gasped at the sudden loss. Cool air replaced the heat of his fingers, and my core screamed for more. Keeping his eyes on mine, he lifted his fingers to his mouth and sucked on them like he was savoring the sweetest treat.

He repeated the torture all over again with his other hand, bringing his fingers to his mouth, and I writhed on the bed, so close to my peak. I couldn't take it anymore.

"I need you. I want you to go down on me." The words nearly stalled in my throat, but I pushed them out. I needed this. I needed to finally let go and let him show me what it was like to not be in control of everything.

"Finally!" His smile turned into a look of overwhelming desire and hunger, and he shoved my skirt up around my waist and lowered his head. Licking my dry lips, I let him spread my legs farther. His stubble scraped against my thighs, and I sucked in a shuddering breath.

Instead of going for a slow introduction, Declan had other ideas and went for complete and total implosion. Like a man starved, he delved into my pussy, his nose nudging my clit. As much as I didn't want to admit it, I knew he was right. What I'd felt before was nothing like this.

Shooting my fingers into his hair, I cried out as my legs jerked and shook. There were too many sensations going on. It was too much, and I tried to close my legs. Overwhelmingly rapturous indulgence plunged me off the cliff into a pool where only my throbbing clit, clenching pussy and his tongue existed.

"Now that I've had a taste, don't think you're going to be able to get me from between these legs. I'm planting a flag. This is the New World, Books." He pumped three fingers inside of me like his tongue wasn't already enough to send me into a spiral of pleasure so fast my stomach clenched and my toes curled.

Writhing, I fell back, my body aflame as he feasted on me. Every nerve focused on the pleasure pulsing from his tongue. He sucked my clit into his mouth, lapping and tugging on it like he did my nipples, and I clamped my legs around his head. It was too much. Too good, almost painful.

"Fuck!" Screaming into the air, I couldn't catch my breath. My heart pounded, and my eyes rolled back in my head. My orgasm built as the waves crested higher until I was seconds away from blacking out.

"Declan—" My voice came out reedy and needy, cut off by a jolt that rocketed through my body as he curled his fingers inside me, rubbing against the spot only I'd been able to find before.

His tongue and fingers were everywhere. They were everything. My body trembled, and there was a thin sheen of sweat covering me. I didn't know if it had been a minute or twenty, but I knew I might die and I was completely okay if that was how I was going to go.

32

DECLAN

Watching Mak come apart under my mouth and my hands was the most satisfying feeling I'd ever felt in my life. Her deep, rich flavor made my mouth water even as I lapped at her pussy and sucked on her clit. She might have thought I was joking when I said this was my new favorite place, but I wasn't.

My cock throbbed in time to my heartbeat, and I was tempted to take it out and wrap my hand around my shaft, to relieve some of the pressure, but this was about her. This was about giving Mak what she needed, and right now she needed me eating her out until she didn't remember her name.

With her thighs clamped on either side of my head, I knew she was close. Her pussy clenched around my fingers as I sucked on her clit. My pride soared as she thrashed on the bed and her cries of pleasure fell from her lips. Lapping up her sweetness, I couldn't get enough. Her grip on my hair tightened to the point of pain, but I'd endure it for the way her eyes blazed into mine.

It was a cross between surprise and the sexiest look on her face ever.

But the scream.

My name on her lips as her back arched off the bed. Every muscle in her body tightened, and I tapped on her clit, sending her even higher. She was in sweetness overload as I ran my tongue up and down her lips, savoring every last drop. Pushing my head away, she collapsed into a boneless, panting heap on the bed, trembling and shaking, gentle moans bursting free from her parted lips.

Triumphant, I stood at the end of the bed and soaked her in, my face covered in the evidence of just how good it had been for her. I would wear that cologne any day. Every day if I could.

Her eyes fluttered open, and she gave me a lazy smile. Her eyes glittered with amusement. I'd turned my girl liquid. Licking her lips, she beckoned me forward. I climbed onto the bed, still fully clothed.

"How was that for you?" Lying down next to her, I ran my fingers through her wild hair.

"It was okay." She shrugged and actually managed to keep a straight face.

"Just okay?" I ran my hand over my stomach.

"I mean, it was passable."

"Passable?" I wiggled my fingers, digging them into her stomach and sides. She jumped and laughed, trying to push my hands away as I tickled her.

"Okay, okay," she said through her gasping laughter and giving in. "More than passable, but I think we're going to have to do a lot of research about this. I don't want to make a snap decision." A mischievous smile turned up the edges of her lips. "But there is one other thing I think we're going to have to investigate tonight." Her hand skimmed down my chest, cupping my shaft. I was rock-hard, but my entire focus was on her. All her. She nibbled on her bottom lip, and I captured it between my lips, nipping her.

"I think that can be arranged." I let her push me over onto my back and get to work undoing my jeans. Tugging them down, my cock sprang out, tapping against my stomach. She wrapped her soft, warm hand around it, and I sucked in a sharp breath.

"I think there's going to be a lot of hard work tonight. Are you up for it?" She stroked me, running her thumb over the crown of my dick, spreading the glistening precum. I resisted the urge to throw her down on the bed and sink inside her. Letting her have her fun was almost as good.

"Tonight and every night. I'm up for all the hard work you can throw my way."

"Good." She smirked and lowered her head. Her breath caressed the tip of my dick, and I fought to keep my eyes open. The hot wetness of her mouth made my eyes want to roll to the back of my head. She took her time torturing me in the best of ways. Mak wasn't afraid to give as good as she got.

She turned me inside out with her mouth, and I sank inside her sweet pussy, driving home how I'd never let her go with each and every thrust. We came together, riding our wave of pleasure wrapped up in one another.

We collapsed into a heap, breathless, sweaty, and satisfied. I wrapped my arms around her and trailed my hand down her back. My heart hammered in time with hers.

Not wanting to break the trance we were under, I couldn't help but ask the question that had been in the back of my mind since the minute she knocked on the door.

"What do we do after graduation? About the med-school program? What about once you're in med school, because if

I know anything about you, it's that you're not going to let this stop you?" Being back together didn't mean the problems from before evaporated.

She pressed her finger over my lips.

"You sound like me now." She smiled with a hint of sadness in her eyes.

"I know you have a lot of plans, and I know things got screwed up. I don't want you to have any regrets."

She shook her head fiercely the second the word left my lips, and my heart squeezed. I ran my thumb over the side of her face. Her smooth skin gliding under my rough fingertips. I was all rough and tumble, and she was sweet and refined. But somehow, we fit together in our perfect imperfection.

"We'll figure it out. No matter what it is, we'll figure it out together. You'll be playing hockey. I'll be in med school eventually. Let's not worry about it now, and Declan..." She paused and dropped her eyes. I tilted her chin back up to meet her gaze.

"What is it?" My throat tightened. Her eyes were full of uncertainty I wanted to wash away.

"I...I love you." She said it with tears spilling down her face. Wiping them off her cheeks, I lowered my head and captured her lips in mine.

"Of course you do," I said, grinning against her lips. Her eyes got wide, and she pushed against my chest and pinched my side. "I love you too." Crushing my lips to hers, she laughed, and I rolled her under me. The soft glow from the streetlights outside cast her in a radiant light, and there wasn't anything in the world that could keep me away from her.

"You're mine now, Books. I was playing the long game. Now you'll never be rid of me."

Lifting her hand, she ran it through my hair. "Who said I wanted to? Maybe now you're stuck with me." She wriggled her hips under me.

"Looks like we're stuck together, and I wouldn't have it any other way." I buried my face in her neck, nipping her until she burst out laughing. Never a better sound in the entire world.

EPILOGUE

I t wasn't often that everyone got together and throwing our college team into the mix meant it was an insane night. The Christmas break was a short window where everything settled into a nice, easy pace, which meant everyone wanted to blow off a little steam. Our team was on fire, victories stacked up one after another on our way to the national championship.

We headed out to the newly opened location of the Bramble Bar. Philly got its own location after New York and LA, which was nice because in the East Coast game of which city gets shown on the map, Philly always disappeared between DC and NYC. We'd practically taken over the place, and everyone was here.

It was a loud and animated re-creation of every night out with the five of us back in high school plus a whole new team of players. Heads turned, and people peered over the booths to see who was trying to shake the place down. A few people came over asking for autographs, but for the most part everyone else kept away.

Ford and Colm had come down from Boston. There

were rumors swirling that Ford might be traded to Philly. Him, me, and Heath playing on the same team would be epic. Ford's younger brother, Grant was there. Colm had brought Olivia with him, and like Emmett had said, she'd certainly blossomed during her senior year of high school. Grant certainly seemed to notice, but he'd always had a thing for her, which drove Colm up a wall.

She'd gotten all dressed up and sat between Colm and Ford. I'd seen the little dance of the chairs she'd pulled off to maneuver that one with Grant and Colm jockeying to stay at her side. Ford and Colm seemed oblivious to how she'd ended up at Ford's side, but I glanced at Emmett, and he gave me a knowing shake of the head. That could cause some trouble.

Heath was in the middle of a retelling of one of his stories when he froze. Standing from the table, his eyes locked on the door to the bar as someone came in. Heath stared at her and stood with his mouth hanging open. Everyone craned their neck to see who'd caught his attention. Slowly he lowered himself back down as the mystery woman settled herself at the bar. *What was that about?*

Mak squeezed my hand under the table, and I glanced over at her, smiling.

"You didn't tell me it was going to be a total sausagefest," she jokingly whispered.

"There's another girl here." I pointed to Olivia, who finished up her pasta and rolled her eyes when she caught mine.

"Another girl whose big brother is about to take her back to the hotel so everyone else can cut loose and get drunk off their asses."

"They think I've never seen anyone get drunk before," Olivia called across the table. "He thinks I'm still twelve."

She thumbed her finger at Colm, who watched over her like a hawk, like she'd only recently learned to eat, and he wanted to be ready to give her the Heimlich at a moment's notice.

"I'm not going to have you here once these guys decide to break in the new bar."

"Then why are you coming back?" she shot back at him.

"I need to make sure nothing gets too out of hand," he said in his best stern-older-brother voice.

"I can walk her back to the hotel." Grant offered and stood from his chair.

Colm shot him a glare. "Not happening." His jaw ticked, and Olivia rolled her eyes. "You need to keep an eye on your brother." He thumbed his finger in Grant's direction.

"She can stay for a bit longer, Colm. They haven't seen Liv in ages," Ford piped up from beside them, and Olivia's eyes got so big and shiny she was practically an anime character as she stared at Ford. "Plus, it's not even nine. Not past her bedtime yet." The anime eyes were replaced with a scowl, and she folded her arms across her chest, mumbling something about a bedtime, she'd show them, and not a child.

"Yeah, let Liv stay," Grant piped up, and Colm shot him a glare and angled himself so Grant would have a harder time seeing Olivia. She shook her head and rolled her eyes.

"Is it always like this?" Mak laughed and grabbed her beer. I was proud I'd gotten my girl to appreciate the acquired taste of beer. She didn't have them too often, but the fact that she'd ordered it all on her own made my heart swell with pride.

Colm took Olivia back to the hotel and made sure Ford kept Grant inside until he returned a little while later. Everyone else finished up their food, and the mood in the bar shifted as the food petered out, the band took the small stage, and the drinks flowed.

Mak dragged me onto the dance floor. The one thing she had to force me to do, but with everything I'd pushed on her, it was the least I could do. It certainly didn't feel like a chore as our hips moved together in a crowded sea of people.

"I thought you said you couldn't dance," Mak said into my ear with her arms wrapped around my shoulder.

"I said I didn't like to dance, not the same thing. You've seen my moves, Books."

She threw her head back, laughing, and I buried my head in her neck, scraping my teeth against her skin.

"I should never have doubted you." Her eyes sparkled with laughter, and she trailed her fingers along the hair on the back of my neck.

"I got everyone rooms, so no need to bang your girl on the dance floor." Emmett butted in and held out a room key, his arms around a woman none of us had seen before.

"How generous of you." I pocketed the key and gave Mak a look that had a slight tremble running through her body. The key in my jeans glowed with possibilities. Hotel sex was one we hadn't tried yet, but I figured tonight we'd break that location in.

The guys were spread out all over the bar, some drinking, dancing, trying to convince the bartender to get the kitchen to pump out another round of those amazing mini tacos.

I caught sight of Heath as he darted off from the group of women who'd surrounded him and made a beeline straight for the bar. He left a wake of despair and pouty lips from the women trying to get his attention. But he wasn't giving them the time of day. He zeroed in on the girl who he'd been checking out from the second she opened the door. He thought he was smooth, but he'd literally stood up from his seat when she opened the front door. Heath was good at a lot of things but being stealthy wasn't one of them.

"Looks like Heath's decided to make a move." Mak watched along with me as Heath slid onto the stool beside her.

"Looks like he has. But I'm not worried too much about him because I think I want to make a move on someone." I ground my hips harder into her, cupping her ass to press her in tighter.

Mak smirked and glanced around. "And who's it going to be on? That cute brunette Heath is chatting up?" She turned her head. "Ohh or maybe the blonde over there? She's pretty cute."

"I've got my eye on a strawberry-blonde who loves to push my buttons and gets under my skin."

"That sounds like a problem you might want to go to the doctor for."

"I think I know someone in pre-med who might be able to give me a checkup." I growled and captured her lips in mine.

"I think I might need a checkup too. You ready to go? I hear there's a freshly made-up hotel room with our name on it." She licked her lips and kept her eyes on mine.

"I thought you'd never ask." Practically carrying her, I had her in the circle of my arms. We rushed across the street to the Rittenhouse Hotel. Racing through the lobby, we flung ourselves into the elevator, both breathing heavily in anticipation of christening the hotel room. Another couple stepped into the elevator with us, and I ran my hand down over Mak's ass, kneading it as the numbers on the small screen in front of us climbed.

Giving as good as she got, her hand slid down the front of my jeans. My eyes bulged as I glanced at the older couple standing less than two feet from us and back at her. Her stifled smile as her hand rubbed harder against me confirmed what I already knew. I'd created a monster.

"You're going to pay for this," I growled, leaning in so my breath skimmed across the shell of her ear.

"That's what I'm counting on." She licked her lips, and I bit back a groan. She was trying to kill me or get me arrested. The other couple got out on the same floor as us, so the speed walk to the room was the last bit of torture before we found our number and burst in the door. I didn't care about the tasteful decor, cream carpet, and bottle of champagne sitting in a bucket by the bed. All I cared about was getting the woman who'd driven me crazy one way or another since the day I met her, in bed.

Barely making it past the closing door, the two of us tore at each other's clothes. Kicking off our shoes, we laughed as my jeans got caught on my foot. Mak laughed so hard there were tears streaming down her face. That was the only way I wanted to see my girl crying. Tears of laughter. My cock approved as it bounced and bobbed with each step, smacking against my stomach.

She walked backward, deeper into the room, with nothing on except for her bra. The small thatch of hair nestled between her supple thighs called out to me. Beckoning me, she glanced to the side and came to an abrupt stop. Her mouth hung open, and she turned back to me.

"Number twenty-one."

My brow furrowed as I tried to think what the hell she was talking about. Following her, I stood beside her and looked at where she was staring. I couldn't hold back a grin so big it hurt my cheeks as I saw the enormous glass shower that overlooked the bed.

"I think we might have to create a few more numbers for the list in this room."

College apartments weren't exactly known for their roomy showers, but this was a shower that could hold a whole marching band. I'd have to buy Emmett some cigars or a bottle of champagne or something, because this was a thing of beauty.

"I don't think I'm going to be able to walk by morning," she said, her gaze riveted to our reflection in the glass.

"Not if we're lucky. I plan on giving you a refresher course on all the numbers we've hit already."

"I think we should have brought more condoms." She peered over at me, and the pounding desire practically vibrated off her. Or maybe that was me because every second she was with me with her delicious body on full display, and I wasn't touching her was pure torture.

Grabbing her hand, I tugged Mak across the room into the glass and slate sanctuary, soon to be sex den. Rushing into the shower, I turned it on to let it warm up. I pressed her up against the cold, hard glass and kissed her while stripping her bra off. There wasn't going to be anything between us until they kicked us out of this room.

Our kisses were ferocious and all-encompassing as I ground myself against her. The tip of my cock nestled between her legs, her wetness coating my shaft as I slid along the seam of her pussy.

"You're so wet already," I growled against her neck.

"Maybe I wouldn't be if someone hadn't been dancing with me like he was ready to fuck me on the dance floor." Her voice came out a shuddering, panting mess as my teeth skimmed over her neck and shoulder. The running water from the shower provided a soundtrack to our newest adventure.

"That's because I was ready. You're lucky we made it to the room. I was ready to knock the food off the table and do it right in the bar."

"I think we can more than make up for the wait." She reached out beside her and took one of the towels off the rack and dropped it onto the floor. The steam from the shower billowed out of the glass partition.

Keeping her eyes on mine, she slowly dropped to her knees and wrapped her hand around my cock. With a smirk on her face, she stuck out her tongue and lapped at the bead of precum on my head. A shiver went down my spine, and I sank my fingers into her hair, piling it up on top of her head.

It was an embarrassingly quick blow job. I think I must have been in her mouth for less than two minutes before I pulled her off me.

"You're getting too good at that." My ribs hurt, my heart was racing so fast.

"I don't think that's a thing," she said, chuckling as I backed her into the shower stall. The steam from the water fogged up the glass. The spray from the multiple shower-heads covered us in a fine mist. Tugging Mak to my chest, I kissed her, plunging my tongue into her mouth as she ground herself against me.

"Never heard the expression, so good it hurts?"

"I don't think so; maybe you should show me." Her teasing smirk was firmly in place. She was always testing me, and I was never happier to teach her a long, hard, wet lesson in my life.

Flipping her around, I pressed her against the slick, wet wall right in front of one of the multidirectional shower-heads. Dragging her hips against my cock, I clenched my jaw. The pleasure racing through me was riding me hard and making my head spin.

She pressed her hands onto the wall as I leaned back, lined myself up with her drenched pussy, and sank into her hot, silky-smooth tightness with one painfully slow thrust.

Her head flew back, and she moved her hips, trying to get me inside faster, but I sank my fingers into her ass, palming her supple flesh, controlling the pace and our movement. The clenching of her core nearly sent me over the edge, but I held back, biting my own lip so hard I tasted blood. Her moans punctuated every wet slap of our bodies together.

"More, Declan. I need more."

"I'll give you everything you need." Reaching around the front of her, I rubbed her clit. Her fingers clawed at the smooth, slick slate wall, and she cried out my name. Music to my ears. She tightened around me, and I threw my head back, my shout echoing off the shower walls. Our bodies shuddered in time together, and I picked her up, sitting on the bench in the stall, our bodies still joined together.

I ran my lips along her wet shoulder as her head lolled back against me.

"I think that would definitely qualify as so good it hurt." Her voice was a little hoarse. "If this was round one, I'm definitely going to be walking like I'm a cowboy in the morning."

I wrapped my arm around her chest, my fingers toying with her wet, hard peaks. "Does this mean I'm your horse?" I laughed, shifting my hips, pushing my not deflated erection deeper into her. She sucked in a sharp breath.

"I guess this means I'm the cowgirl."

I shot my hips up again and she moaned. Her fingers

dug into my thighs as she swiveled her hips and I tried not to pass out.

"I'm okay with that. Are you ready?" She smirked over her shoulder.

"With you? Always."

****

Thank you for reading SHAMELESS KING!

I hope you love Declan and Makenna as much as I loved bringing their story to life. For another day with them, I've got an extended epilogue for you!

Don't miss it!

Have you read the FREE Prequel, Kings of Rittenhouse?! If not, grab your copy today!

Heath and his mystery woman are right around the corner! Don't miss Reckless King available now!

She walked into my life with a sexy smile and wicked tongue. One night was all she was looking for, but the universe had other plans. Now we're thrown back together, unable to keep our attraction at bay even though it could mean disaster for both of us...

One click Reckless King or read it for FREE in KU!

Looking for another sweet and steamy sports romance read?

The Perfect First - Reece + Seph

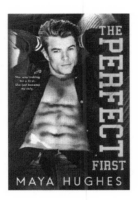

The Second We Met - Nix + Elle

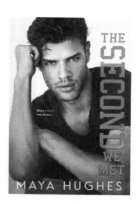

EXCERPT FROM ALL HIS SECRETS

She's the one woman I should stay away from, but I can't help myself...

He was insane. Not eccentric. Not unconventional. He was fucking insane. Who gives away money like that, just so someone doesn't lend me a bed to sleep in? A bed that probably wasn't even available. I kept running over it in my head, and it didn't make sense. There was only one conclusion.

Rhys Thayer had lost his mind. I'd decided that during the car ride across town and cemented it in my mind as we rode up in the elevator to his penthouse apartment. The elevator only had one button. PH. This elevator was nicer than most places I'd slept over the past year. The warm wood and brass covered the entire thing floor to ceiling. There was even a mini chandelier hanging overhead.

I wondered if I could just camp out in there overnight. Being in the confined space with him wreaked havoc on me. Rhys stood perfectly still, but reminded me of a caged animal. Power poured off him in waves as he tapped away on his phone like I wasn't there. Like he hadn't stalked me to get me here.

After what felt like centuries, the elevator doors slid open and he stepped out, leaving me plastered against the back of the elevator. The brass handrail warming up under the death grip I had on it. But I didn't have much of a choice about where to go. I knew the shelter proposition wasn't going to fly and I really didn't want to have to find a random place to sleep, so a penthouse wasn't the worst place to end up tonight. I didn't know exactly what Rhys had in mind. He seemed pretty adamant about my coming. *Was this just for Esme?*

"Don't make me come in there and get you, Melanie," he said, as he shook his coat off and laid it across the table by the door. I tentatively stepped out, my white-knuckled hands wrapped around the strap of my bag. I still didn't know what I was doing here. Well, other than the fact that

I would have had to sleep on a park bench tonight, if I hadn't come with him, and the fact that he didn't seem inclined to let me go. The hulking security guy stood beside the couch.

The patter of small feet came down the hallway and Esme launched herself into the room and wrapped her arms around me for the second time that day.

"You came!" she said, her face buried in my stomach. "Daddy said you'd be coming over today. I'm so happy!" I threw a glance over my shoulder and Rhys quirked his eyebrow at me, as if to say, he was right, wasn't he? *Did anyone ever tell him 'no'?* Lord knows I'd tried.

"Hey, Esme. How was your day, kiddo?" I asked, crouching down in front of her and tousling her hair.

"Good, really good now that you're here. Daddy said he'd be able to get you to come, but it was so late and I didn't believe him."

"Your dad can be pretty convincing when he wants to be, kiddo," I said, and Rhys chuckled before disappearing down the hall.

"Come see my room," she said, tugging me along.

"Only for a minute, Esme. You know you're supposed to be in bed. It's so late right now."

I spent a few minutes in Esme's room, with her showing me pretty much every toy a kid could ever ask for. Her room was bigger than Jeanine's apartment. It wasn't until she let out her third yawn and her blinks got slower that I suggested she get back in bed. I kept checking the doorway, and had even ventured out a few steps into the apartment to look for Rhys, but he'd disappeared.

Esme climbed into bed, a book under her arm, and I tucked her in. Faint memories from a time I'd tried to forget flittered through my mind as I sat on the edge of the bed and read her the bedtime story. As I turned the last page, her soft snores made me smile. She wore herself out.

"See, you're a natural," came a voice from behind me. I yelped, nearly throwing the book across the room, and glanced down at Esme. She didn't move a muscle. Rhys leaned against the doorway, shadowed by the darkened hallway. "Come with me, I'll show you to your room," he said, before disappearing back into the hall.

I stood up, unsure my knees would hold me, and followed him into the dark hall.

My room. A place for me. I wondered if the nightmares would follow me there.

How was I going to tell him I shouldn't stay? I couldn't stay. *Where else did I have to go?* Maybe just for a few nights, until I figured things out. As much as he thought I was a natural, I'd had to fight episodes of panic throughout the short visit I'd shared with Esme. She was so happy. So incredibly happy with everything in her room. She loved showing it to me. She didn't have a care in the world, and my heart ached for all the kids out there like me growing up, kids who would never know this level of peace, comfort, and ease. She had more at six than I'd ever had in my entire life, except for the one year that still haunted me. It made things easier that way. Better to pretend it never happened than be crushed that it had.

Even with that jab in my gut, and pang in my chest, watching her in her own little world prancing, dancing and laughing, so happy made me smile. I pushed away my own pain and reveled in her joy. She was a great kid. A kid who deserved a lot better than me looking after her. But I didn't know how to convince her father of that.

I trailed behind Rhys, his muted steps reverberated through me like anvils dropping. His pull made me want to lean into him, speed up my steps, until I could breathe him in. The other part of me wanted to make a run for it and never look back. I could tell he wasn't a forgiving man and I was bound to disappoint.

He led me through a couple of turns before he opened the door in front of him and flicked on the lights. My breath caught as I stared past him into the room. The plush cream carpet looked soft enough to sleep on. There was an over-sized reading chair next to the window in the corner, piled with green and blue pillows.

The floor-to-ceiling windows showcased the entire city, like a moving picture frame. And there was a new coat laying across the bed. It was purple like mine, but that was where the similarities ended. Everything about it screamed elegant, warm and comfortable.

He pushed the door open wider and motioned me inside. Cautiously, I poked my head inside. Rhys didn't move, so I brushed against him as I made my way past. Every cell in my body was completely aware of every point of contact our bodies made. His freshly laundered smell hung in the air as I passed through his wake. I made it to the other side, nearly gasping for air, but I couldn't push down the temptation to look back. When I did, he was so close our lips almost touched. The heat from his body against my back caused me to shiver as he spoke.

"This room comes with the job. It's not much, but I hope it will do," he said. His minty breath caressed my ear. The heavy, foreboding press of his body against mine made me wonder if I'd ever been around a man before. He was a man unlike any I'd ever encountered, and I didn't think I'd ever encounter anyone like him again. The pulsing pounding raced through my body like nothing I'd ever experienced. He hadn't even touched me, not really, and I was already addicted. I wanted him to touch me. I wanted his hands on my body, running across my skin, tickling the flesh between my thighs.

I bit my lip and put my hand against the wall to steady myself and took a step away. His heady presence was enough to make me forget everything that had ever worried me. Make me forget anything but the two of us in this room. Him standing so close to me, his eyes boring into me, devouring me. It was so easy to forget who I was outside of these walls when he looked at me like that. I couldn't afford to forget. Things like this didn't happen to me. Nothing good ever happened without me smashing back to earth more bruised and battered than before. I'd already had enough damage to last me a lifetime.

"I brought your bag in. Come with me and I'll show you the rest of the apartment." He slipped out of the room and I felt like I could breathe again. I was torn between locking the door until morning and following him wherever he wanted to take me. But that didn't seem like a request and I had no doubt he'd be coming after me if I didn't comply.

"Here's the gym." He pointed through the half glass door. A treadmill, free weights, a few weight machines and other standard gym equipment was lined up neatly against the mirrored wall. I'd almost walked past when a dancing blue light caught my eye.

"There's a pool?" I whirled around. My eyes must have been as big as saucers. He chuckled. The sound made me smile wide.

"There is a pool. Do you want to see it?" He pushed the door open. I wasn't even going to try to play it cool.

∽

I sat on the edge of the pool with my pants rolled up and my feet dangling in the water, staring at the lights of the city.

"The apartment certainly has its perks," he said from behind me, his hands shoved in his pockets. I couldn't have imagined a place like this existed high above everything going on down in the grime of the city. The floor-to-ceiling windows wrapped around the whole apartment. I was a bird perched on a ledge outside, watching everything pass by. It certainly made the city feel a whole lot calmer. Like anyone up here was the master of their domain. Maybe that was why Rhys came across that way, so in control of everything. When you were staring down at the city street watching everyone scrambling from your tranquil perch, how could you not feel like you owned everything as far as you could see?

"Ready to continue the tour?" He held a big fluffy towel out to me. I grabbed it and dried my feet. I'd forgotten I still hadn't seen the whole place.

Everything in the apartment fought for my attention. There were lamps with stained glass lampshades. The book-shelves were filled with leather bound books, I imagined cost more than I could make in a lifetime. The artwork on the walls looked like it belonged in a museum, and when I read some of the nameplates below a few of the frames, I saw I wasn't far off. On loan from the MET. *Who the hell could just borrow something from the Metropolitan Museum of Art?* Rhys Thayer, that's who. Every room held something unlike anything I'd ever seen, and the most intriguing of them all was Rhys himself.

Every glance, every brushed touch, every word had me on edge. The heat behind his gaze should have sent me running from the room, but it didn't. It wasn't like the leering of someone like Roy. Rhys stared at me like he wanted to possess me, not use me. His gaze held the promise of things I'd never experienced before, and my mouth watered to try them all. I had never had someone look at me like that. Like I was someone they couldn't wait to get their hands on. Like someone they needed to be close to.

I just didn't know how long it would last. *Was I just a passing infatuation? Did he sleep with all the other nannies? Look at them like he looked at me?* I wouldn't believe that I was someone so special that it made him sit up and take notice. So why did I want to be near him when he had the power to destroy me with a word. I guess I hadn't yet learned my lesson about flying too close to the sun.

I'd been programmed to be hurt. People don't last, and he's so far out of my league it's not even comprehensible. Regardless, if I wanted to do this job right, I shouldn't start it out by sleeping with my boss. But the temptation was real and raw, pounding in my chest like a signal drum of impending war. A war of the wills, and I wasn't sure I was strong enough to win.

We finished the tour when he showed me to the kitchen.

"Wine?" he said, moving behind the counter.

"Sure," I said, following him.

"No, have a seat," he said, gesturing to the living room.

I watched him in the reflection in the glass, the city lights surrounding him, making him seem even more like a mirage. He moved efficiently around the kitchen, opening, and closing cabinets and drawers. He knew where everything was. I imagined he'd have a staff crawling all over this place, taking care of his every whim but other than the guy who drove us to the building, I hadn't seen anyone else in the apartment. Every so often he caught my eye in the reflection and held me pinned there, in his skin-tingling gaze, until he decided to break the connection. His choice, every time. Each time he looked away I had to remember to breathe again. Remember my name. His gaze lingered, and it was like a fiery embrace wrapped around me, my skin singed by his vision.

"Here you go," he said, holding out a glass of chardonnay. He hadn't even asked what I liked. *How did he know I hated red?* My hand wrapped around the cool, smooth glass, momentarily brushing against his, and that energy that pulsed between us remained unspoken, but I knew he felt it.

I turned and mumbled a "Thank you." *Keep it together, Mel. Keep it together.*

"What do you think?" he asked, walking over to the couches and sitting, stretching long legs out in front of him, and his arm out over the back. He was sin, wrapped in a mixture of masculinity and refinement. *How many other women found themselves treading water in the wake of his power?*

"This place is amazing," I said, taking a gulp of my wine and sitting in a chair across from him. My leg nervously bounced up and down and some of the wine sloshed onto my hand.

"It serves its purpose. And about the job? You start tonight." he said, his eyes on me as he tipped his crystal tumbler back, sipping the dark amber liquid inside.

"I...I still think you're making a mistake. I don't think I'm going to be able to give Esme what she needs," I said, apparently trying to talk myself into homelessness. The urge to say *yes* sat on the tip of my tongue, but every time I looked at him I forgot my name, forgot to breathe, and forgot how to talk. And I knew this would send me down a path from which, I might never recover, a path where the world was spread out for me on a platter and then snatched away. I knew where I'd end up. More bruised, battered and even more shattered than when I started.

"Esme has the best teachers, tutors and other specialists she could ever need. What she doesn't have is someone she feels comfortable enough to talk to, and be as free with as I've seen her be with you. For now, that's all she needs," he said, leaning forward.

"There are some things in my past," I said, taking a sip of wine.

"I know. I've already read your file. There's nothing in there that concerns me."

"But—" I said, trying to decide how I felt about that. He'd already had me researched, dissected, and analyzed. It made sense, a man like him didn't make an offer like his, to come live in his house, without vetting someone first. I wondered how deep that research went. *Did he know everything about my past?*

"There is nothing in there that concerns me, Melanie. Don't worry so much. And I took the liberty of calling the diner. You won't be going back there," he said, taking another drink like he hadn't just taken away the steadiest thing I had in my life.

"What the hell? I didn't say I'd take the job. I didn't say I wanted to quit the diner," I said, jumping up. It wasn't his place to interfere in my life like that.

"You didn't have to. It's not like you'll have the time, if you're going to be with Esme." I took a deep breath. It was a shitty job, but it was still the only job I had. I rubbed my hand against my temple. This was insane. He was insane. Swirling his drink around in his glass like he didn't have a care in the world, and he didn't, did he? He held the power, and I was fucked, and not even in the way I'd like to be.

What choice did I have now? I didn't have a place to live, a job or any money.

For now. This was a temporary situation. I could handle him—for now. Keep him at bay—for now. At least knowing I was on shifting ground would make it easier to prepare for what happened once everything fell out from under me. Maybe I'd be able to grab onto the ledge when the time came, and save myself. I cleared my throat. Better get down to business if I was walking into this ring of fire.

"How much does this job pay?" I plopped down in my seat, resting my elbows on my knees. I took a sip of my wine to draw his attention away from my shaky hands. Rhys stared at me for a few seconds, an assessing look that made my stomach clench. He grabbed a piece of paper and pen from the coffee table, his hand flying across the notepad.

He got up and stood in front of me, my eyes level with his shining belt buckle. He held out the piece of paper between two of his fingers. He flicked them up and down, waiting for me to take the paper, and I imagined those two fingers inside of me doing the same exact thing. My pussy throbbed as I glanced up at him and took the paper from his hand, careful not to touch hm. I unfolded it and choked on the sip of wine I had in my mouth. The wine burned on its way down the wrong pipe as I hacked and coughed. Rhys took the glass of wine from my hand and gently patted me on the back.

"Per month," I wheezed, as he thumped my back.

"Per week," he said, chuckling. I'm sure I looked like I was having a fit. He handed my glass back and I chugged the contents. This could change my life. Even if I only stayed for a few months, I could finally catch the break I'd always needed to do things with my life. Maybe go to college, find a nice place to live. Living a life, instead of running from one. Forever caught in the trap I'd been stuck in since I was born.

"Okay. I'll take it," I said, my voice barely above a whisper, gazing up at him. He took a step closer, still towering over me, the hungry look back in his eyes, causing the wings of hundreds of butterflies to go crazy in my stomach. I licked my suddenly dry lips. He briefly closed his eyes, tipping his head back.

"Thank you, Melanie. You've made me very happy," he said, his hand coming up, meeting the side of my face. I hated how making him 'very happy' made me very tingly inside. I wanted him happy. I resisted the urge to nod my head like a good little girl. He'd come into my life, turning it upside down and disrupting the sliver of normalcy I'd created, but I wanted his approval. I felt it deep down, like his existence wasn't as perfect as I'd imagined. Every so often I caught a glimpse of him, the real him. His rawness didn't come from a life of perfection. He had cracks and he let me see every single one.

His hand hovered an inch from my skin and I ached to rest my cheek against his palm. To savor his hands on me, in a way beyond a polite interaction. Then he dropped his hand completely, holding it out for me to shake. I slid my hand into his and the second our skin touched I knew I was in trouble. Big trouble. Because the energy that pulsed between us wasn't something I could deny for long, and from the look in his eyes, I don't think he wanted to, either. It was a force that threatened to consume me.

I'd been through so much shit in my life, I was ready to finally make a choice about which ledge I leapt from. I'd been pushed off a cliff so many times before I even had my footing. This time I knew exactly where I stood—at least I hoped I did. I could already tell the fall from Rhys' cliff would hurt more than most. It would be from so much higher than I'd ever dreamed of diving, but I knew no matter what happened, my life would never be the same.

All His Secrets is available now and FREE in Kindle Unlimited!

You can also get the Extended Epilogue if you missed it the first time around!

ALSO BY MAYA HUGHES

Kings of Rittenhouse

Kings of Rittenhouse - FREE

Shameless King - Enemies to Lovers

Reckless King - Off Limits Lover

Ruthless King - Second Chance

Fearless King - Brother's Best Friend

Heartless King - Friends to Enemies to Lovers

Fulton U

The Perfect First - First Time Romance

The Second We Met - Enemies to Lovers

The Third Best Thing - Secret Admirer

Manhattan Misters

All His Secrets - Single Dad Romance

All His Lies - Revenge Romance

All His Regrets - Second Chance Romance

Under His Series

Under His Ink - Second Chance Romance

Breaking Free Series

Blinded - Second Chance Secret Baby Romance

Mixed - Enemies to Lovers Romance

Served - Enemies to Lovers Romance

Rocked - Rockstar Romance

Standalone

Passion on the Pitch - Sports Romance

CONNECT WITH MAYA

Sign up for my newsletter to get exclusive bonus content, ARC opportunities, sneak peeks, new release alerts and to find out just what I'm books are coming up next.

Join my reader group for teasers, giveaways and more!

Follow my Amazon author page for new release alerts!

Follow me on Instagram, where I try and fail to take pretty pictures!

Follow me on Twitter, just because :)

I'd love to hear from you! Drop me a line anytime :)
https://www.mayahughes.com/
maya@mayahughes.com

Made in the USA
Monee, IL
22 May 2020